OCT - - 2019

PRAISE FOR *THE LINE BETWEEN*

"VERDICT: Lee's perfectly crafted dystopian thriller will keep readers up all night and have them begging for a sequel."

—*Library Journal* (starred review)

"A tight, fast-paced thriller, with a winding, twisty plot and an intrepid protagonist.

—*Booklist*

"A fast-paced and deeply human story. Tosca Lee has put together a terrifying apocalyptic scenario, made all the more real through the eyes of a protagonist who comes to life on the page."

—Patrick Lee, *New York Times* bestselling author of *Runner*

"*The Line Between* blurs the line between science fiction and terrifying real science. Tosca Lee gives us a cautionary tale that is beautifully written and deeply unnerving!"

—Jonathan Maberry, *New York Times* bestselling author of *V-Wars*

"The perfect blend of spellbinding and heart stopping, *The Line Between* is an absolute must-read. Tosca whips up a thriller that is emotionally wrenching yet utterly believable, the kind of story that is sure to leave readers breathless and begging for more. This well-written, carefully plotted tale is apocalyptic fiction at its finest!"

—Nicole Baart, *New York Times* bestselling author of *You Were Always Mine*

"Everything you want in a thriller: suspense, intrigue, and, best of all, a truly captivating protagonist to cheer on. Throw in a white-knuckled race from Chicago to Colorado over back roads that this author obviously and respectfully knows well. This one's a slam-dunk that'll keep you reading, non-stop until the very last sentence."

—Alex Kava, *New York Times* and *USA Today* bestselling author of *Breaking Creed*

"[A] moving dystopian thriller . . . Lee gets readers to invest in the characters, particularly her well-defined and sympathetic lead."
—*Publishers Weekly*

"Relevant and frighteningly real, *The Line Between* is an infectiously good read. Be prepared to lose sleep."
—Brenda Novak, *New York Times* bestselling author of *Face Off*

"Tosca Lee nailed the twists and turns in this masterfully crafted thriller."
—Steena Holmes, *New York Times* and *USA Today* bestselling author of *The Forgotten Ones*

"Tosca Lee's *The Line Between* is terrifyingly close to a future reality. An utterly immersive tale of apocalyptic cult manipulation and all-too-possible infectious epidemics, this story will have readers holding their breath on every page and dearly wishing for their own basement survivalist shelter. Perfect, chilling entertainment."
—Lydia Kang, bestselling author of *A Beautiful Poison*

"An edge-of-your-seat, nonstop, apocalyptic rollercoaster of a thriller! As only she can, Tosca Lee pulls the reader in and refuses to let go until the final heart-pounding page!"
—J.D. Barker, international bestselling author of *The Fourth Monkey*

"Wynter's daring escape draws the reader into a maze of intrigue and false realities, as a bona fide apocalypse grips humanity. This frighteningly topical page-turner from Tosca Lee is a wild ride that will leave you breathless."
—Maria Frisk, producer, Radar Pictures

"A tremendous thrill-ride that is sure to linger long after you turn the last page. With compelling and memorable characters, this is a true run-for-your-life, end-of-the-world, amazingly realistic tale full of twists and turns that will have your heart pounding."
—E. C. Diskin, bestselling author of *Broken Grace*

ALSO BY TOSCA LEE

Firstborn

The Progeny

The Legend of Sheba

Iscariot

Demon

Havah

A

SINGLE

LIGHT

A NOVEL

TOSCA LEE

HOWARD BOOKS

NEW YORK   LONDON   TORONTO   SYDNEY   NEW DELHI

Howard Books
An Imprint of Simon & Schuster, Inc.
1230 Avenue of the Americas
New York, NY 10020

First Howard Books hardcover edition September 2019

HOWARD and colophon are trademarks of Simon & Schuster, Inc.

For information about special discounts for bulk purchases, please contact Simon & Schuster Special Sales at 1-866-506-1949 or business@simonandschuster.com.

The Simon & Schuster Speakers Bureau can bring authors to your live event. For more information or to book an event, contact the Simon & Schuster Speakers Bureau at 1-866-248-3049 or visit our website at www.simonspeakers.com.

Interior design by Jaime Putorti

Manufactured in the United States of America

1   3   5   7   9   10   8   6   4   2

Library of Congress Cataloging-in-Publication Data
Names: Lee, Tosca Moon, author. Title: A single light / by Tosca Lee. Description: New York : Howard Books, [2019] Identifiers: LCCN 2018056282 (print) | LCCN 2018056943 (ebook) | Subjects: | GSAFD: Suspense fiction. Classification: LCC PS3612.E3487 (ebook) | LCC PS3612.E3487 S56 2019 (print) | DDC 813/.6—dc23

ISBN 978-1-4767-9864-6
ISBN 978-1-4767-9866-0 (ebook)

For Kaya. I love you.

(Future world, you're in good hands.)

A
SINGLE
LIGHT

DAY 14

I miss ice cream. The way it melts into a soupy mess if you draw out the enjoyment of eating it too long. That it has to be savored in a rush.

I miss the Internet, my cell phone, and Netflix. I was halfway through the first season of *Stranger Things* when the lights went out.

I miss the sky. The feel of wind—even when it carries the perfume of a neighboring pasture. The smell of coming rain.

But even fresh air is a small price to pay to be sane and alive. To be with the people you love.

The ones who are left, anyway. My five-year-old niece, Truly. My mom's former best friend, Julie, and her sixteen-year-old daughter, Lauren. And Chase—my (what? boyfriend?)—who has made it his mission to keep me safe since we met three weeks ago.

We're five of the lucky sixty-three who have taken shelter from the flu-borne pandemic in an underground silo west of Gurley, Nebraska.

I used to hate that word—*lucky*. But there's no better way to describe the fortune of food and water. Amenities like heat, clothing, and a bed. Not to mention an infirmary, gymnasium, library, hydroponic garden, laying hens, and the company of uninfected others. All safe and living in relative comfort due to the foresight of a "doomsday prepper" named Noah, who thought of everything—including the pixelated walls and ceiling of the upper lounge aglow with a virtual meadowscape of billowing grasses and lazy bees beneath an artificial sky.

We spent the first four days confined to two of the silo's dorm levels with the rest of the last-minute arrivals, waiting to confirm the rapid tests administered upon our arrival. Mourning the loss of Julie's husband and Lauren's father, Ken, and my sister, Jaclyn—Truly's mother. Stiffening at any hint of a cough across the communal bunkroom, fully aware that there is no fleeing whatever we may have brought with us; the silo door is on a time lock, sealed for six months.

By which time the grid will be back up and the disease causing fatal madness in its patients should have died out with the flu season . . .

Along with most of its victims.

Luckily (there's that word again), the tests held true and we emerged from quarantine to find our places in this new community.

That was nine days ago. Nine days of meeting and learning about the others, of feeding chickens on the garden level, starting a formal children's school, and assuming new responsibilities on the kitchen, laundry, and cleaning crews.

Of speculating about what's happening in the world above as we watch the electric sunset after dinner.

That first week I helped the children make calendars to hang by their beds so they could color in a square each night until Open Day—which is how I realized the scene in the atrium lounge is always attuned to the same sunny month: June.

If we had come here in June, would we be looking out on a snowscape more closely resembling the December weather above?

Yesterday was Christmas—the first one I've observed in fifteen years. I caught Julie crying and knew she was thinking of Ken, and wished, for the thousandth time, that Jaclyn was with us as Truly and I decorated a construction-paper Christmas tree.

She asks questions at night. About why I took her away from the compound we grew up in. Why her daddy couldn't come. Questions I answer with lies.

I TAKE A seat on the floor near the end of the L-shaped sofa in the atrium, one of the last to arrive. It's become regular practice for the community to gather on the upper level beneath the pixelated stars after the children are asleep. To sing songs everyone but me knows the words to as Preston, who used to run a bait and tackle shop, plays the guitar.

But mostly to share what we know about the disease. To mine hearsay for information in the absence of any real news, which is a scarce commodity.

Especially down here.

The chatter is lively tonight. I gaze up at the constellations I had no names for (I'd been taught it was a sin to see anything in the heavens but God) until the night Chase and I brought a sky map up from the library below and spent an hour lying on the floor, tracing their shapes in the air.

I rarely speak at these gatherings. My story of growing up in a religious commune, while apparently fascinating, has little to offer these discussions.

Julie, however, is the widow of the former field epidemiologist who caught the disease while traveling with the CDC team that linked its spread to the flu. As such, she's routinely peppered with questions.

"Do they have any idea of the virus's origin?" Rima, our resident nurse and one of the first people here, asks. Her adult son, Karam, told me yesterday she used to be a doctor when they lived in Syria. "Is it a bird flu, or swine?"

"Forget the origin," Nelise, a retired rancher who oversees the hydroponic garden with an obsessive fixation that could give even my OCD a run for its money, says. "How long till there's a cure?"

She's asked the same question every night since we were cleared to leave quarantine.

"Too long for anyone sick," Julie says. She's changed in the three weeks since I left her in Naperville. The woman who suffered no idiots is gone. She's thinner, her complexion ashen as the lusterless gray taking over her once-blond roots.

But I know there is no cure. That the best anyone can hope for is a vaccine. That the fatal disease eroding the sanity of North America emerged with a caribou carcass from the melting Alaskan permafrost to infect a herd of pigs and mutated when an infected slaughterhouse worker also became ill with the flu.

I know this because I carried the index case samples myself to the man who is, at this moment, involved in the creation of a vaccine.

Truly's father.

"Winnie?" Piper, our resident fitness instructor, says, startling me. It's what Truly calls me, the name I gave on our arrival—the closest I dare get to my real name, which I will never speak again.

Piper is the thirty-something wife of Jax Lacey (also known as Jax Daniels for the cases of whiskey he brought with him), who preps meat in the kitchen—including a few hundred pounds of frozen game he shot himself. It's apparently delicious, not that I would know; meat wasn't allowed in the compound I grew up in.

And these days I'm glad to be vegetarian.

I glance at Piper and then follow her gaze across the room,

where Chase has just emerged from the tunnel connecting the subterranean atrium to the silo itself. The short crop of his hair has grown an inch in the three weeks since we met, and he hasn't shaved for days. I like the rogue scruff even if it does obscure his dimples, but the tight line of his mouth worries me.

"How did you two meet?" Piper asks as I slide over to make room for Chase on the floor.

She thinks we're married. That my last name isn't Roth, but Miller.

"Oh, it's a long story."

I can't say that it was while fleeing with the stolen index case samples.

Or that I'm wanted for murder.

I wouldn't have even revealed my history with the cult I grew up in except I couldn't risk Truly, whom I took from there just fifteen days ago, contradicting my story. At least the only people who've seen my picture on the news were those who had generators—and then only as long as stations managed to stay on air.

For now, I'm banking on the hope that by the time the lock opens and we emerge from the earth like fat cicadas, the hunt for me will be forgotten as the fugitive Wynter Roth becomes just one of thousands—possibly tens of thousands—missing in the aftermath of the disease. We have time to plan the rest.

169 days, to be exact.

In the meantime, I like to tease Chase that he's stuck with me, which is more fact than joke. But at least he seems okay with that.

"What'd I miss?" Chase says.

"Piper wants to know how we met," I say. I note the way she's looking at him, taking in his fighter's physique and olive skin. The mixture of ethnicities and striking blue eyes that would snag anyone's gaze for a second, appreciative glance.

Chase chuckles. "The short version is Winnie's car broke down while she was learning to drive—"

"After getting kicked out of that cult, right?" Piper says.

"After she had gone to live with Julie's family, yes," Chase says, stretching his legs out before him. "So there she was, stranded on the highway without a valid driver's license. In Julie's stolen Lexus."

I roll my eyes. "It wasn't stolen."

It kind of was.

He leaves out the fact that it happened the morning after the grid went down as panic dawned with the day. That I barreled my way into his car—and his life—out of desperation to get the samples to Truly's father at Colorado State.

"Ooh, so you're an outlaw," Piper purrs, glancing at me.

More than she knows.

I'm relieved when Nelise starts back in about the time she caught a cattle thief on his way to the auction house with two of her cows.

It always goes like this at night: speculation about the disease, and then stories from before. Some meant to impress. Some to reminisce. Others to entertain.

All of them pointless.

We will never be those people again. Julie, the Naperville socialite, whose money can't buy her a single meal or gallon of fuel. Chase Miller, the former MMA fighter and marine, unable to combat the killer running rampant within our borders. Lauren, the popular high school junior who may never see her friends alive again.

Me, just starting over in the outside world, only to retreat from it more radically than before.

Today, a hospice center janitor is our chief engineer. An insurance broker heads up laundry. Julie runs a cleaning crew. Reverend Richel preaches on Sundays and is the only one Nelise trusts near the tomatoes. Chase works maintenance and teaches jujitsu. Delaney, who ran a food bank in South Dakota, plans our menus. And Braden, who flipped burgers at Wendy's, oversees the cooking.

I teach, as I did the last five years of my life inside the Enclave, and rotate between kitchen and cleaning shifts. I look after Truly. I am her caretaker now.

Micah, the computer programmer whose son, Seth, has become Truly's new best friend, glances at his watch. At the simple gesture, conversations fade to expectant silence.

At eleven thirty-five exactly, the scene on the curved wall before us breaks, a shooting star frozen in midflight. And then the night sky vanishes, replaced by lines of static before the screen goes dark. A moment later it glows back to life, pixels reconfiguring into the form of a face.

It's larger than life, the top of his head extending onto the curved ceiling. I've grown fond of the gray whiskers on his dark-skinned cheeks, the gaps between his front teeth. Even the rogue white hairs in his otherwise black brows that I wanted to pluck the first time I met him.

They are as endearing to me now as the man himself.

Noah.

He's a man resolved to save his own soul by saving the lives of others and one of the few people here who knows my real name. This is his ark.

But he is not with us. The time lock meant to keep intruders, chemical weapons, or nuclear fallout at bay requires someone from both the inside and outside to set it.

Noah sits in an office chair, plaid shirt peeking through the neck of a tan fleece jacket. The clock in the round wooden frame on the wall behind him shows just past five thirty. The usual time he records these briefings.

"Greetings, Denizens," he says, with the calm assurance that is as much a part of him as the creases around his aging eyes.

"Hello, Noah!" Jax calls as similar greetings echo throughout the room.

"If you can hear this, knock twice," Noah says with a grin. Chuckles issue around me. Last night it was "If you can see me, blink twice." It's a running joke; the atrium is three stories below-ground and video communication is strictly one-way. Our messages to the top have consisted of nothing more than a digital "all is well" and "thank you" once a week since Day 1.

"What news we have is sobering," Noah says. "Our ham radio operator reports dire circumstances in cities. Shortages of water, sanitary conditions, medicines, food, and fuel have led to more riots, fires, and the kinds of acts good men resort to when desperate. The death toll of those dependent on life-support machines will climb steeply in the days and weeks to come as those devices shut down, I'm sorry to say."

Preston, sitting across from me, rubs his brows as though his head hurts, and Julie sits with a fist to her mouth. I know she's thinking about her grown sons in New Mexico and Ohio. About her mother, already sick by the time she and Lauren fled the city for her house. Who turned them away without opening her door.

I think of Kestral, who first told me about this place. Whose return to the religious compound I grew up in must have induced a few coronaries given that our spiritual leader had told everyone she was dead in order to marry my sister. I hope Kestral's safe. That even Ara, my friend and enemy, is, too.

"The greatest shortage after food, water, and fuel, of course, is reliable information," Noah continues. "We are in the Middle Ages once more, operating on hearsay and what radio operators report. What I can tell you is that the attack on the substation in California three weeks ago appears to be the act of terrorists working in conjunction with the cyberassault on the grid in order to prolong the blackout. The consensus is Russia, though there are those celebrating in pockets of the Middle East and Pakistan and groups claiming unlikely credit."

"What about the attack on the CDC?" Nelise says.

"It's got to be them," Preston says.

"How is it possible we've harbored Russian terrorists in our country and not even—"

"Shh!" several others hiss as Noah continues.

"The president has not been heard from since his radio address last week. Foreign borders remain closed to Americans, and our neighbors to the north and south have sworn to vigorously defend their borders in an effort to stem the tide of Americans attempting to enter Canada and Mexico illegally. They don't want us there, folks." He hesitates a moment, and then says, as though against his better judgment: "There are reports that an Alaskan ship full of Americans was deliberately sunk when it wandered into Russian waters."

Piper glances from person to person with a wide-eyed stare. Chase sits unmoving on my other side, jaw tight. There was news of a missile strike in Hawaii hours before we entered the silo. But that turned out to be only a rumor.

"There's talk of aid from our neighbors and allies in the form of food, fuel, generators, relief workers, and engineers. How much and how quickly remain to be seen. I imagine sharing information toward the creation of a vaccine in exchange for help manufacturing it will be a part of that discussion. Our knowledge of the disease will be the best bargaining chip we have," he says, gazing meaningfully at the camera with a slight nod.

"What knowledge?" Nelise says, too loudly. She's unaware that not only does Noah know about the samples being used in the production of a vaccine but two of his crew helped us get them over state lines in the middle of a manhunt. His pause is a silent acknowledgment of Chase and me.

"Meanwhile, we hear it may be March before the first power grids come back online. By which time we hope to have not only vaccinations but your favorite television shows waiting when you all reemerge. I will, of course, keep you apprised as we learn more. Hey, Mel—" he calls, leaning out in his chair. "Remind me to get a television, will you?"

Quiet laughter around me.

Noah looks back into the camera and smiles.

"We are well up here. You may be interested to know we've acquired our first acupuncturist, as well as a zookeeper specializing in reptiles. We are fifty-three in number. As you might guess, the bunkhouse is full, as is the main house. Packed to the gills. There's a long line for the showers—those of us who grew up in houses with only one bathroom never knew we had it so good."

He chuckles, and then says, more somberly, "I'm sorry to report that we have had to close our gates. I hope the day does not come that we have to defend them. And so our number stands at one hundred and sixteen souls above- and belowground. Too few, at the risk of being too many."

He pauses, and I hate the disappointment that's etched into his features. It causes his lip to tremble as he looks away.

Gazes drop to hands and laps around me. Julie swipes at her eyes.

A few seconds later, Noah continues: "Five of our number have assembled a country band. Which leads me to say that I hope you're making good use of the keyboard and guitar in the library. Perhaps when you return to the surface we'll enjoy an old-fashioned summer jam—" His attention goes to something below the edge of the screen. "We have someone who wants to say hello." He turns away in his chair and reaches down.

When he straightens, there's a dog in his arms—a brown and white mix of churning feet and floppy ears panting happily at the screen.

"Buddy!" I shout happily at sight of the puppy Chase rescued during our journey west. A round of "aww" circles the chamber. I wish Truly was awake to see him. It'd been difficult to leave him topside, but in the end, practicality won out over the comfort of his presence.

Chase laughs and glances at me. "Can you believe how big he is?"

"You won't believe how big this fella has gotten," Noah says, and Chase points at the screen as Noah steals his words. "Artemis the cat, on the other hand, has become strangely thin despite the fact that I fill her bowl repeatedly throughout the day." Chuckles issue around me as Noah lifts one of Buddy's paws and waves.

"We're signing off for now. I wish you a good night's rest, a happy Boxing Day, as it were. A holiday I'm fond of for its—"

The screen freezes, Noah's face separated into two disjointed planes by a line of static.

We wait, collective breath held, for the video to buffer and finish.

The screen goes blank instead.

DAY 15

We stare at the empty wall and then at one another as though someone will interpret its meaning. I catch a glimpse of Micah's watch, the arms barely separated on its face. Just past midnight.

No one moves.

"What happened?" someone finally says. The question is directed at Micah.

He frowns. "My guess is the message was too big and cut off. Or just froze the system."

"It was longer than the others," Nelise says, looking around. "It was, wasn't it? Longer."

"But what's wrong with the screen?" Jax says, as Nelise launches into a discussion about how this is normally the time she turns in for the night and she hasn't even brushed her teeth yet.

Micah shakes his head. "I don't know. Maybe the dog was trying to get down and hit the keyboard."

"But it isn't live!" Preston says.

"I don't know!" Micah says. "It could be a dozen things from a cable going bad to his laptop's battery dying. Or the computer itself freezing up."

"From the cold?" Jax says, with a weird look.

Micah closes his eyes and takes a breath on reopening them. "Hasn't your cable box ever glitched up and just needed to be re—" The wall flickers and darkens. "Look! There. It's back."

The stars return in sectors, the night sky rebooting itself by constellation: the Little Dipper. Boötes. Ursa Major. Hercules. Draco.

The North Star, last of all.

We loiter another half hour, waiting—I'm not sure for what. A follow-up message of "oops" and "all is well"? To check the stars' carousel journey across the sky?

For it to go offline again?

But it doesn't.

"Come on," I say, my fingers twining with Chase's.

"I SHOULD BE up there," he murmurs that night, his arm beneath both our heads. I start to say everyone's gone to bed by now, and then realize he's not talking about the atrium, but about topside. And though I know why he's saying it, it's hard not to take it as some kind of rejection. After all, I'm down here.

"You will be," I say. "There'll be plenty of work to do by summer. Think of it as the second shift."

"Feel so frickin' useless down here," he says.

"Sorry."

I say it, but I'm not. I'm *glad* Noah insisted Chase come below. Because unlike Truly and me, who had the benefit of an early dose of antibodies her father created to protect the two of us when we thought Chase was dead, Chase—like Julie, Lauren, and everyone else in this silo—has no such immunity. It's the reason I situated myself like a human wall between them and the rest of the last-minute arrivals those first days of quarantine. If anyone should be above, it's me.

Except I have Truly to take care of now.

"I need you," I say. "If it's any consolation."

When he doesn't respond, I roll away until his arm tightens around me.

THE NEXT EVENING we gather early beneath the waxing moon. For once, there is no discussion about the disease. Just Preston playing the guitar as everyone but me sings "Stand by Me" and "American Pie," and then "Sweet Caroline" ("bah bah bah!"), which stayed with me for two days the last time they sang it. ("So good! So good!")

There's a forced levity to our assemblage tonight, determined and hopeful as Preston pumps his fist in the air during the chorus.

We've done our best to get through the day, going through the motions of chores while simultaneously seeking and shunning the clock. Willing its arms to move faster. Anxious for Noah's appearance and the reassurance that everything's okay.

At 11:34, Preston puts down the guitar and we lift our gazes to the wall and wait for Noah's appearance. For laugh lines to crinkle his eyes as he tells the story of Buddy tangling in a computer cord when he scampered after the cat. Or the system lagging after his long-windedness as he vows to keeps tonight's message brief.

We won't complain.

Someone shifts on the squeaky leather of the L-shaped sofa.

At 11:36, Micah checks his watch.

Rima, sitting on the floor in front of me, glances over her shoulder, the LED moon shining above her head.

"What time do you have?" Preston says, leaning over to compare with Micah.

"Same," Micah says.

I glance at Chase, who frowns. Across the room, a few people begin to murmur.

Finally, Nelise blurts, "Well, he wouldn't just forget us!"

"Of course not," Preston says.

"Maybe something happened," Piper says. "He said they had to close the gate. Maybe people were trying to get in and they had to fight them off. Maybe they still are."

Chase lifts a palm. "Let's not get dramatic. The most boring answer is usually the accurate one."

"I'm not being dramatic," Piper snaps. "You heard what he said about what's going on. Anything could be happening!"

"He also said all is well," Chase says.

Nelise swivels, turning on Chase. "Noah's messages are like clockwork. Have been since Day One, when you were still in quarantine."

"Noah knows how to take care of himself—and anyone else with him," Micah says. "I'm sure everything's fine."

"Maybe something happened that he had to tend to," Delaney says. "Something broke down. Personality differences that had to be mediated. He's only one man, for crying out loud."

Nelise shakes her head. "He's got plenty of men to—"

"Did he actually *say* he'd be sending a video every night?" Julie asks.

"No," Rima says from across the room. "He said he would send word that all was well after the door closed. None of us knew how until the door shut and the screen came on."

"He did say in the last message he'd keep us apprised," Preston says.

Micah shrugs. "If the system's down from whatever caused the problem last night, he could still be working on it."

"Then what do we do?" Nelise demands.

"There's nothing we can do." He gets to his feet.

"Where are you going?" she says.

"To bed."

Nelise gives an incredulous chuff as Delaney and a few others rise from the sofa around her.

"Wait," Reverend Richel, whom several of the others call Carolyn, says. "What if a message comes and we're not here?"

Preston lifts a hand. "I'll stay up, just in case."

Jax volunteers to take over at 3 a.m. Delaney says she'll come up after she's made the oatmeal we eat twice a week for breakfast. It sits in a big pot on the stove next to a bowl of reconstituted blueberries, nuts, and stevia, and everyone just helps themselves.

Finally, we follow the others into the silo and down the spiral stairs through the library, Nelise still asking questions of anyone who will listen.

"What do you think happened?" I whisper when we're alone in our quarters after checking on Truly, curled up with Lauren in the older girl's bed.

"Probably some technical issue, like Micah said," Chase says, yawning. "Or maybe there was some minor crisis. You pen a bunch of strangers in together and all kinds of issues can break out. We're probably missing some really good fights."

But I've lived the vast majority of my life in community with others in the name of safety from the outside world, and fights were unthinkable.

No, the damage we inflicted on one another was far more insidious.

THAT NIGHT, I dream of Noah, his kindly face on the titan screen. But as he talks, his skin begins to lighten. His hair, gray and tightly cropped, lengthens in dark curls. The crow's feet disappear as his brows lower until he's glaring at me from the wall.

It's coming, he says. His eyes glitter with unnatural light. With laughter.

Magnus. My sister's husband and leader of New Earth. The Interpreter of God who preached the coming apocalypse as he tried to seduce and then rape me. Who shattered my faith, and my peace along with it.

The man I killed.

DAY 16

I sit up in the darkness.

My heart is racing, thumping in my ears.

I glance toward the frosted partition of our small, private quarters, but the lamp that emulates sunrise in the main dorm outside is still dark.

Careful not to jostle Chase, I slide from bed, pad out to check on Truly, Lauren, and Julie.

"Can't sleep?" Julie whispers, startling me. I shake my head.

She gets up, throws a shawl over her pajamas, and follows me up the eight flights of back-and-forth cold metal stairs to the dining hall, up the spiral staircase to the library, and through the tunnel to the atrium.

Jax sits on the sofa in animated conversation with Delaney, a bottle of Jack Daniels on the table between them. At our arrival, she shakes her head.

"Nothin' yet," Jax says, his words slightly slurred.

I prepare for the school day. Wake Truly at seven thirty.

"Morning, sugar booger," I say, nuzzling her as she wraps her arms around me. But the fringe of panic is there. The old familiar sensation like the bass of a car in the lane beside you at a stoplight: thrumming up your spine, taking over the rhythm of your heart. The same heart that believed when the disease broke out that the cataclysm was here. That despite all the ways Magnus proved himself a fraud, he managed to be right all along.

And now you're going to Hell.

I help Truly dress and wash her face before taking her upstairs for breakfast. All the while reminding myself that the dread clawing at my gut is only the PTSD and my special talent for obsession. That I expected this after running out of meds before we got here and declining a substitute from the silo's limited pharmacy, which Rima warned could make my symptoms worse or take up to six weeks to work—if it worked for me at all.

The world is not ending. I know this because I delivered the samples being used even now to create the vaccine.

Magnus wasn't just wrong. He's dead today by his own hand.

I only supplied the weapon.

I smile during school. Make Lauren, the oldest student by six years, retake the precalculus test I wrote for her that she failed yesterday despite her argument that she'll never need to use it.

"No other kids are in school right now," she says, shoving it away.

"You don't know that."

"Yes, I do. They're too busy trying to find food and water and wondering if their friends or parents are alive!"

Seth, Truly, and the others look between us in the silence, pencils poised over their homemade worksheets, eyes far too somber.

"My mommy's dead," Truly says, going back to work matching uppercase and lowercase letters. She looks so much like Jackie sometimes it makes my soul ache.

"Mine is, too," Seth says.

"Mine, too," I say softly.

Lauren studies the table between us. A minute later, she slides the test closer and bends over it.

THERE ARE NO songs that night as we crowd around the sofa. Just Piper reaching for Nelise's hand as Reverend Carolyn lays an arm around Rima's shoulders, all of us focused on the artificial night sky. It's cloudy tonight, the haze obscuring Ursa Major, diffusing the glow of the moon.

The video never comes.

DAY 29

It's been two weeks since we last heard from Noah.

Yesterday, Micah sent another message to the surface. It said only: "Is all well?"

No response.

DAY 37

By now we have no expectation that the moon emerging from the clouds over Preston's head will transform into Noah's screen likeness.

We steal glances at it anyway.

"I understand there've been concerns," Preston says, trying to regain the control over this discussion that he lost in the first five minutes. I'm having a hard time concentrating on him; there's a square of dark pixels that doesn't match the sparkling wash of the Milky Way around it.

Chase whistles, the sound piercing and shrill. A few of those closest to him—including me—grimace.

"Please!" Preston says. "We can't decide a course of action if we can't have an orderly conver—"

"Did we get any response to our message yesterday?" Nelise shouts.

Micah shakes his head. "No. At this point, we have to assume there's been a mechanical failure."

Rima's son, Karam, raises his hand. "What if something happened like an attack on the compound? What if Noah needs us? We owe it to him if he does. Whatever might be happening, there's more of us here than up there—" he says, pointing.

"You have to subtract eight children," I say. He glances at me, and then concedes the point with a slight nod.

"Noah's a contingency planner and he knows how to handle himself," Chase says. "The man's a Vietnam vet. Give him some credit. I guarantee you he's knocked some heads in his day."

But even as he says it, I know he's worried, too.

"The key phrase being 'in his day,'" Jax says.

"Guys," Piper says. "We're saying this like we can just decide to leave. Hello? We can't."

"There's got to be a failsafe," Braden says. "Noah was too smart to just 'set it and forget it.'"

"Then why doesn't anyone know about it?" someone else asks.

But as the conversation careens toward chaos, I'm thinking about the New Earth religious commune where I grew up. How my own sister kept to a Penitence cell once she realized she'd gotten sick to keep the disease from spreading like fire behind those walls and killing her own daughter in the process.

There is no failsafe.

Nelise stands up. "We need to find out what's going on!"

"Do we?" Micah says from the edge of the room.

Nelise blinks. "Well, I want to know!" She turns to Rudy, who used to own the largest insurance office in Alliance, Nebraska. I know this because he made sure to tell us—several times—as he presented each of us with "Rudy Bryant, CLU" pens our first night out of quarantine. "Don't you?"

"It sure would be nice," Rudy says, crossing his arms. His jowls get larger when he sits like that. "And I'd be frankly surprised if Noah didn't plan for circumstances like this."

"I think he did," Micah says.

Rudy arches a brow. "Then you *do* know how to fix this?"

"No," Micah says.

"Son, you just said—"

Micah points in the direction of the stairwell leading to the locked entrance above. "That door isn't going to open for 146 more days no matter what. And that's exactly the way Noah wanted it—for our safety. And, worst case, for the survival of our kind. Which is why we all came down here: to be sealed off from the virus wreaking havoc on the surface until the danger passed and a vaccine became available. It was part of the deal. And we took it."

"But the video feed malfunctioned," Rudy says angrily. "Something's clearly not working!"

"The feed isn't vital," Micah says. "I'm not even sure it's helpful."

"How can you say that?" Piper asks.

"Is it helpful to know how many are dying?" Micah asks, looking around. "Does it encourage or lift your spirits? No. It only adds to the anxiety that's going to deplete your immune system before you walk out of here in just over five months."

"But it's the truth!" Nelise says, looking at him like he's out of his mind.

"It won't prepare you any better than focusing on your health and staying strong willed," Micah says. "We should all be putting in regular hours on the gym level. Spending less time on idle speculation and more on the maintenance of our life-sustaining equipment, garden, and bodies."

"Walking out into nuclear winter ain't gonna help our immune systems none, either," Jax says.

"Wait, what?" Braden says.

"He's joking," Chase says.

"Am I?" Jax says. He isn't smiling.

"If we walk out into nuclear winter, nothing's going to matter anyway," Micah says.

WELL THAT WAS uplifting," Julie mutters as we convene in Chase's and my private quarters late that night. "You okay?" she asks, studying me.

But I don't want to talk about the anxiety gnawing at the pit of my stomach.

"Please. I've lived with imminent doom before."

Julie glances at Chase. "You don't really think—"

"Jax is an idiot," Chase says under his breath. "That's what I think."

Despite Jax apologizing for his comment at the end of the conversation, the procession downstairs to the living levels had been somber.

"Micah didn't help," I say. Though he did manage to steer the conversation away from trying to get out.

"No, he didn't," Julie says. "Does that man *ever* smile?"

"Only around Seth," I say, remembering the way Micah grinned the first time Chase and I met him when we stopped over on our way to Colorado. He's changed since the doors closed.

We all have.

Julie turns to Chase. "So is it possible, what they were saying?"

Chase shakes his head. "What would be the point? We're already down. No one's going to risk retaliation from an ally when our economy, infrastructure, agriculture—everything—is already obliterated. We're a third world country right now."

"That's what I was thinking, but the world is a crazy place filled with crazier people than before," Julie says.

I exhale slowly. Draw a stabilizing breath.

"Unless you're seeing something I don't, Noah's comm going out doesn't change anything," Chase says.

"No," I say. "We stick to the plan."

DAY 44

It takes a lot of work to survive. We perform maintenance on the silo's generators, commodes, air filters, pumps. Test the water and air purity. Scrub the showers so prone to mold. Inventory supplies.

Act cheerful around the children.

I create a hopscotch grid with some masking tape and teach Truly and her friends to play. Read from *Charlotte's Web* at night.

It looks like normal daily life, but it's not. Though after fifteen years in a walled compound, two-and-a-half months trying to adjust to life on the outside, and four days as a fugitive, I don't know what normal is.

In a way, nothing's changed. I can tomatoes—a job I used to despise at New Earth. But I'm the only one other than Nelise who knows how, and she's too busy midwifing green beans, spinach, cucumbers, and bigger organic strawberries than we ever produced in the compound.

In another way, everything's changed.

The recycled air feels brittle. The silence of this place, one of its most calming features our first days here, is tinged with the tension of resolute survival . . . and the aimless wait for something that never comes.

Or can't come fast enough.

I steal time with Chase—as much as two people who live with sixty-one others can. In addition to jujitsu, he now teaches fighting technique and self-defense two hours every day.

Because when the door opens, we might need it.

The plan is simple: once the silo opens, we get to Wyoming. Maybe by June the world will have forgotten me, but it's a chance I can't afford to take. I have Truly to protect, and that means obscurity. Nestled away in a cabin belonging to a buddy of Chase's—the place he was headed to when I barged into his Jeep and his life.

Noah has said he'll have a vehicle and supplies waiting for us. When those doors open, if I can find a way to thank him unseen, I will. I hope I can.

But if not, we'll separate only as long as it takes for Chase, Julie, and Lauren to visit the nearest vaccination center and receive immunizations.

And then make our way west.

DAY 51

I repeat myself sometimes. Have to ask Julie to tell me when I do it. Meanwhile, my day-to-day is one long series of repetitions that begin at the table: oatmeal for breakfast one day. Malt-O-Meal the next—chocolate. I never had that growing up, and the novelty of eating anything chocolate for breakfast would normally strike me as slightly rebellious. Today, it's just one more vacuum-packed reminder of Noah's forethought that makes me wonder why we don't have a periscope on the world above.

When I say as much to Chase, he shakes his head. "I think he saw a lot of things he wished he never had. Maybe he didn't want that for anyone else."

Which isn't reassuring.

The children ask what it'll be like when we leave. If they'll have to go back to regular school again. How big Buddy will be when we emerge. If there will be presents waiting since they didn't get any at Christmas.

I give answers I have no way of knowing. Yes. Forty pounds. And if they're very good.

It's different than the picture the five of us paint in hushed

brushstrokes, alone: chasing Buddy. Digging for worms. Fishing the
Green River gorge for wriggly rainbow trout.

Which makes Truly giggle.

She doesn't realize she'll have to learn to eat fish. That it may
make her sick at first, or even horrify her. That she'll do it in order
to survive.

Only in private do I ask what we'll do if the cabin is filled with
squatters. How we'll find food beyond fish and wild game. There's
a book of edible plants in the library. We pore over pictures of wild
asparagus, raspberries, and dandelion greens, memorize prepara-
tions for thistle root and daylilies, the characteristics of safe and
unsafe mushrooms.

I've suggested, in moments alone with Truly, that it might be fun
for us to make up new Wyoming names.

"I like the name Charlotte," Truly said yesterday, coloring a
picture I drew of a cabin on a lake surrounded by wildflowers. A
fresh beginning for our makeshift family filled with sunshine and
hope.

Until night comes and the conjecture begins. About what's happening above us. If the first batches of vaccine are ready. How many
pharmaceutical companies around the world have dedicated themselves to its nonstop production.

"It's too soon," Julie says. "It'll take months, even with the aid of
the UK, maybe Switzerland or France."

Jax starts in on his regular rant about all the countries that
owe the United States favors, how there better be foreign troops
defending our ports and asses for once by the time we get topside. He's drunk; his wife, Piper, pretending to protest as he shows
Chase—and by extension, me—pictures she sent him from her
junior year abroad in the Philippines six years ago, which mostly

consist of her on the beach. I look on with interest, not because I'm fascinated by her in a string bikini, but because I dream of seeing an ocean like that.

"Even our allies," Jax says, jabbing a finger at his phone's screen. "You don't see refugee camps for Americans there. Ever. Do you, Karam?" he says, unable to resist poking his favorite bear.

"Gosh, it's late," Chase says, ready to stave off another argument; last night he had to drag Jax off to the showers to cool down.

CHASE IS QUIET that night. And I know he's worried about his family, whose names I've only recently learned, and friends he's known far longer than he's known me.

I ask him to tell me about growing up in Ohio. Why he enlisted in the Marines. The girls he dated—including Jessica, whom he was with for two years.

He grimaces and rolls away when I mention her name. "I really don't like talking about her," he says. "Can we just chalk that one up as an expensive lesson?"

"Expensive?"

"She never gave me back the ring," he says, sliding a hand beneath his head.

I blink in the darkness.

"I told you we were engaged," he says. And then: "Didn't I?"

"No," I say slowly.

"Oh. Well, does it matter?"

"No. It doesn't matter." But as I say it, I feel tipped slightly off-axis. And even though it's true that none of us are who we were before, I'll still obsess about it through the night and spend tomorrow biting back questions, by which time he'll have forgotten we even had this conversation.

Things are different between us than they were during that frantic trip to Colorado, the memory of which is like so much white
noise to me now. When we knew every conversation might be our
last. When we were all each other had.

I lie awake long after his breath evens with sleep, unsettled. Certain that he means to go with us to Wyoming. Realizing I have no
idea how long he plans to stay.

DAY 72

"Chase," Micah says, out of breath as he strides into the dining hall, where Chase and I are the last ones eating a late tomato soup and reconstituted "cheesy pasta" lunch sprinkled with fresh basil from the garden.

Chase lowers his fork, instantly alert. "What is it?"

"You'd better come," Micah says.

I get to my feet and follow them as they take the stairs two at a time. Up to the library, where alarmed and angry voices issue through the tunnel from the atrium.

We shove past Sha'Neal, who cleans on Julie's crew, and her husband, Ezra. Emerge into the false sun of the atrium to find Jax red-faced, tendons standing out from his neck as Preston grapples him backward.

"You hurt her, I swear to God, I'll kill you!" Jax shouts, snot running down his nose. Movement from the corner of my eye. Braden, backing along the wall behind the pool table, Piper clutched in his arms.

A butcher knife pressed to her neck.

Behind him, the door to the stairwell that leads to the sealed entrance above hangs open for the first time since the day we closed it.

"Calm down!" Preston grits out.

"Hey, Braden," Chase says, palms lifted. "What's going on, man? Talk to me."

"We need to get out of here," Braden says, breathing hard.

"I found him trying to tamper with the main door," Micah murmurs.

A high keen escapes from Piper, the mascara she insists on wearing every day running down her cheeks.

"We need someone to go up. Find out what's happening up there!" Braden says. "For all we know there could be a war—a—a ballistic missile. A nuclear strike!" His facial expression twists. "Man, don't look at me like I'm crazy! Jax said the same thing himself!"

"If that's the case," Chase says, "you really, really don't want to go out there. We're safe down here, okay?"

"What if our air system fails? What if the door doesn't open? We'll starve to death—we're gonna die!"

"Please! Please don't hurt her," Jax says, his threats having subsided to pleading.

"It'll open," Preston says, practically hanging on Jax, his arms wrapped around him. "Tell him, Micah."

"It's a different system," Micah says. "One has nothing to do with the other. But if you tamper with it, if you start shoving that knife around the edges trying to get it to open now, you could damage it. For all we know, he already has."

I turn to Micah and mouth, *Shut up*.

"Open it," Braden says. "Just for a minute. We can close it again if it's bad. I just need to know. I need to see! I can't take this—this waiting. I can't!"

"All right. Calm down, buddy," Chase says. "Let's see what we can do. Okay? But you've got to let go of Piper. That's the deal. We can't do anything like this. Let her go, and we'll figure out the door. Right, Micah? We can open it for just a look, right?"

"Uh, sure," Micah says.

"You're lying!" Braden says. "He wants to keep us here!" He points at Micah with the knife.

In a flash, Chase is flying over the pool table. Someone screams as his hands collide with Braden's wrist and the knife goes skidding across the floor.

"Move!" he shouts, dragging Braden down, arm around his neck. Instead, Piper falls to the floor with them, kicking and clawing her way out of Braden's clutch as the two men roll into the wall. Chase doesn't let go until Braden's form slumps. Three seconds later, the fighter once known as Cutter Buck releases him and gets to his feet.

"Is he dead?" Piper cries.

"No."

"Don't let him go!" Jax shouts, dragging Preston forward.

"Too long and he might not wake up," Chase says. He turns to Micah. "What do we want to do with him?"

Micah blows out a breath and glances at Preston, who slowly lets Jax go. But before he can answer, Piper lurches across the floor.

Flash of metal.

I shout: "No!"

With a scream, she sinks the knife into the back of Braden's neck, yanks it out, and drives it deep again.

Chase whirls around. "What the—"

He leaps back as she lashes out at him, swinging wildly with the knife, blood on her hands, her face.

"Piper!" Jax gasps.

I bolt to the rack on the wall behind her, jerk out a cue stick. Upend it and rush in swinging. Chase's eyes go wide and he leaps out of the way as the butt connects with Piper's head—*crack!*—and sends her sprawling sideways.

Jax howls and shoves past me. Falls down to gather his wife in his arms as Chase kicks the knife from her hand.

"Oh, my God," Micah says, hands going to his head as he turns away.

I throw the cue away from me onto the green felt of the pool table. There's a fresh red smudge on the thick end.

A pneumatic gurgle issues from the floor.

"Sweet Jesus," Preston says as I grab the throw blanket off the sofa. There's blood everywhere behind the pool table, soaking between panels of the laminate wood floor.

"Get the doctor!" Chase says, whipping off his shirt and dropping to a knee to press it against Braden's neck.

"Yes. I'll—I'm going," Preston stutters as voices issue from the tunnel. I throw the blanket over Braden and then stiffen, recognizing Lauren's laughter.

"Don't let them in here!" I shout.

A rush of movement—Preston, hurrying toward the tunnel. "Get Rima! Don't come in. Just get her!" With a curse, he shoves past them as Micah yells at him to hurry.

"He's bleeding out," Chase mutters.

Piper groans as Jax sits back on the floor, rocking her.

"Baby," he cries. "What did you do?"

By the time Rima rushes into the room, it's too late.

We are no longer sixty-three, but sixty-two.

DAY 73

We have nowhere to bury a dead body.

The next morning, we wrap Braden in plastic and prop him up in the back of the kitchen's walk-in freezer as Reverend Carolyn says a few words.

"I'll never eat anything that comes out of there again," Julie murmurs as the Reverend leads us in prayer.

But now there's the question of what to do about Piper, who spent the day locked in a custodial closet.

"She can't just roam free!" Nelise says that night. "God knows what she might do next, and I don't trust him." She points to Jax, pacing off to the side.

Piper sits in a chair brought in from the library, cleaned up and eerily quiet, her hair drying in ropy strands, bound hands resting in her lap.

Jax stops. "He had a knife to my wife's throat!"

"How do we know that kook didn't damage the door in his attempt to get it open? That he hasn't killed us all?" Rudy demands.

"From what I can tell, it's fine," Micah says.

"How do you know?" Rima asks.

"I don't. But it doesn't look damaged."

"It was self-defense," Jax says. He turns to Preston, and then to Chase "*You* saw! He was raving. He would have killed her!"

"No," I say, my voice garnering surprised glances. "He wouldn't have. Because he was out cold. Your wife stabbed an unconscious man *in the neck*. And I do not want her around my niece—or any child."

"She needs to be locked up!" Nelise says.

"Noah thought of many things," Chase says. "But a jail isn't one of them."

"I suppose we could rig something up," Irwin, the former hospice center janitor, says.

"She was sleeping with him," someone blurts out.

Heads turn in the direction of the voice, seeking the person it came from.

Delaney.

The room goes still.

"Uh . . ." Preston says awkwardly.

"Your wife," Delaney says, staring point-blank at Jax. "Was sleeping with Braden."

Jax comes to stand beside his wife. "That is a lie!"

Piper stares at her lap.

"It isn't true," Jax says. He crouches down and takes Piper's hands. "Baby, you have to tell them." When she doesn't respond, he looks desperately around the room and stops at me. "What about her?" he says, pointing.

"What about her?" Chase says.

"She tried to kill my wife!" Jax says.

"Jax," Chase says and shakes his head as though to say *just don't*.

"It's true," Micah says, turning to regard me. "She could have killed Piper."

"Have you lost your ever-lovin' mind?" Julie says.

"Hold up," Chase growls, getting to his feet. "Piper killed Braden. She stabbed him in the back of the neck. We're all clear on that, right? And she took a swing at me before Wynter neutralized her the only way she could have. What part of that did you *not* see?"

"I said it's true that she *could* have," Micah says. Preston gives him a sidelong glance.

"Oh. So you're just being an ass," Chase says. "I get it."

"I'm saying it's possible she might have had a vendetta against Piper."

"*What?*" I give a harsh laugh.

"She's openly flirted with Chase for weeks," Micah says.

I roll my eyes. "Everyone flirts with Chase. Including you."

"How do you know she hasn't given my wife permanent brain damage!" Jax yells, throwing a hand out toward Piper. "Look at her. Does she seem right to you?"

"She never seemed right to me," Sha'Neal mutters.

"I examined her," Rima says. "She's traumatized and likely has a concussion, but she'll be fine."

"A person can't be held responsible for damage they may cause stopping a killer," Karam says and turns to me. "You did the right thing."

"I agree," Ezra says. "We're all here for one reason: survival."

"The way I see it, anyone who robs another member of that doesn't deserve to survive themselves," Rudy Bryant, CLU, says, pointing at Piper.

"Hear hear!" Nelise says.

"Wait, what?" Julie says, looking at them like they're both crazy. "You can't be serious."

Nelise straightens. "If it means protecting the rest of us—"

"If you're saying what I think you are, you're talking about murder!"

"Not murder. Justice," Rudy says.

Reverend Carolyn gets to her feet. "And who's going to carry that out?" she says angrily. "You?"

"Whoa!" Chase says. "We are *not* having this conversation."

"I think all options deserve to be on the table," Rudy says. "Maybe there's a reason Noah didn't build a jail."

"Because he believed better of us!" I say, stunned we're even talking about this.

"We're already past that," Rudy says. "There's a murderer among us!"

I feel the color drain from my face, and it takes me a minute to realize he isn't referring to me. By which time he's involved in a heated debate with Delaney.

"Let's all take a deep breath," Preston says. "Irwin, how long before you can rig up some kind of holding cell?"

"Few hours?" he says, looking around uncertainly. "Day at most."

"I propose Irwin and his crew get to work and we let the authorities deal with Piper when we get out."

Ezra barks a laugh. "Authorities? What authorities? No one's going to be prosecuting anyone for crimes that happened during the blackout for a long, long time."

"Then we let Noah decide," I say. "If he wants to turn Piper out based on what she did, it's up to him. His silo, his decision. Can we all agree on that?"

"Turn her out to—what? Hurt someone else?" Karam says, raising his palms. "I'm not advocating for capital punishment here. I'm just saying that seems irresponsible on our part."

"We don't even know if Noah's alive," Rudy says.

"I promise I'll look after her," Jax says. "I'll never leave her side. She won't harm a soul."

"She already has!" Nelise says.

"There's only one moral choice here," Julie says, as though not believing her ears. "Separate her from the rest of us for our safety and that of our children. And then decide what to do after Open Day based on what we know then."

"Obviously your morality and Rudy's are completely different," Micah says.

"Well he's wrong!"

"I say we take it to a vote," Rudy says, crossing his arms.

"Fine," Julie says, angrily. "Then let's get this over with. All in favor of jail?"

Chase, Preston, and I raise our hands, as do Delaney and a dozen and a half more.

A few others hesitate.

"Are you kidding me?" Julie shouts at them. "What is wrong with you?"

"What if the doors don't open on time?" Ivy, our resident barber, says. "We'll need the extra rations. Has no one noticed that there's sixty-three of us—"

"Sixty-two," Micah says.

"That there were sixty-three," she says, ignoring him, "but there are only beds for sixty? That when we reassigned quarters to make room for the new arrivals, two children ended up with makeshift cots?" She looks at me.

"What are you getting at?" I challenge. But even as I say it, I realize she's right; Truly has never had her own bed, having slept with Lauren since we left quarantine, where she slept with me.

"This ark was only designed for sixty," she says. "Sixty beds. Rations for sixty."

Delaney hesitates. "True—but the gardens are producing more than expected. Isn't that right, Nelise?"

The other woman doesn't respond.

"We also have more meat because of Jax. Plenty to get to Open Day. For all of us."

"That's right!" Jax says. "I've fed you all. You owe us!"

"I've got a kid, too," Sabine, who works kitchen prep, says. "And you might say that Piper will never be able to harm anyone else, but I can't take that chance. I won't."

I sit forward. "Sabine. That is not what I—"

"We'll assign a guard," Chase says. "Piper won't escape."

"I'll do it. I volunteer," Reverend Carolyn says. "Sabine, I promise Evie will be safe."

Sabine sits back. "Sorry."

"I'm just curious, how are you planning to explain two missing people to your daughter?" Julie says.

"I'll say they died."

"If we go down this road," Chase says, "we will not come back."

"Can you at least give this decision a few days?" I say. "We're all in shock. Everyone's afraid—for themselves, for their children, about what's going on above us . . ."

"For God's sake," Julie says. "We're talking about a life!"

"No," Ivy says. "We're talking about sixty-one lives, including eight children. We can't afford to live with a killer among us."

"Just give this a week. She'll be locked up and under guard," Preston says. "You have my guarantee."

"What's a week, if we know we're safe?" Delaney says.

"Seven days I won't let my daughter out of my sight," Sabine says. "That's what it is."

"It's nothing until she kills someone else," Nelise says. "Or it takes us an extra month to find a way out because the door won't open and there is no food. We still don't know what Braden did to the door!"

"Three days!" Reverend Carolyn says, trying to speak over the others. But no one's listening.

"Three days!" Chase shouts. "If only to prove this isn't a lynch mob!"

"Why should she get three days?" Nelise says. "Braden didn't."

"Not for her," I say. "For you. So you don't do something you'll regret!"

But it's too late; their minds are made up.

"All in favor?" Rudy says, his baritone carrying throughout the room.

I stare around us in disbelief as hands raise, one by one.

Piper's, last of all.

"I killed him," she says simply, her voice strange. "I wanted him dead."

"No," Jax cries, gathering her in his arms, his sobs tearing at my heart. "No!"

MY MIND IS still reeling when Chase pulls me aside in the tunnel after the others have gone below. Even from here I can hear Jax pleading, his choked words drifting up the spiral staircase of the silo's upper levels.

"What have I done?" Chase whispers, eyes wild, fingers digging in his hair.

"What do you mean? You had no idea what she was going to say!" Piper had gone on at length after the vote about how Braden had grown increasingly unstable and threatened to tell Jax about them when she tried to break it off—and then threatened to hurt Jax when she said she'd tell him herself. In the end, he'd snapped, and so had she. She'd recounted it all in that same detached tone after the vote, her expression distant and childlike at once as Jax covered his face and wept, rocking where he sat. "Chase, it isn't your fau—"

"*I said your name!*" he hisses.

I blink. "What?"

"When I was refuting that ridiculous claim that you tried to kill Piper. I didn't even *realize* until after I'd said it. I called you 'Wynter'!"

"Are you sure?" I ask, thinking back through that horrible debate. Because I didn't notice.

"Yes." He turns away with a curse. Slams a fist against the tunnel wall.

"Stop," I say. I've never seen him like this. "Come on. How many people who actually heard the broadcast would even remember my name? Especially in the middle of a conversation like *that*?"

He lowers his head and shakes it. "I hope you're right."

THAT NIGHT WE watch in horror as Ezra and Rudy walk Piper into the freezer, zip-tie her hands to a shelf post, and leave her, shutting the door behind them.

It's too quiet. Too peaceful. Too painless for those who demanded it.

On the way down to the chain-link pen cleared in storage for Jax's "well-being and observation"—meaning the peace of mind of those afraid to sleep around him—Jax breaks free of his escort, flees up the stairs to the kitchen freezer, and jams the latch from inside.

DAY 74

The lies we tell ourselves.

That we're civilized. That we are sane.

This place was supposed to protect us. But concrete walls cannot keep out the fear infecting the ark with its own form of lunacy.

The maintenance crew works feverishly for hours to get the freezer open.

By which time we're down to sixty.

DAY 81

It's storming in the atrium, a dark bank of clouds on the ceiling pelting the LED meadow with rain. Except for a dead patch of pixels the size of someone's head on the right side of the screen. It's less obvious in the storm, but shows up in stark relief with each flash of silent lightning.

I've quit coming up here in the morning, when the sun rises promptly at 5:19. The real sun doesn't rise this time of year until 7:00, and then not as a molten orb but a wan disk against the late winter sky. I used to think of this room as a fake window to the real outside. But now I know it isn't a window at all—just a lie on a repeating loop.

I'm sick of the blue sky and flowing grasses. The butterfly that appears for exactly fifteen minutes every sunny afternoon. The stupid bee with the same route through the same white and purple flowers. The rain is the closest thing to the snow I imagine above us blanketing the lunatic world white. I miss the drifts, the smell of wood fires, the ice storms that turn trees into standing chandeliers.

By now, every infected person I encountered before we came down here is probably dead. And many of those infected since then are, too.

I finish outlining the week's lessons and glance over at Truly, asleep on the sofa next to me beneath the churning clouds.

It's four o'clock. The younger kids are napping after school as work shifts break until dinner.

Two nights ago Chase and I argued. He said he'd seen Micah and the others talking. That they fell silent whenever they saw him.

I know what that feels like.

"Why'd you and your fiancée break up?" I had asked.

He blinked at me as though I were mental.

"Don't you think we have more important things to talk about?" He was planning to confront the others, to get them alone. Threaten them if he had to.

"No. Promise you won't," I said. I told him the best thing he could do was be predictable. Dependable. And barring that, invisible.

"That isn't the Wynter I know," he said, searching my face as though for a trace of someone else.

I gave a harsh laugh. "Wow. Really? Three whole months and you know me?" I said, irritated that he wouldn't answer my question about his fiancée. Two months ago, we'd told each other everything.

Or so I thought.

"Better than most people, yeah. Maybe better, even, than you do."

"Then you'd know I spent *fifteen years* of my life living behind walls like this."

"It wasn't living, Wynter," he said, shaking his head in a way that only made me angry.

"No," I said. "But it's how I survived."

We haven't spoken since.

I glance at Truly, unwilling to wake her. Brush away the tendril of fine hair matted to her forehead. She's always been a sweaty sleeper. And is the only thing down here that makes me wish time would stop, or at least slow to a crawl.

"You know, when Micah told me . . ." someone says from across the room. I jerk, startled, and glance up to find Preston standing near the tunnel. I hadn't heard him come through. "I didn't believe him."

Something about the way he's moving . . . Too carefully.

"Told you what?" I say as Truly murmurs and rolls over, roused by my sudden movement.

"That Noah's harboring a fugitive."

"What?"

"But then, this is no news to you, is it?" he says, coming toward me as two more figures emerge from the tunnel behind him.

Karam.

And Micah, carrying a phone.

I get to my feet, pulse ratcheting. Position myself between him and Truly.

"I don't have any better idea what Noah's doing right now than you do," I snap.

Micah tosses me the phone—an object most people down here, Julie and Lauren included, cling to for the solace of their playlists, videos, and photos. Some even have movies stored on them that they trade with others.

But when I look, there's no playlist or movies on the screen. Instead, a news article with a photo that never loaded, an error message in its place.

MURDER SUSPECT DISAPPEARS WITH PROMISING RESEARCH

It's dated December 6.

Chase was right.

"It's the last news that ever got pushed to this phone," Micah says.

"Okay . . . ?" I say, forcing my shoulders to shrug.

"What do you have to say about that?" Preston asks.

"Preston, I have no idea what you're talking about and I'm busy planning school for our kids," I say, indicating Micah and me with one hand as I thumb the article closed with the other, knowing it cannot reload.

"I think your teaching time is over," Karam says, looking not at all pleased to be involved in this conversation until he tilts his head, gaze fixed on something behind me. "Hello, Truly. How was your nap?"

I whirl around to find her sitting up, hair mussed, looking from me to Micah.

"Good," she says groggily. I gather her up, her little body warm, her head sweet-smelling against my neck as she wraps her arms around it.

"It's time for us to get cleaned up for dinner," I say, heart pounding against my ribs.

"Just one question," Micah says.

I look wildly around, my gaze snagging on the pool table, and the rack of cues behind it.

Karam shakes his head faintly, as though saying I'd never make it there in time.

"What's Winnie short for?"

"I told you—"

"Not you," Micah says. "I'm asking Truly."

My lips pull back from my teeth. "You leave her alone."

"Truly? Seth wanted to know," Micah says. "What's Winnie short for?"

"We're leaving," I say. But as I start toward the door, Preston moves to block my way.

"Truly!" Micah says.

"Chase!" I shout toward the tunnel and the library beyond it. Knowing that if he's in the maintenance room above it he'll hear me through the stairwell. "Chase!"

"He isn't there," Karam says, coming toward me.

I go stone still. "What have you done?"

"He's being detained in storage."

Where Jax's cell was meant to be—ten levels below, accessed by sealed stairwells.

"Wynter," Truly says in my arms.

"What's that, Truly?" Micah says.

She lifts her head.

"Shh-shh. We have to go," I say.

"Wyn-ter," she says again, in two distinct syllables.

"Yes, it's winter outside," Micah says, pointing upward.

"No. That's Winnie's name," she says.

"Oh, is it?" Micah says.

Our eyes lock.

In an instant, I'm running for the tunnel. They grab me, hauling me backward, Truly wailing as Micah tries to take her. Silent lightning cracks overhead.

"Don't you touch her!" I shout as Karam and Preston drag me toward the sofa. "Take your hands off of her!"

Micah pries her from my arms, and he might as well be tearing off one of my limbs. I scream and she starts crying, a handful of my hair in her fist.

"You hurt her and *I swear I'll kill you*," I say, voice rasping like that of a woman possessed.

Sharp pain in my neck. For a weird, disjointed moment, all I can think about is that stupid bee. That somehow it's escaped the screen and stung me.

Before the room goes dark.

I'M AWARE OF voices, raised in argument.

Of cold concrete beneath my cheek.

Truly.

I shove up, but can't move my arms and flop back. Find my hands zip-tied around a pole. I grab it and push to my knees, head spinning—and then double over and puke on the floor. It isn't much, just a wet spot on the concrete, mostly bile.

"Obviously neither one of them knew!" someone says. Nelise. "Or why would she tell her to come here? And why would Noah let her stay? No. Impossible."

"Why not just check her ID?" Delaney.

"We couldn't find any." Karam.

I cough and then spit as one voice rises over the others.

"You have no idea what you've just done. So help me, the day our justice system is functioning again, I will not only turn you over to federal authorities—and see your ass deported—but make sure she hits *each* of you with every lawsuit money can buy!"

Julie.

"For what? Restraining a murderer wanted by the federal government? I don't think so." Preston.

I lift my head, which feels like it weighs a hundred pounds, and sit back on my heels. Look unsteadily around.

We're no longer in the atrium but gathered in a storage area partitioned by chain-link fence, the one pen not stocked with pallets of canned food and totes of freeze-dried stroganoff looking vaguely like a fight cage. But it isn't a fight cage. It's Jax's cell.

And there, pacing inside it, is Chase.

"D'jou—*drug me*?" I manage to get out, the words cottony and foreign in my mouth. At the sound of my voice, Chase strides to the fence directly in front of me and crouches down, clasping the chain link.

"Hey," he says. "You okay?"

And then I remember the summer storm. The lightning flashing as Truly wailed and Micah pried her from my arms.

"Truly. Truly!" I say, searching the assembled Denizens, their faces moonlike and round in the LED light.

I find her snared in Rima's arms, the doctor crouched down beside her.

"Winnie!" she cries, straining against Rima, the sight, the sound of her tearing at my heart.

"Truly, can you tell us what you told me earlier today?" Micah says, leaning over to peer at her.

She shakes her head. "No!"

Chase grabs the chain-link fence. "Micah, leave her alone!"

"Truly . . ." Micah tries again.

"You. Get away from her," I say very quietly. Homicide in my voice.

"Tell them," Julie says, and I realize she's talking to me. "For God's sake, tell them!"

Chase gives the chain link a sharp rattle. I turn and find him staring at me with a warning in his eyes.

Rudy comes to stand in front of the cage. "If you have something to tell us, *Winnie* . . ." He pauses for effect. "Now would be the time."

I've been here before. Except this time I'm not standing at the open gate of the religious community I grew up in but kneeling thirteen stories underground, facing not the loss of my eternal salvation, but a short walk into a freezer.

I clasp the cold metal of the pole. Haul myself to my feet.

"My name," I say, "is Wynter Roth."

Chase releases a harsh breath behind me as those before me exchange glances.

"Truly?" I say, looking at her.

Rudy lifts his hand. "She's not the one—"

"Shut up!" I say. "Truly? What's your mommy's name?"

She looks up through her lashes. "Jackie," she whispers.

"And what's your last name?"

"Theisen," she says, eyes roving over the assembled others.

"How does your mommy know me?"

"She's your sister," she says, the words a soft whine.

I give her a small smile. "Truly, what's your daddy's name?"

"Magnus."

"Is he the leader of New Earth?" I ask.

She nods. "He's God's Ter-preter."

I ignore the quizzical glances and turn to Micah, my head pounding. "Take her upstairs. I'll tell you the rest."

I SPEND THE next hour recounting life in the Enclave, shut off from the outside world. How Magnus's first wife died and he married my sister, Jackie. How he tried to take me as a second wife. My failed escape, witnessed by the community, which Jackie orchestrated so Magnus would have no choice but to cast me out.

That I went to live with Julie and her family. How I learned Kestral—Magnus's first wife—was not dead at all, but living here with Rima, Micah, Nelise, and the others who arrived before us.

Nelise's eyes go wide as she exchanges a look with Karam.

"Two days after you came through here," Micah says, "Kestral left without explanation."

"She went back to Iowa," Chase says. "We met her on the road outside the compound after Wynter retrieved Truly."

"If what you're saying is true, it seems that'd be the *last* place she'd ever want to go," Preston says.

"Magnus was sick," I say. "She knew it was safe."

It's a lie. Magnus was sick, but she couldn't have known; he'd been infected for only a few hours.

It occurs to me that I never knew exactly why Kestral went back. Whether it was to confront Magnus, appear to the community as proof of his lies, help me get Truly out . . . or a combination of all three.

"Kestral never said anything about a Magnus," Nelise says. "Or any of this."

"She did to Noah," I say. "Which is why he believed me when I told him about Magnus's illegal business deals, including those with his former partner, Blaine—who conveniently died two weeks after delivering a set of stolen animal samples to Magnus. The same ones Magnus sent my sister to deliver to a third party. He threatened to kill her if she failed. She brought them to me instead."

"Stolen animal samples?" Delaney says, looking lost.

"Of the pigs that first contracted the disease," I say.

"You mean—"

"Rapid early-onset dementia." The disease ravaging our nation.

"All these nights we've been talking about it, asking where it came from . . . you're saying you knew all along?" Sha'Neal says, her voice going up an octave. "You and"—she looks at Julie and then Chase in turn—"you and you?"

"Wait," Nelise says. "Why would anyone want those?"

I look at her like she's stupid. Mostly because, other than being a botanical savant, she is.

"Uhh . . . a vaccine?" Julie says, sarcastically.

"Or good old-fashioned biological warfare," Chase says, his forehead pressed against the chain link.

"Excuse me," Rudy says. "But nobody's talking about the issue, which is the fact that this woman is wanted for murder! What about the murder?" he demands.

"There wasn't one," I say. "Magnus reported that I stole 'research' from an off-site New Earth lab and killed Jackie in the process. But the last time I saw Jackie, she was alive. Sick . . ." I pause, swallowing back emotion at the memory of that night. The sound of her heels on the pavement as she ran down the street will haunt me the rest of my life. ". . . which is why she couldn't take them to Colorado or rescue Truly herself. But alive."

Micah glances down, scrolls through a set of screenshots of the article I thought I deleted. Reads: ". . . *potentially life-saving research was stolen in a violent break-in at the New Earth lab in Ames that claimed the life of Theisen's wife, Jaclyn.*"

"Except I've never heard of an off-site lab. And I would never harm my own sister," I say.

"It's all she talked about!" Julie says. "Trying to get Truly and Jackie out of New Earth and somewhere safe!"

"So she gives you the samples. Then what?" Preston says.

How do I tell the story of those five days? On the run after Julie's SUV broke down. Stuck in a snowstorm with Chase, whom I had to convince I was not a terrorist. Crossing into Colorado after I thought Chase had been killed.

How do I tell it without saying whose daughter Truly really is?

"Julie's husband, Ken, would have been the perfect person to give them to," I say. "It's the reason Jackie brought them to Illinois. But Ken got sick while traveling with the CDC team. So I took them to a Dr. Ashley Neal at Colorado State—someone Jackie met while working the New Earth ministry in Ames, where he did his graduate work."

It sounds so simple, stated like that. "I took them." May they never know how frickin' hard it is to travel hundreds of miles in the middle of a blackout without enough gas when you're wanted for murder.

"After the attack on the CDC, the National Guard flew him and the samples to the University of Nebraska Medical Center in Omaha. I assume by now he's in England or Switzerland or wherever the companies are that have agreed to help make it."

"Unfortunately, Noah's not here to corroborate her story," Micah says. "And without the Internet I can't verify the identity of Dr. Neal, if he exists, or anything else she said."

"I'm telling you the truth!"

"So after this Dr. Neal left for Omaha, you drove back to Iowa and kidnapped your niece," Rudy says, frowning.

"Her father was infected," I say. "I'm her only surviving family."

I don't say that he infected himself—with a vial he thought was a vaccine meant for Truly.

"Why didn't you take the samples to the authorities, or the CDC?" Preston says.

"You ever tried walking into the CDC with stolen samples at the outset of a pandemic?" I say.

"But then at least they would have had them! It would have been a small price to pay to save—"

"I'll tell you why! Because Dr. Neal knew my sister and trusted me. Because Colorado is a lot closer than Atlanta, where I had less chance of getting through the city alive, and if I had, who knows what would've happened to them in the attack!"

Rudy shakes his head. "I—this is . . ." He laughs. "This is very elaborate. And all a bit much. Don't you think?"

"No one could make this up!" Chase says.

"As Micah pointed out, there's no way to verify any of this," Preston says.

Julie's face is white. "She's told you the truth!"

"Yes," Nelise says. "She admitted she's wanted for murder!"

Ezra turns on Julie. "You seriously believe one man could dupe the government into hunting for an innocent—"

"That man?" Julie says. "Absolutely. I wouldn't put anything past that lying, manipulative psychopath. He had money. Friends in high places!"

"Be that as it may, I don't think any one of us feels safe with a wanted murderer living among us," Rudy says.

"No," Reverend Carolyn says. "We can't go through this again. Just keep her locked up until Open Day!"

"We're talking about our children's safety!" Sabine says. "My *daughter's* safety!"

"Stop!" Chase shouts from behind me. "She's telling the truth!"

I glance over my shoulder in time to see him close his eyes with a curse. When he opens them, his expression is terrible.

"I can prove it," he says.

DAY 82

Karam returns ten minutes later, a small object in his hand.
Chase's phone.

He hands it to Micah.

"43832," Chase says, clutching the chain link.

Micah taps the code in, kneels down, and frowns as he thumbs through to a notepad of saved files.

The same ones Chase found on the USB drive in the carrier the samples were in the night he confronted me.

Articles about the "Bellevue 13"—the first patients linked to the same location. Obituaries of the two slaughterhouse workers and the farmer, whose pigs dug up the caribou carcass infected with the disease. The home page of a gourmet pork supplier. A roster of vendors offering samples at a Redmond, Washington, Baconfest.

"Go to my photos," Chase says.

Micah glances at him and, after a few taps, pauses.

"What is it?" Rudy asks, trying to peer over Micah's head.

"A photo of some medical slides. Labeled 'Porcine boar tissue and soil, Fairbanks, AK, PrP'"—he frowns—"and what looks like a specimen bag." He looks up. "Someone get Rima."

Julie goes after the doctor, who took Truly upstairs.

"The 'PrP' stands for *prion*," I say, repeating what Ken told me in what might have been his last lucid conversation before I summarize Ashley's explanation in Colorado. "The virus triggers rapid misfolding of proteins in the brain, which causes dementia. It's like mad cow, only faster. But instead of tainted meat, which normally causes the disease, the virus is now being spread by influenza A."

Rima returns with Julie.

"Truly's with Lauren," Julie says to me, as Micah gestures Rima over and shows her the image on the phone.

"Can you tell what this is?" he says.

The doctor tilts her head, studying the picture. "Some kind of sample . . . of a pig's brain from Alaska. One that apparently died of prion disease." She looks up, clearly confused. "What does this have to do with anything?"

Micah taps the files back open. "What do you make of these?"

Rima studies them with a frown, swiping slowly from one to the other. And then she abruptly looks up.

"This would suggest a prion disease caused by a virus. But— I've never heard of such a thing," she says, shaking her head. "These files show the progression of the initial outbreak. Where did you find this? If this is causing the rapid early-onset dementia, those samples contain all the antigens necessary to produce a vaccine!"

"She claims she took these to a veterinarian at Colorado State," Micah says.

"Perhaps not so strange a choice, given that it's a zoonotic disease—one spread from animals to humans. I assume many veterinary schools contain prion research labs," Rima says, glancing strangely at me. "The most important question is, where are they now?"

"At the university medical center in Omaha," Micah says. "Or so she claims."

Rima looks at me, her large brown eyes startled. "If that's true . . . then this woman is a hero."

"Or a very good storyteller," Rudy says. "For all we know, she sold the samples to China, is hiding out here with her accomplice and orphaned niece until the sick die off and the banks are back online to accept the transfer from her offshore account."

I stare at him. "*What?*"

"The only storyteller here is you!" Julie shouts.

"I bet she's in on it!" Rudy says, pointing at her. "Tell me, *Julie*— what's your cut?"

"*Excuse me?*"

"She didn't know anything about it!" I say, frightened now. Not just for myself and Chase, but for Julie. Horrified at the way the others are looking at her now, sizing her up as though seeing her in a new light. I glance at Chase, still clutching the chain link, wondering why he isn't saying anything. But he just drops his head and shakes it side to side.

"She had no idea Jackie came to the house," I say. "I lied when I left—I said I was going back to Iowa."

"You saw the files! What more do you need?" Julie says.

"It doesn't prove that she took them where she said, or that they're in Omaha or Switzerland, or anywhere," Preston says.

"I don't care about a bunch of pig samples." Sabine.

"Well you ought to!" Julie.

"What I care about is my little girl being locked underground with a murderer." Sabine's voice breaks as she says it, her lips trembling. "We came here to be safe!"

"Why would I kill my own sister?" I ask, incredulous.

"Oh, I don't know," Sabine says. "Maybe for a bunch of pig samples worth millions of dollars? People kill their own flesh and blood for far less every day!"

"I find it hard to believe our government would initiate a manhunt without proof of wrongdoing," Rudy says, shaking his head.

Sha'Neal stares at him like lobsters just crawled from his ears.

"The only thing she's proven is that she had the samples at one point," Nelise says. "But she can't prove she's not a murderer!"

"Micah," Chase says. "Open the locked file dated December fourth. You'll need my thumbprint."

I turn and give him a questioning look—what else can there be?

Micah scrolls for a minute and then moves to the pen and holds the phone to the chain link. Chase presses his thumb to the button, his expression chiseled in stone.

I'm trying to think what file he could mean. I didn't even meet Chase until the morning of the fifth. But when I try to catch his eye he refuses to look at me.

My stomach twists as Micah reads in silence, his expression grim.

"What is it?" I ask, my voice shrill. "Chase, what's in the file?"

Micah walks over. Turns the phone toward me. Studies me as I glance at it.

It's a screenshot of a text conversation.

—*Got a job for you.*
—*What, who, how much?*

—Wynter Roth, 22, at the attached address in Naperville.
  30k.

I reread the exchange.

Job?

How much?

". . . been working as a bounty hunter for nearly a year," Chase says. "I had a guy who sent me jobs."

I turn and stare at him, unable to reconcile the Chase I know with who he's claiming to be.

Micah swipes to the next screen.

It's a photo of a girl in bright red lipstick. It takes me a moment to recognize her.

Because she is me.

It's the photo Magnus took the second time he made me accompany him from the Enclave—that time to a local bar. I recognize the lipstick he put on me himself in the backseat of the car.

I can't breathe. My hands are shaking.

"I know for a fact she didn't kill her own sister," Chase says. "That they parted ways after Jackie delivered the samples to Wynter at the apartment over Julie's garage, where she was staying."

Micah swipes to the next photo—and the next, and the next.

They're fuzzy, but I'd recognize the woman in the first one anywhere: Jackie. Knocking at the door of the carriage house apartment.

Me, answering it.

Jackie, running down the stairs.

Me, taking the carrier of samples down to the Lexus in the garage attached to the house.

My knees buckle, the world tilting beneath me.

I've slept next to this man. I trusted him with Truly . . .

"I told Wynter I'd come from Ohio. But I'd been living the last eight months in Chicago. Which is how I got there so fast and saw the exchange."

"You bastard!" Julie spits. She runs at the pen, slamming her hands against it.

"Well, uh," Rudy says awkwardly.

"I couldn't do it!" Chase says, as Julie pounds on the chain link over and over again, the rattle echoing through the entire lower level. "I couldn't take her in. I knew something was off from the beginning. And once I found out she was—"

"Did you kill my sister?" I say in a terrible voice. *Did you kill Jackie?*"

"No," Chase says, looking at me at last. His face is pale. "I swear to you. I was on you the whole time. The pictures will prove it. I don't even know where she went."

"You liar!" I shriek.

The shock of Magnus's picture has given way to the horror of that night. My sister, sick, at my doorstep, carrying a case of samples. Jackie, saying she loved me before she ran down the street the last time I saw her.

The sound of her heels on the pavement.

I slump against the pole as my vision closes in, my ears ringing— and then double over and retch.

"I said it was too bad Noah wasn't here to corroborate her story," I hear Micah say. "But now I think it's possible that he did."

"How?" someone asks.

"The night of Noah's last message he said our knowledge of the disease will be the best bargaining chip our country has. I thought it a cryptic statement at the time, given that our only 'knowledge' was a rising population of infected. But it makes sense if he knew we in fact had specialized information the public was not aware of."

I glance up, dully, as he looks straight at me. "I think she's telling the truth."

At that, Chase releases a long breath and sinks down to his knees.

HE TRIES TO talk to me after.

I scream at him till my voice gives out.

DAY 90

I refuse to leave my quarters. Spend all day sleeping or coloring in bed with Truly. Step out only long enough to take one or both of us to the bathroom or to bathe Truly.

Julie tries to get me to eat. Says I need to get up and move.

But I am, inside, my thoughts racing a hundred miles a minute as I replay every moment of those first days with Chase in my mind, over and over again.

The first time I saw him on the highway, head banging to the same song playing on my radio. Did he engineer that, too? The grill that fell out of the truck in front of me and blew out the radiator in Julie's car. Was that driver working with him? The way he grimaced and then agreed to let me ride with him as though against his better judgment. The night he showed me how to make a proper fist.

The first time he held my hand.

The way he was so careful around me that I finally told him to quit treating me like I was fragile.

I had treasured his response. "There's a big difference between fragile and exquisite," he'd said, before excusing himself to sleep across the hall.

Where I joined him.

I replay it all in stark, painful detail. Forward, backward. Frame by frame.

Again and again.

None of it was real. But it felt like it. Still does when I go back to that moment.

Of course it does. For as much as I confessed in Penitence to wanting to kiss boys, I'd never had a boyfriend. Never been alone with a man other than Magnus, let alone slept next to one.

Too naïve to see he was playing me.

I'd been the perfect target.

DAY 93

"Wynter," Julie says when she comes to take Truly for lunch. "You have to eat."

I don't answer. I'm in the middle of a snowy Nebraska road the night Chase pulled over to rescue Buddy. Seeing all over again the way he cradled the shivering puppy inside his jacket, fingers scratching those floppy ears.

Remembering how I'd sobbed in the car, afraid for my sister—sick, alone, and on the run. The way he'd laid Buddy in my arms as though knowing I needed him.

I can't reconcile it. Start the moment over again, more slowly.

Julie sighs and brushes the hair from my eyes. "If you don't, you're going to have to try a new medication. So you need to get up, comb your hair, and come down to the dining hall. Okay?"

I nod.

"We'll be downstairs waiting for you."

I nod. Promise to go.

But obsessing is exhausting and I fall asleep instead.

WHEN I OPEN my eyes, I know something's changed in the room. It isn't the light, which is on dim, or the feel of the bed, or my limbs, heavy with sleep on top of it.

"Truly?" I murmur, arm sweeping across the other side of the bed. It's empty.

I turn over in a panic.

And find myself staring up at Chase.

He lifts his palms the way you do with wild animals, his eyes darting from my face to my stringy hair and dirty T-shirt.

I scrabble out of bed. "What are you doing here? Get out!"

He looks different. The beard on his cheeks unkempt. New bags beneath his eyes.

"Trust me, I wouldn't be here if it wasn't some last resort," he says. "Julie and Rima are worried about you. I am, too. And you're scaring Truly."

"Don't talk to me about trust," I say. "Don't say 'trust me' to me ever again."

"Wynter, please just listen to me," he says, backing up.

"Oh, I've listened plenty. And trust *me* when I say there's *nothing* more from you I want to hear."

But there is.

I want him to say this was a ploy to protect me from the others. But he can't, because he has that picture of me in the lipstick taken by Magnus himself. Which means Chase could only have gotten it from whoever hired him on Magnus's behalf.

I want him to say he'll make it right.

But he can't.

In which case I just want this to stop hurting.

"How was I supposed to tell you?" he says. "You didn't trust me—or any man, for that matter—from the beginning."

"So it's my fault?" I say, incredulous. "You're right. It is. I trusted you. And look what a mistake that was."

"I got captured trying to get you to Colorado! If that isn't trust-worthy, what is?"

"How do I know those people weren't your buddies? That you didn't do it to say I was long gone and get them off your tail once you'd decided you wanted to be with me and come back looking like a hero?" I say, voice rising. "As part of your plan to live happily ever after in a relationship built on a lie!"

"You *know* that's not true! How many bounty hunters have you ever seen with a helicopter? For God's sake—it was the National Guard!" He stops, looks around the room. I follow his gaze from the open dresser lined with half-full water glasses to the clothes on the floor, books, and crayons on the bed. The place looks ransacked—a far cry from my knee-jerk tidiness.

"'Highway to Hell,'" I say, unable to help myself. Of all the questions, this one has tormented me the most and is the one that matters least. But I need to break free of the spin cycle happening inside my mind. "Was that real?"

"What?" he says weirdly, his brows drawn together.

"You, singing along to the same radio station that I was listening to that day."

He knows what I mean. It was the first time we ever locked eyes—when I caught him singing in his car in the next lane. Awkward and endearing. He'd grinned. I'd sped past. A chance encounter, one of millions anyone might have in a lifetime.

Until I saw him at the truck stop.

"Yes, that was real!" he says. "One of those crazy things I took as a good sign. And it was. Just not for the purpose I thought. For something better."

"Were you working with the guy in the truck? Whose grill took out my radiator?"

"Come on, Wynter," he says, sounding tired.

"You owe me this much!" I say desperately.

He tilts his head, studying me. "You're obsessing," he says with strange revelation. "Wynter, you have to stop."

But I can't stop. Not until I figure it out.

I just don't know what "it" is.

"The guy in the truck," I repeat. "Were you working with him?"

"No! How could I have planned that?"

"You tell me."

"I couldn't!"

I laugh. "How am I supposed to believe you?" But a part of me really is asking.

"I'm telling you the truth! It was a job. Nothing else—until I couldn't do it. I couldn't take you in. Because I knew what you were doing was right and I wanted to help you. More than that. I wanted to *be* around you. I wanted to be *with* you. Because I—"

"You should have told me!"

It's a demand, and a plea. For him to somehow, magically, undo it.

"How?" he shouts. "You would have never let me help you!"

"Get out."

"And then when I found you again in Iowa—"

"Get out!" I grab the lamp off the stand and throw it at him.

He ducks. The lamp crashes against the wall.

"I'm sorry, Wynter," he says, and lets himself out.

I GET UP and move, trying to outpace the tendrils of my own mind. Knowing at some point I have to think about the future.

Of all the things Chase said, one stuck the most:

You're scaring Truly.

Late that afternoon, I wash my hair and get dressed. Walk down to the infirmary, where Rima rises from her desk at my arrival.

"I want the medication," I say.

DAY 123

I look away as we pass in the stairwell, even as I feel Chase stop and turn behind me, as though wanting to say something.

I keep moving, heels echoing on the metal grate.

"You should come train," he says. "Open Day is less than two months away."

I stop, shake my head with a brittle little laugh. "So what? You figure you've got two months to make everything right?"

"No," he says, moving onto the landing below me. "I know I can't. You're right, I blew it. Seeing you like that . . . I'm glad you seem to be doing better. You should come train unless it'll trigger you. For Truly's sake. And after Open Day I promise you'll never have to see me again."

The words feel like a sucker punch.

"I'll think about it," I say and hurry upstairs.

Open Day. It's all anyone can talk about now, including Julie, who's been fretting about our plans. Obviously Wyoming is off the table—a thing I hated explaining to Truly and swore I would never forgive Chase for, though Lauren took it the hardest. And we don't dare return to Chicago. Not yet, anyway.

"We can't stay here. Even if no one aboveground recognizes you, I don't trust anyone down here," Julie said last week.

It's something I've been pondering for a month, running through every scenario I can come up with in my head. Always landing on the same solution.

"We'll ask Noah to help us get set up someplace else," I said.

He's done so much for us already I hate to ask for more. But what other choice do we have?

"What if something did happen?" Julie said, finally broaching the topic last night. "To Noah, I mean."

"Noah's a survivalist. Besides. Who's going to take out an armed compound?" I said. Because the thought of anything happening to Noah could only mean Magnus was right about good disappearing from the world.

AT DINNER THE others speculate that the grid has to be back up by now. It's been four months. Ivy and a few others have begun taking their cell phones to the atrium, though they've never had luck finding a signal.

"The frequency's too high to reach us down here," Irwin says. "Too much concrete, too much ground."

"For all we know, the country's running again, the last of the sick are dying off, and everyone else has their vaccine already," Nelise says loudly. "By the time we get out we could be two months behind everyone else."

"You say it like we're in prison," Sabine snaps. "We're the lucky ones. Remember?"

"It's too early for vaccines," Micah says. "Especially with the disease making foreign inroads from any city with an international airport. Or American tourists. If everything we've heard is true, they'll need millions of vaccinations—not to mention the man-

power to organize distribution and aid workers to set up vaccination sites."

Either way, Nelise is right about one thing: without communication from above, they're all in stasis. Unable to plan whether to stay
here as long as the ranch can support them, or head home. Unable
to know when or how to resume their lives.

What's left of them, anyway.

As for me, it's all reinvention from here as I prepare to protect
my makeshift family.

The only people I have left.

THAT NIGHT I return to the gym to train with Chase and the others.

DAY 170

"Wynter."

I glance up from the table in the library where I'm surrounded by seven children and Lauren, who feels less like a child and more like a somber young adult to me these days. It's just after lunch and I'm beginning to rethink my assertion about the importance of keeping routine these last two weeks, as all they want to talk about is Open Day.

Sha'Neal pauses on the spiral staircase, out of breath. And I know by the look on her face that something's wrong.

I get up, not missing the glance she flicks toward Lauren and back to me.

"Keep working," I say, hurrying after her.

I follow her to the dining hall, where the spiral staircase ends, and across the room to the closed stairwell as she yanks open the door. The minute it shuts behind us, she spins toward me.

"It's Julie. She slipped in the kitchen carrying a rack of cutlery. Stabbed herself in the side."

And then I'm running down the stairs past the living quarters and gym.

I burst into the infirmary level, with its curtained-off rooms, the locked cabinets of medical supplies. The middle workstation is empty, a plate of food abandoned on the desk.

Movement from the corner of my eye: Delaney and Chase easing a form onto a padded table in an examination bay as Rima grabs a pair of latex gloves.

I hurry toward them, catch my breath at the sight of the blood smeared on Julie's pants and what I can see of her arm.

She gasps as her head touches the table. Curses—loudly.

Then I see the folded towel Delaney's holding against Julie's side.

It's soaked in blood. I'm instantly taken back to the day that Piper stabbed Braden. The blood soaking through Chase's shirt as he pressed it to Braden's neck.

"How bad?" I ask.

"Bad enough," Chase murmurs, grabbing the pillow at the top of the bed and shoving it beneath Julie's feet.

"Delaney, stay right there," Rima says, snatching a pair of shears from a metal tray.

Chase backs out of the way, dragging his arm across his forehead as Rima starts to cut away Julie's shirt.

"Wynter?" Julie says, her eyes shut, her face scrunched up in a grimace.

"I'm here," I say, moving around Delaney. I grab Julie's hand. Her fingers are sticky.

"Where's Lauren?"

"The library."

"Don't let her see this."

"I won't," I say, glancing back at the door, where Sha'Neal nods and slips back out.

"Everybody out except Delaney," Rima says.

But I don't want to leave her. My fingers tighten on hers.

"I'll be fine," Julie says.

Chase draws me back by my upper arm. I let her go. Stumble backward until he can pull the curtain, blocking her from sight.

I turn to look at him in a stupor. "How did you—what were you doing there?" I say. "Did you have anything to do with this?"

"Of course not!" Chase says.

"What were you doing in the kitchen?" I demand.

"I go to lunch late! Delaney leaves a plate for me after she puts the food away. I was there when it happened."

The stairwell door opens, and I prepare to intercept Lauren. Except it isn't Lauren who comes through, but Brit, who interns with Rima in between shifts.

She dashes past us and swipes the curtain aside.

Delaney emerges a few seconds later, hands held out before her, arms and sleeves covered in blood. Too much to clean off in a sink.

I leave with her, if only to make sure none of the kids see her on the way to the shower.

BY THE TIME Lauren and I get the green light to visit Julie, she's got fifteen new stitches, a tube in the back of her hand . . . and she's smiling as she slurs her words.

"Mom," Lauren says weirdly, after lifting her head from Julie's shoulder, where she buried it with a sob as soon as we arrived. "Are you *high*?"

"She going to be okay?" I ask Rima.

"Can't you tell?" she says wryly. "She's okay now."

I give a slight smile, but it's weird seeing Julie like that. So *relaxed*.

"She caught herself on her hands or she might have punctured her colon." She pats me on the shoulder. "Don't worry. She'll walk out of here on Open Day."

DAY 177

"You've got six days to get better," I say, tucking the blanket around Julie's shoulders.

She smiles slightly, her eyes closed. Her lips are pale.

She's been shivering off and on for half an hour, seeming to forget at times I was there as Rima checked the growing patch of red skin around Julie's stitches.

When I emerge from the curtained room, Rima draws me away so Julie can't hear us. Not that I really think she's listening.

"What's happening to her?" I say. It's been a week. She was supposed to be walking around by now.

"My only guess is that she punctured her colon after all. I didn't see anything, but without exploratory surgery I easily could have missed it. In which case, it's probably closed up now."

"Then why isn't she getting better?" I demand in a whisper.

"The wound's infected." She looks at me with those dark eyes of hers, and I think twenty years ago—before war tore her country apart and she took on the life of a refugee—she must have been beautiful. "I've upped her antibiotics, but what we have might not be powerful enough. If the infection reaches her bloodstream and she becomes septic . . ."

"Septic," I say, not understanding. "What does that mean?"

"If that were to happen," she says, too carefully, "her organs could begin to shut down."

"You mean . . ." The heat drains from my limbs. "There's got to be something you can do!"

"Believe me when I say I'm doing the best I can with what I've got."

"Will she make it six more days?"

She bites her lips together, brows lifting over the bridge of her nose.

"I hope so," she says, with a small smile. "You know Julie. She wouldn't go without a fight."

It's enough for me to latch on to. Until she adds: "But you might want to prepare Lauren if things don't improve."

THE REST OF the ark is busy taking inventory. Of supplies. Of the food we have left. The number of days it will last.

Just in case the door doesn't open.

The personal items they brought with them in case it does.

I sit in the silence of the infirmary, detached from the activity above us. Knowing there's no way we'll be able to leave when the door opens.

Unwilling to think of the consequences for Julie if it doesn't.

DAY 179

Lauren dozes where she sits, arms folded beneath her cheek on the edge of her mother's bed. Truly curls against me in her sleep on a bed in the next bay over.

We were supposed to be packing our few possessions. Anticipating our first breath of fresh air. The sight of the setting sun. The full summer moon.

Instead, I've just spent two hours listening to Lauren's sobs. To her pleas for her mother to get better, her promises to be a better daughter. To take care of her. To make her proud.

Knowing, in days to come, I will have to convince her that there was nothing she could do. That none of it was her fault. Even as the old anxiety over my own mother's death keeps me awake, heart drumming against Truly's cheek.

The door to the stairway creaks open, and I hear Rima in whispered conversation. Lift my head just enough to see through the gap in the curtains that she's speaking with Karam.

He nods to his mother, who has attended Julie around the clock the last three days, relieved by Brit only long enough to shower and catch a few hours' sleep. And then he comes to stand at the break in the curtain.

"Wynter," he says. "Can you come up?"

He was the first of the others to approach me in private, months ago, and say he didn't know. That he was sorry for how everything went—and thank you. His dark brows knitting together as he asked if I'd like to meet him for dinner some night in the library. Which I did, once, for an awkward hour before declining his invitations ever since.

I want to say no. Want to give everyone who sent him the finger.

Instead, I slide from bed, careful not to wake Truly, and toe into my sneakers.

Before following Karam to the atrium.

DAY 180

The stars are falling.

After avoiding the atrium for months, the sight of that wall is a shock: entire blocks of screen gone dark. Others filled with nothing but static, so that the night sky looks like one of those tile puzzles revealing only clues of the picture beneath.

The others look uneasy, though they've saved a place for me. At least they won't have to tolerate my presence much longer.

Chase gives me a quiet nod from across the room, his blue eyes more vivid than I remember beneath those well-formed brows—an effect, perhaps, of his new beard. Or perhaps of the hair that now curls past his ears. He's leaner than he was—not thinner so much as more defined. But of course he is; he's spent hours inside the gym every day.

Then again, so have I.

We've changed—all of us. Our chins are sharper, our skin paler, our arms wirier, and waists trimmer.

Only Rudy Bryant, CLU, looks the same, except that he now has a ponytail.

Preston clears his throat. "Wynter, thank you for joining us. How's Julie?"

"Not well," I say.

"I'm sorry to hear that. With hope, we can get her the help she needs on Open Day."

"If she makes it that long."

Gazes drop away. As they should. As I want them to, because I'm angry. Not at anyone specifically—except Chase. And myself. Because whatever happens, I should be nothing but grateful to have Truly with me. To have sheltered her these last six months in comfort and safety.

Instead, I feel robbed. Of the picture that we created and that I clung to those first weeks—not just of a new start in Wyoming but of a future I could look forward to for the first time in my life.

Someone coughs and the silence grows uncomfortable.

"With that day in mind," Preston starts again. "We wanted to consult you on what the health protocol should be on our reemergence. If there's anything extra you learned during your time with Dr. Neal in Colorado."

"Assume anyone you come in contact with above is infected," I say. "Wear your mask and gloves. Don't accept blood transfusions from anyone who might potentially have been exposed—which is everyone. Try not to require surgery from a hospital that operated on someone infected. Which would be all of them. Oh. And know where your meat comes from."

They sit forward as they listen. A few of them take notes.

It hits me then: time might have stopped for Julie, Lauren, Truly, and me, but Open Day is three days away. A matter of hours. Everyone else here is preparing to exit, making plans to continue life on Noah's ranch above or to attempt a return home.

After months of knowing exactly what my life and routine will look like for the next week and month and month after that, I have no idea what my life may look like three days from now.

Except that we will not be able to leave until Julie recovers . . . or dies.

And I will never see Chase again.

"This raises a big question for me," Ezra says. "Of how and when we want to go up. Because if there's a chance of anyone other than Noah being up there—"

"We'd just come back and lock the door," Nelise says with a shrug.

"Does it lock without engaging the time mechanism?" Brit asks. "We have limited supplies. We can't go another six months."

"*I* can't go another six days," Sha'Neal mutters.

"No," Micah says. "It's only designed to lock by agreement from inside and outside, both."

"We have to leave eventually," Preston says. "Do we know what time of day it's supposed to open?"

"It should open the same time it closed," Micah says. "Five p.m."

Preston reaches over and stands up a whiteboard I recognize as the one we use for school. I can still see the chart I made to show the kids' progress through a series of individual assignments just faintly beneath his swift erase job.

He writes *5:00 p.m.* on the board. "Obviously, it'll still be light out," he says, and adds *light* beside it.

I get up to leave, step past several people sitting on the floor, who crane to see around me. I move past the pool table, averting my eyes from the spot where Braden died, and am about three feet from the exit that leads up to the time lock when I hear something.

I pause, gaze resting on the padlock Ezra installed after Braden forced the door open to tamper with the vault entrance above.

It comes again: a brief siren blast from above, like the one at the car wash Julie used to frequent, that told you when to drive in, and when to exit . . .

Or the alarm that sounded every five seconds before the time lock engaged six months ago until it was a single undulation of sound.

The discussion across the room grows louder, someone saying, "What if the strike on Hawaii wasn't just a rumor—what if Jax was right and we walk out into nuclear winter?"

"What if it doesn't open at all?" someone else says.

I move closer and then press my ear to the door as Chase comes over.

"What is it?" he asks.

"Listen."

He stands beside me, head tilted against the cold metal surface until it comes again.

"Hear that?" I ask.

He frowns and then straightens and gives a shrill whistle, startling the others to silence.

"Hey," he says. "Anyone know how long the siren's been going off?"

Micah comes around the edge of the group, looks from me to the door, and then presses his ear against it.

An instant later, he says, "Irwin, get the key."

By the time Irwin returns, the siren has turned into one ongoing alarm. He removes the padlock and throws open the door.

For an instant, the sound is deafening.

And then it stops. The grind of gears fills the sudden silence, rumbling down the metal stairs.

Chase steps through the door onto the landing.

"What's happening?" someone hisses as Micah brushes past me to join him, the two men staring up at the dark stairwell above.

A heavy click sounds from above.

Followed by the unmistakable slide of a bolt.

DAY 181

The echo of that bolt thunders down the stairwell as fluorescent lights flutter to life on the concrete walls.

Karam and Preston step past me to squint up through the four flights of metal grate.

"This—this isn't right," Micah says, backing into the atrium, obviously flustered. "It's too early."

"Maybe Noah calculated each month as thirty days," I say.

"No," Micah says. "I set the system. I built it for Noah, taking each month and even leap year into consideration—"

"Look," Delaney says, pointing.

I follow her finger as Micah whirls around.

The LED wall is blank. Not just the malfunctioning sections, but the entire thing.

But all I can think about is Julie. Now that the door's open, she might have a chance.

"I'm going up," I say.

"Whoa," Chase says, stepping back into the atrium. "Are you crazy? We don't know what—or who—is up there right now."

"Then we go out and look," I say.

"It's the middle of the night," Karam says. "Our flashlights will be seen by anyone on patrol."

"We don't need flashlights," I say, impatient. "We know the ranch well enough to get around."

"And to risk getting shot by anyone up there not expecting us—including Noah's own people!" Chase says.

"Julie is dying! She needs medicine we don't have to survive!"

"I know!" He rubs his brow as though it hurts.

"Micah, is there any way Noah would know the door's open?" Preston asks. I picture the barn directly above us and wonder the same thing; the silo entrance is concealed behind a nondescript wooden door at the end of a line of horse stalls.

Micah nods. "There's in the systems control center an indicator. Assuming it works, he would notice that it's off."

"Where's the control center?" I say.

"In the basement."

"It's late," I say, too conscious of the minutes ticking by. As though time, ground to a sluggish crawl these last few months, began to accelerate the instant that door unlocked. "He might not see it till morning."

"What was the Open Day protocol supposed to be?" Chase asks.

"Noah said he'd be waiting when it opened," Micah says. "To let us know it was safe and escort us up top."

"Then we wait for Noah," Chase says. "Give him a chance to sound the all clear. Till then, we get a team in place to defend the door in case someone other than Noah comes through."

"I'll open the weapons locker," Irwin says.

Ten minutes later I'm crouched behind the end of an overstuffed chair in the library with the pistol I checked in six months ago, a clear view of the tunnel, and a round in the chamber. Straining in tense silence for any sound from above. For Noah to call out his Denizens.

Anyone other than Noah himself—or his men, Zach and Mel— will never make it past Chase, Nelise, and Karam, stationed in the atrium, their weapons trained on the door.

Five minutes.

Ten.

Twenty-five.

A soft shuffle in the atrium—someone shifting position. A knee pops. I straighten my legs, move my weight off my heels. A sibilant whisper drifts up through the spiral staircase six feet away from me, where several others crouch in the dining hall below. The rest wait in the closed stairwell a level below, ready to bar it with an ax handle if all else fails. The same ones so eager to leave an hour ago, driven back underground.

I glance at the library clock. Forty-five minutes.

"Wynter," Chase says softly, his voice carrying through the tunnel.

I lean out far enough to see him kneeling against the end of the sofa.

"Get Micah."

I pad over to the stairwell, grab the rail, and lean over. Point to Micah. Gesture him up.

I wait for him at the tunnel and, once he's in, follow him through, not fully emerging into the atrium, but crouching right there at the end. I note Karam leaning out from the other end of the sofa, fore-arm on his knee. Nelise sitting against the panel connecting two of the pool table legs, her own legs bent in front of her, a shotgun across her thighs.

Chase straightens and nods toward the stairs.

"Is there any way we can lock the door from within?" he asks softly.

"No," Micah murmurs. "And even if there was, I wouldn't trust it—obviously something malfunctioned. Personally, I don't even like having it shut like this."

"You think it could reengage?"

If the lock reengages, Julie's as good as dead.

We all are.

I move into the atrium past the pool table.

"Jam the bolt channel," I say, grabbing a cue from the rack. I've refused to touch any of them since that terrible day. But now as I consider the cue's graduated circumference, it seems like a thing redeemed. "Cut the right girth from this."

"What if there was a bomb?" Nelise says.

Chase hesitates. "We do have a Geiger counter and ten Tyvek suits."

"I'll do it," Micah says, fumbling with his glasses.

His response surprises me, and I hand him the cue with a new splinter of grudging respect.

"I'll cover you," Chase says.

Twenty minutes later, they emerge from the tunnel looking like yellow astronauts, a device with an attached wand in Micah's hands.

Nelise moves into position at the stair door, ready to close it behind them and reopen it when they knock. I take Chase's place at the end of the sofa.

For a minute, there's just the soft, hollow ring of their steps up the metal grate. They kill the lights. Nelise shuts the door.

A few seconds later the groan of hinges echoes down the stairwell outside.

Silence.

As we wait, the old anxiety begins to gnaw at the base of my skull like a rodent flushed out of hibernation.

What if it's true? All the sermons Magnus preached on the destruction of the earth, the end to come?

Stop.

I squeeze my eyes shut but can already feel the breath tightening in my chest.

Where's Noah? Why isn't he here?

A loud, hasty knock. My eyes fly open as Nelise throws wide the door—and closes it as soon as the second yellow form is through.

On reaching the atrium, Micah and Chase pull off their masks.

"No radiation," Micah says, out of breath, as Chase drops back against the wall to the side of the stairwell entrance, pistol ready.

"Only thing we have to worry about is anyone who heard the noise," Chase mutters. Nelise doesn't even bother returning to her post under the pool table, but trains the shotgun, hip level, on the door right where she stands.

"Maybe the wooden door in the barn muffled it," I say.

"No," Micah says. I can practically hear him sweating.

"Why? Was it open?"

"It isn't there."

I don't understand. "You mean they took it off?"

"No," Chase says. "The whole barn. It's gone."

2 A.M.

My arms and legs ache. My back and neck do, too. But my urgency for Julie's sake hasn't abated. If anything, it's gotten worse every minute I've forced myself to stay still.

Finally, Chase gestures to Nelise, who stays in position as Karam gets up and follows him to the tunnel.

"Time for a new plan," Chase says.

A few minutes later we're gathered around a table in the library, talking in hushed whispers.

"I think Wynter's right," Preston says. "We go under cover of darkness."

"In the dark you can't see booby traps, you can't see holes in the ground," Chase says. "Let alone guards who might have night vision."

"Who's gonna have night vision?" Sha'Neal asks as though he's lost it.

"Hunters," Delaney and Ezra respond in unison.

"And crazy militia types," Delaney says.

"Jax has a nightscope on his rifle," Irwin says. "It's upstairs in the locker. Showed it to me the day he checked it in."

Chase glances around. "Who's our best shot here? We got any more hunters?"

"It's been a decade or more for me," Rudy says, slowly shaking his head.

Karam, who has taken over my position at the end of the tunnel, relays the question to Nelise. A few seconds later, he turns back and shakes his head.

"It's gonna be you," Irwin says to Chase.

Chase nods. "I need a couple volunteers."

"I'll go," Karam says softly from the tunnel.

Preston lifts a hand.

"Me, too," Ezra says.

Chase stands. "Let's gear up."

But I don't think I can take another hour of sitting helplessly by while Julie's own flesh poisons her blood.

"One of them should be me," I hear myself say.

"We're good," Chase says over his shoulder.

"Chase!" I say, as loud as I dare.

"No disrespect for women's lib and all that," Ezra says, "but there's a big difference between a man and a woman's ability to defend themself."

"Can you defend yourself against a cough?" I say. Chase looks me in the eye at last. Gives a barely perceptible shake of his head, as though to say, *Don't*.

"You get into it with someone infected, they don't need to kill you—just spit in your eye. I'm the only one here with antibodies to the disease."

Rudy does an honest-to-God double take. "Excuse me?"

Chase drops his head with a soft curse.

"How's that possible?" Delaney says, looking around.

"I got an early dose from the man I delivered the samples to. Which means I can defend myself better than any of you."

I don't mention that I dosed Truly after retrieving her from the New Earth compound—a gift from the father she's never laid eyes on. Or that Ashley warned me I may have only slightly more protection from the disease than anyone else.

Midway down the last flight of stairs to my quarters, Chase comes barreling after me. Grabs me by the arm.

"Look," he says. "If you're trying to put yourself in danger to somehow spite me—"

I spin back and hiss: "Spite you? This isn't about you! Which means when I get out there I expect you to have my back!"

He straightens, squinting. "You think I wouldn't?"

I brush past him without answering.

Downstairs, I quickly change, tie back my hair. It's grown over the last six months, past my shoulders again.

Down four more flights of stairs, I push through the infirmary door, stride to Julie's bay, and pull aside the curtain. Find Rima hooking up Julie's IV to a fresh bag of fluids, Lauren asleep in the neighboring bed with Truly.

"Door's open," I say, out of breath.

Rima looks from me to the entrance I just came through in confusion.

"What does she need?" I ask. "The medicine we don't have. What does Julie need?"

"What do you mean, 'open'?" Rima says.

"The silo door malfunctioned—or something. It opened early."

Rima's expression goes from shocked relief and the first smile I've seen from her in weeks—to fear. "Did you see Noah? Did you find out what—"

"No. We're going up to look. What does she need?" I nod at Julie.

"IV antibiotics," Rima says. "Piperacillin-tazobactam or vancomycin . . . Possibly aztreonam and daptomycin." She pulls a pad and pen from her pocket and writes swiftly. "In these two combinations if you can. It'll be a powder."

"How much do we need?"

"As much as you can get." She tears off the sheet and hands it to me.

"Keep an eye on the girls?" I ask.

"Of course," she says.

And then I'm flying up the stairs.

3 A.M.

By the time I return, the air in the atrium has noticeably changed. It's more humid. Downright balmy. Especially near the stairwell.

Karam and I don surgical masks and gloves hastily colored with a black marker by Delaney, who fastens a holster—another find from Jax's trove of gear—around my thigh. The latex feels alien on my fingers as I tug down the navy blue stocking cap given to me by Sabine and slip a penlight into my pocket. Snap the magazine in my pistol as Karam press checks his.

Chase and Ezra wait near the stairwell with some kind of tripod structure as Irwin wraps black tape over the illuminated displays of two walkie-talkies.

"I set the VOX to its most sensitive level," Irwin says. "But you may still need to press the button to speak," he says, showing us the round button on front. "Push to talk—the entire time you're talking. Remember: when you're talking, no one else can."

He hangs the clip from the waist of my jeans and fits me with a headset, twisting the bud into my right ear.

"Testing," Chase says, and Karam gives him a thumbs-up. He

repeats the word more quietly, again and again until Karam shakes his head. "That's the level," he says and turns toward me. "Your voice is softer. Use the button every time. Stop at the bottom of the last flight until I tell you to go."

He hefts Jax's rifle off the pool table as Ezra grabs the tripod.

And then Chase leads us up the stairs.

I reach for Ezra's shoulder ahead of me as the light from below disappears, pistol in my other hand. Karam, at my side, clasps me by the elbow. The last thing I see is the sheen of sweat on his forehead.

On the final landing, I sense more than see Chase raise the rifle in the dark. Hear his and Ezra's methodical steps up the metal stairs. Ezra spraying the hinges. The soft groan of the heavy vault door and then . . .

Crickets and cicadas in full symphony. A sound so beautiful I want to weep.

I can just make out Chase crouched against the dark sky, pivoting in as wide an arc as the cement frame will allow. Tapping Ezra, who raises his gun.

The next instant, they're out, dissolving into the darkness.

I can smell the night. Practically taste the humidity. A firefly glows into a single pinpoint of light, disappears, and seems to reappear in two places at once.

There's another scent, too, though I can't quite put my finger on it.

Soft static in my ear. "Antenna is up," Ezra says.

"I hear you loud and clear." Irwin.

And then silence.

Karam and I wait on the stair.

I count to 60, to 120.

360.

I wonder where the moon is, the stars. Search for Ursa Major, trying to orient myself.

Hiss of static. "Farmhouse is dark," Chase says quietly.

That short sentence ratchets my pulse against my eardrum.

I tell myself of course it's dark. It's the middle of the night.

Chase's voice comes through again: "Shed's intact."

A minute later: "No one at the gate. No sign of patrol."

His last sentence unnerves me the most. There were four men in two trucks patrolling the section last December, and others stationed around the perimeter fence.

Where is everybody?

"We're coming back."

A few seconds later Chase and Ezra reappear just beyond the door.

"Ezra," Chase says without lifting his head from the stock of the rifle.

"In place," Ezra says.

"Karam."

He moves ahead of me, crouching four steps from the top.

"Yup."

"Wynter?"

I touch the button on the walkie-talkie. "Ready."

I chamber a round. Take the stairs on the balls of my feet.

Step out onto an uneven surface, the humidity instantly clinging to my clothes, my skin.

The smell hits me then.

Ash. Like a dank hearth.

Twenty feet to my right, a pile of rubble hulks in the darkness.

What happened here?

I crouch beside Chase on wooden debris.

Thumb off the safety.

The Quonset building sits between the barn—or what's left of it—and the farmhouse, and even from here I can see that the sliding metal door is open, the interior dark.

We keep to the grass along the gravel drive. Forty yards out, Chase crouches, scope trained on the building. Gesturing for me to wait, he moves to the side of the entrance.

A beat, and he steps inside.

My heart trips in my chest as I wait.

"Anything?" Karam asks.

"Place has been cleared out," Chase says.

He emerges from the darkness.

"Fog coming in," he murmurs. "Another twenty minutes and I'm not going to have clear sight of the road."

Hiss of static. "Wait till dawn?" Ezra inquires.

I touch the button. "No. We go now."

"We're going," Chase says. And then turns to me and whispers, "Stay with me."

I lay a hand on his shoulder. A second later, we're moving toward a giant locust tree in the direction of the farmhouse. It's the closest I've been to him in months, even in training, and the sense of him, so familiar, triggers sadness in me.

Followed by anger, my new old friend.

A furious flapping in the grass somewhere to my right sends me skittering back. I raise the pistol as Chase snaps around. The sound stops. Comes again.

"Just heard something," Ezra says.

"Injured bird," Chase says.

"You see it?"

"Looking at it right now."

We reach the north side of the house, turn our backs against the brick. He gestures toward the east side and I nod in agreement, not wanting to hazard the wooden porch.

We duck beneath a set of windows to the corner. Chase rounds it, rifle raised. Sweeps the scope back across the yard where a set of solar path lights ought to be glowing. And then I'm following him, low, toward the back door where we stop just short of its frame.

It's ajar.

Chase slings the rifle over his shoulder and draws his pistol. Reaching across, he pushes the door open and pivots into the entrance. A beat, and he moves into the house.

I wait, heart slamming in my ears. Anticipating raised voices, a shot. Gunfire.

Because I'm certain by now anyone we run into here won't be Noah.

"House is clear," Chase says.

I step inside the mudroom past an open closet. An old washer and dryer. There's garbage strewn on the floor.

Chase comes back, closes the door behind me as I thumb the safety on the pistol and holster it.

"Won't lock," he murmurs.

I move to the windows, draw every shade I find as Chase goes to check the front door. A moment later, he's got his cell phone out, the screen turned down to a dull glow. He holds it up.

"Anything?" I murmur.

"Nothing. Could just mean the tower's not working."

I take out the penlight, move through the living room into the bedroom, beam trained on the floor. Close the curtains.

Scan the room.

The bed is rumpled. No, it's filthy—covered in garbage. Open cans, plastic bags. A syringe or two.

I move into the bathroom, which has no window. Try the light switch.

Nothing.

I check the medicine cabinets, the cupboards. Find a pair of nail clippers and some empty pill bottles.

It's been cleaned out of anything useful.

Back in the bedroom I search the open drawers of the dresser. Find a dead mouse.

Static in my ear. "Found the office," Chase says. "Downstairs."

I retrace my way through the living room to the kitchen, take the stairs just past the pantry down to the basement. Find Chase shining his flashlight inside the open door of a room set back in a bay so that when the metal door is shut, it's flush with the concrete wall.

"Looks like a converted storm shelter," he says when I peer inside. A bank of security monitors occupies the south wall over a panel of master switches, gauges, and indicators. All of them dark except one, shining like a red eye in the darkness. I recognize the clock on the opposite wall from Noah's video comms.

Chase steps over a mass of tangled cords spilled—or yanked—from the open cabinet beneath the control panel like the intestines of an eviscerated creature, shards of what sounds like glass crunching beneath his feet. He sweeps his flashlight over the single live indicator. Unlike the other items on the panel, it isn't marked; the label's been torn away.

"The light's on," he says. "There's just no one to see it."

Outside the office, I shine the beam of my flashlight down the length of the subterranean chamber and stare. To call it a basement is an understatement. It stretches so far I can't see the other end. But that isn't what has my attention.

The space is filled with row after row of metal storage shelves. All littered with boxes, rubber totes, and their lids.

I stride to the closest unit, grab a tote, and slide it toward me. It's empty. I sweep down the row past empty plastic bags, turn over a box filled with packing peanuts. Scan the shelf below it.

"What are we searching for?" Chase says, moving to the next unit.

"IV antibiotics."

I fumble through a container of eyeglasses. Shine my light on the bin beside it, turn it around.

INSECT REPELLANT

"They're labeled," I say.

"Kids' shoes . . . Baby clothes . . ." A minute later, Chase says, "Here! Medical supplies."

I hurry over, seize the nearest bin. GAUZE. It's empty. I move on and find sutures, surgical glue, bandages—their labels, at least, if not the items themselves.

We finally locate the medicines. Pull each tote off the shelf to peer inside.

ASPIRIN. COUGH SYRUP. PENICILLIN.

Empty.

Every single one.

Not that it would matter, because there isn't one for IV antibiotics.

Static, and then: "Guys, there's something out here."

Karam. I'd forgotten about him and Ezra, guarding the entrance to the silo.

"Something or someone?" Chase says.

"Not sure. I just heard something running toward the trees."

I fumble around in a last, desperate bid, tearing bins from the shelves before kicking them out of my way.

"Wynter."

I turn to find Chase's flashlight trained on a break in the wall. No, a passage. "I bet that leads to the bunker in the shed."

It was a charmed place to me once, the veritable underground hotel of buried shipping container rooms outfitted in kitschy furniture and antiques. Magical not only for its gravity-assisted showers on the ground floor but for the single night we spent together there.

I push the memory away and start off, but he catches me by the arm, his eyes on that dark opening. And I realize that anyone in the house when Chase first came in could have escaped down here.

My nape prickles, and this time I move toward him, glancing over my shoulder as he covers our retreat, pistol drawn.

Upstairs, we turn off the flashlights, the darkness instantly stifling, the house I once found so welcoming ominous for its emptiness and unknown corridors. Chase holsters the pistol and unslings the rifle. Moving to a back window, he lifts the rifle and nudges aside the shade with the muzzle. Peers through the scope at the shed less than fifty yards away.

"What is it?" I whisper.

"Door's cracked open. Can't tell if there's anything moving inside it through this fog."

"Which door?" Ezra.

"Shed. We're coming out the front."

I look around the kitchen in the darkness with a sense of desperate frustration. Where's Noah? What's happened here? Where did everyone go?

Just then a sound issues up the stairs beyond the pantry. An echo from the basement, like wind howling through a loose-fitting window.

Or a croon.

The hair stands up on my arms.

"What the—" I pull my pistol and move backward into the living room.

"Time to go," Chase says, positioning himself on the other side of the door.

Pistol trained on the opening to the kitchen with one hand, I reach for the knob with the other. Unlock it.

"One. Two . . ."

I yank it toward me, hidden behind it. Chase moves out onto the porch, rifle raised.

"All clear," he says. "Let's go."

We hurry down the steps into the milky haze suspended in mid-air. Blunting sound.

We've made it fewer than twenty yards when Chase stops and turns, rifle pointed toward the corner of the house.

"Chase."

"Go!" He pivots toward the front porch.

And then I understand: anyone following us from the direction of the shed will come around that corner. Unless they come up through the house and out the front door.

I run for the locust tree. Am almost there when I hear something beyond it, shuffling along the ground. At first I think it's that bird.

Until it growls.

I freeze. Pistol trained in front of me. Looking for eyes, but in the absence of light there is no glint. Belatedly realizing I left my penlight in the basement.

The sound again, a coughing snarl.

"Chase," I say, as loudly as I dare so the VOX picks it up, not wanting to take a hand from my gun. "There's something—"

Flurry of movement, coming right at me. "Chase—"

"Wynter, drop!"

I don't question. My knees buckle, finger off the trigger as I fall flat to the ground.

A shot rings out, whizzes overhead. Punches into something.

A terrible flurry of scratching and clicking teeth. A clod of damp earth smacks me on the cheek.

And then silence.

"Get up," Chase says. He's running. "Go! I'm right behind you. Ezra, we're coming in!"

I claw to my feet and launch myself forward. Sprint for the concrete ramp rising from the earth to frame the silo door.

"Ezra," I pant.

"I see you."

And now I see him, too, moving away from the entrance enough to let me pass.

I stumble over a broken board and land heavily on the metal grate, the sound reverberating down the concrete well as Karam grabs me in the inky blackness before I can tumble down the stairs.

Ten seconds later, Chase and Ezra pull the door shut and I wish we could lock it behind us.

"Noah's gone," I say, breathing hard. "Everyone's gone."

"How far does the sound of a rifle shot travel?" Ezra asks.

"Not sure," Chase says. "But if anyone nearby didn't know we were here before, they do now."

5 A.M.

By the time we reemerge, fog has settled like a fine shroud around the ranch known as the old Peterson place, granting it an eerie, in-between feel. In but not quite of this world. Caught in a twilight before dawn that feels like the one before night.

Far too quiet. As though the air itself is listening.

For a minute it actually feels and looks like the New Earth Magnus preached about. Primordial and charged with newborn electricity.

Until I take in the splintered boards beneath my next step. The great heap of rubble that used to be the barn.

Ezra, Karam, Micah, and I move out in careful silence, determined to learn what happened to the others. To take stock of our surroundings, assess threats and options.

Nelise and Delaney guard the silo entrance. I gesture Micah to wait where they can cover him. He's the only one of us not armed, having claimed he'd be more of a liability than an asset with a gun in his hands.

Chase, crouched on the top of the concrete ramp above the doorframe, squints through the scope toward the house and then lowers the rifle with a curse. I know he's anxious to learn who—if anyone—was out here earlier. But night vision doesn't help in fog.

Static. "You see this?" Ezra murmurs in my ear and I wonder who he's talking to.

I move around the heap, impatient to get going. Because I need to know what's in the bunkhouse beneath the shed. Have promised myself that I will figure something out today. That I will get Julie what she needs by this afternoon—nightfall, latest.

I find Ezra and Karam staring at the pile, a piece of twisted shrapnel in Karam's hands.

When I follow their gazes, I stare, too.

At the mass of mangled white-and-red metal protruding from the debris. It's burned black in some spots. Crumpled like a cheaply made toy crushed by an angry child. A buckled roof collapsed over a rounded nose.

No, not a roof. Wings.

The wreckage of a plane.

"Looks like an old Cessna Agwagon," Ezra says. "Used for crop dusting."

"Wonder what this is about," Karam says, kicking the corpse of a turkey vulture. The instant he does, it flutters, sending him skittering back.

"What the—"

It goes still. The next time he nudges it, it doesn't move.

"Look," he says, pointing around us.

There are three more like it littering this side of the heap.

Ezra climbs up onto the wreckage.

"At least we know what happened to the barn," Karam says.

"I'm guessing the pilot was sick," Ezra says. "Judging by the fire, he wasn't out of fuel."

Static, and then: "There a body?" Chase.

Ezra shines his flashlight into the cockpit, the door of which is hanging open. "Well, there was at some point. Can still see blood in some places. Whatever happened, the body's gone now."

I touch the button on the walkie-talkie, though Ezra's only ten feet away. "Remember what I said about surgical instruments. If that pilot was sick and you cut yourself through your gloves . . ."

"Roger," Ezra says, moving to jump back down. But as he does, he slips. Grabbing the edge of the cockpit door, he skids out onto the stub of an amputated wing and regains his balance. For a nervous moment, he studies his latex-gloved hands. No one bothered to color them black in anticipation of sunrise. With a grin, he holds them up to show the gloves intact.

"Clear back there?" Chase.

"Clear," I say. "We're coming back."

I've barely got the last word out when Ezra drops down to the ground. A beat later, he screams.

Ezra pitches forward, hands over his mouth. Karam and I run toward him at once.

"Who's that?" Chase demands. "What just happened?"

Ezra rolls onto his back, grabbing his foot and wincing in agony. The toe of his sneaker flops to the side, shorn almost completely off.

Along with his toes.

I turn away, arm across my face.

"Ezra stepped on a metal shard," Karam says. "Oh, yup. It's bad. I'm bringing him back. Irwin, send for Rima."

I help haul Ezra to his good foot. Slide a shoulder beneath his arm and look fixedly away as Karam pans the debris at our feet and then swiftly collects several objects and drops them in Ezra's pocket.

Chase curses. "When the sun comes up and this fog clears, we have no cover between us and whatever's out here."

"I'll go," Delaney says.

We get to the entrance. Ezra grabs the concrete frame. The instant he's hopping past Nelise onto the landing, Delaney emerges, gun pointed toward the ground. And then Micah, Karam, Chase, and I are moving toward the house, Delaney covering our backs.

Just past the locust tree, Chase stops. Rifle over his shoulder, he circles back, scanning the ground, pistol naked in his hand.

And I know he's looking for the animal he shot.

"It should be right here," I murmur. The grass is bent every which direction and I remember the clatter of the animal's teeth, the convulsive spasm as it died.

But there's no sign of it.

Chase shakes his head. "Must have crawled off and died somewhere else."

We cross slowly toward the northeast corner of the house, the fog tinged incrementally lighter than before, grass dampening the hems of our jeans. From here, I can see the pallid metal of the shed. There's a dark truck parked at an odd angle just to the right of it, missing its front wheels.

We circle wide to the long side of the shed, having rehearsed this—on paper at least—an hour earlier. For a minute I have the strange sensation that I'm swimming rather than skulking through the fog. It's fatigue, I know. But I can't shake the thought that Chase, Micah, and Karam look like specters. And that it feels like premonition.

I don't want to be here. Don't want to go into that shed or see the state of those bunkers. And I don't want Truly, Lauren, or Julie near them, either.

I touch the button on the walkie-talkie. "Chase, did you see any vehicles earlier?" I whisper.

"A UTV near the gate. I assume it doesn't work or they'd have taken it."

"Let's go look. Maybe it just needs fuel." Which we have. "Or one of you can fix it. Maybe we can get it working, take Julie into town."

Karam glances at me.

"And what? Leave the rest of us like sitting ducks?" he demands.

"I'm talking about saving a life!"

Chase gestures us angrily toward a windbreak.

"Look," he says, as soon as we've retreated behind a line of spruces. "We have to secure the bunkhouse and basement. Then we figure out how to get Julie the help she needs."

"You don't need me for this!" I hiss as Micah glances nervously around.

"The whole point of you being here is that you're immune," Karam says, eyes narrowed. "You volunteered to go in!"

"'Scuse me," someone cuts in. Nelise. I'd forgotten she was on the frequency. "Ezra passed out. And I'm guarding the entrance and everyone below by myself right now. Wynter, I'm sorry to say that if Julie can't wait another few hours, she ain't gonna make it anyway."

I lower my head, calculating the direction of the fence. Where the UTV might be. But finding it won't be enough if it needs gas from the silo's storeroom. And I'll need help getting Julie topside and into the vehicle, as well as someone to hold on to her while I drive.

"The minute the ranch is secure, we find the UTV and do whatever it takes to get it working," I say, looking from Chase to Karam, and then Micah. "If Julie dies and you didn't do everything you possibly could, it's on your heads."

"Agreed," Micah says. Karam doesn't respond. Whatever he's thinking, he doesn't say.

By the time we cross to the front of the shed, the sky is the color of new denim. Fog to the east tinged an uncanny shade of red. The color of blood in water, which does nothing to settle my unease.

So eerily quiet.

Chase pulls a flashlight from his belt and nods to Karam. The next instant they're pushing their way inside the shed in a rush of motion.

"Anything?" Chase.

A moment later: "Nope."

"Clear here."

"Clear."

I gesture Micah in ahead of me, pistol drawn. Step in after him and grab the edge of the door. The instant Delaney's through I lean my weight into sliding it shut, wheels screeching along the track. It closes and Delaney turns the latch handle, driving the bolt into the concrete floor. Unlike most sheds, which are meant to keep things inside, this one is also meant to keep others out.

Micah turns on the lantern, holds it up.

The interior tells a story similar to that of the basement: the far shelves, once stocked with white plastic buckets, are empty. The tubs of hygiene supplies and towels that lined the adjacent wall sit askew or tumbled onto the ground.

I find the bank of light switches, which should work; the fixtures in the shed are solar. I try them all. Nothing.

Moving to the tubs, I peer in each one. Like the bins in the basement, they're empty except for garbage: a few MRE containers, cans that once contained food. Tuna, by the smell of it. I cover my nose. Kick the last tub over.

A hiss sounds from the corner, followed by a rhythmic growl.

"What's that?" Micah says, stumbling back.

I grab the lantern and shine it toward the opossum.

I saw plenty in the Enclave—along with the requisite mice and occasional raccoon. The last few weeks I was there, I spent hours wondering how they got in. Wondering if I could follow the same way out.

Karam's studying a door that, by all appearances, leads to a side room. It reminds me of the wooden one in the barn that obscured the silo entrance.

"Ready?" he asks.

Chase raises his pistol, braced against the hand holding the flashlight, rifle slung over his shoulder. "Let's go."

Karam gives the silent count, hand on the door handle.

Throws it open.

And then he's following Chase down a set of plywood stairs.

A moment later Chase gives the all clear. I descend behind Micah and his lantern as Delaney closes the door behind us and locks it.

The motion-sensor light in the stairwell sputters on and then fades with the last of its battery. Down the hallway a second one flicks off and back on as Chase disappears into and steps back out of one of the shipping container rooms. Looking at the sliding doors to my left, I can't help but remember the night Chase and I spent here.

I push the thought aside as I take the lantern from Micah, enter the room to my right, and begin searching the open drawers of the antique dresser. I look under the bed and inside the pocket door closet at the far end of the room. Find nothing but garbage, a discarded Rolling Stones T-shirt, a toothbrush, an issue of *People* magazine. Relics of lives abandoned and forgotten. Squalor compared to the luxury of our laundry, clean facilities, kitchen, and library.

Each room tells a different tale: from sweat stains on the mattresses to the MRE wrappers in the back corner of the closet to the old traveling trunk I remember from before. It had been filled with toys. There's a blanket in it now, giving it a manger-like appearance.

"Anything?" Micah says from the hallway outside the fourth room, the others—including Chase—not daring to touch the objects down here.

Someone—a little girl, I imagine—left a broken butterfly necklace beside the bed. I pick it up, consider giving it to Truly. But then
notice the purple Sharpie on the floor, the array of butterflies drawn
on the corrugated metal wall beside the headboard. I return the
necklace to the nightstand, the tarnished chain pooling beneath the
upturned charm.

"No," I say. No clues to where they went. Or why. Only who they
once were.

In the last room—a larger family suite made of two containers
side by side—I find a tear-off calendar like the one Julie's husband,
Ken, used to have on his desk with a Far Side cartoon for every day
of the year.

I carry it out to the hallway. "Look at this. The last day is March
twenty-first." Beneath the date it says, in bright, whimsical art,
"Today Is Going to Be a Great Day!"

I wonder why it was left behind—unless whoever owned it just
got sick of being lied to.

"Some of the food wrappers in the shed seem a lot more recent
than that," Chase says, stationed at the far end of the hall, gun and
flashlight both trained around a corner I never knew existed.

"I used to have one of those calendars." Micah shrugs. "And I'd
forget to tear the pages off for weeks at a time."

"People who live in community would never leave a place in
this condition," I say. "Not if they actually worked in it to survive the
unthinkable and respected their leader."

I should know.

"So the most recent inhabitants were squatters." Karam.

Noah's been gone for months.

5:30 A.M.

There's a narrow turn just off the end of the hallway that I do not remember from before. Not that we did more than explore the rooms themselves, enthralled with their knickknacks and antique, mismatched furniture, the shipping containers cut open and laid side by side to form two double-wide suites at the end. As we get closer, I see what looks like a dark bookcase, labels fixed to the front of the shelves: TWIN SHEETS, PILLOWCASES, FULL SHEETS, EXTRA BLANKETS.

Chase shines his flashlight at the floor. It's scratched where the case has been moved.

"Never realized Noah was this paranoid," Delaney murmurs.

"It's not paranoid. It's smart." Karam.

We move single file through the passage, which feels more like a concrete channel. West, toward the house, and emerge in the exact spot Chase pointed out earlier this morning.

"Place looks ransacked," Delaney says as we navigate the chaos of toppled rubber totes.

Part of the mess is mine.

Inside the office, Micah tries several switches. When nothing happens, he pulls a folding knife from his back pocket and snicks the zip tie around the bundled cords. After searching for several seconds, he pulls out one in particular. Follows it toward the wall.

The end of it comes away in his hand.

It's been cleanly severed.

"What is that?" I ask.

"The communications feed from the silo. The reason our messages weren't received."

"Who would do that?" I say.

He traces the sticky backing of the missing label beneath the red indicator. The only live thing on the panel.

"Noah," he says quietly.

"*What?*" Nelise, in my ear, and I both say at once. Karam just looks at him like he's talking gibberish.

"Obviously he left. Everyone left," Micah says.

"They abandoned us," Delaney says from her post outside the office.

"I don't think so." Chase.

"I don't, either." Micah.

"You think someone forced them out," I say.

"Maybe," he says. But his frown says no. And then he's searching the console, pulling down security screens, tugging components from the cabinet above. They dangle from cords like bungee jumpers, a few of them falling onto the control panel with a clang before crashing to the concrete floor.

"What are you looking for?"

"Guys." Delaney.

"The security footage drive." Micah.

"Guys, I thought I just heard something."

"Something like what?" Chase says, stepping out.

Across the room, Micah's murmuring to himself, saying something ought to be here. It comes through on the VOX, hogging the channel.

"Micah, shut up," Chase says.

I grab Micah's arm. Hold a finger to my lips. When he doesn't stop, I grab his walkie-talkie, yank the cord from it.

Chase: "You hear it again?"

Silence.

"No—wait . . ." Delaney says. "No. It's gone."

"Let's go," I say. And then, when he doesn't move: "Micah."

He doesn't answer, searching frantically, yanking down anything within reach.

"What's that?" Karam says, pointing. I follow the line of his finger to the cabinet, which is mostly bare thanks to Micah. There's a black splotch against the back wall, darker toward the corner, as though emanating from the point where the cords were fed through it. At first glance, it looks like black mold spreading across the Formica.

No, it's not mold. It's singed.

"I think we know what happened to Noah's video feed," Chase says.

Once, when I was thirteen, lightning struck the Enclave's laundry. It left a char like that—in addition to a black hole in the corner of one of the dryers.

"He knew we were coming," Micah says. "That we'd need answers. Instructions. How to find him after—"

"Micah, it was lightning," I say.

"Yes, I know!" he snaps, gesturing with one hand toward the fuse box set in the adjacent wall. Now, in the light of the lantern, I see the umbra around its edges. "The feed might have fried, but the strike should have triggered a backup system for the security monitors . . ."

He stops. Looks around. Steps back and takes in the cords snaking across the floor, and then feels along the underside of the panel. Pauses. And then slides out a black component that looks a lot like the cable box in Julie's living room.

At the thought of her my pulse spikes.

"We good?" Chase asks. This time Micah nods, cradling the box in his hands as Karam reconnects his earpiece.

Upstairs, the kitchen looks even more abandoned in dawn's diffused light. The plates on the counter picked clean by unseen rodents, the cupboards open, pots spilling from one, the door hanging off its hinges.

Micah, Delaney, and I crouch at the top of the stairs, waiting for the all clear. A breeze stirs the tendrils at my nape, and now I remember leaving the front door open as we ran out through it earlier this morning.

A snuffling flap issues from the direction of the porch just as Karam follows Chase around the frame of the arch into the living room.

"Who's there?" Chase shouts.

"Don't you move!" Karam yells in reply.

I push Micah against the wall. Feel, more than see, Delaney tug him down a step toward her as Chase passes through my line of vision.

A split second later I hear his heel find the porch, his arrival greeted by a low, snapping growl.

"What's happening?" Nelise.

A shot cracks the air.

Karam runs out after him.

When no answer comes, at first I wonder if Chase didn't fire the shot, but took it instead.

I try to school my breath. Force myself to stay put, where I've launched forward onto one hand, ready to sprint like a runner. The pistol in my other hand.

The silence is terrible.

"Chase," I say, loud enough not to have to push the button, my voice hoarse. And then: "Karam!"

"Was that one of you?" Nelise. "We heard a shot!"

I launch forward. Am across the kitchen when static hisses in my ear.

"That was us." Chase. He walks back inside. "Some kind of co—"

He turns as I come through the arch. Holds out a hand, trying to ward me off.

Too late.

I see it. Not the thing on the porch, but the figure on the couch.

Flesh rotting away from the bones, the skull picked clean of all but gristle.

I stifle a scream, raise my forearm to my nose.

"Some kind of what?" Nelise says.

"Coyote," he says, as Karam comes in and strides off toward the bedrooms, pistol raised. "By the way, I think we found the pilot."

"Clear," Karam says, reemerging from the back.

Micah and Delaney appear at my side.

"Oh, my God," Delaney says, turning away. An instant later I hear her retching in the kitchen as Micah turns up the lantern and moves toward the sofa.

It's far worse in the light, blackened and charred, tendons like jerky.

It's the head, though, that's the worst. The back half of the skull is missing.

As horrific as the corpse is, far more unnerving is the fact that I know it wasn't here two hours ago.

"What is that?" Karam says, pointing.

There's something metallic blue and slender protruding from one of the sockets where an eye should be.

My penlight.

5:45 A.M.

The fog is burning off with the sunrise by the time we emerge from the house to find the UTV gone.

Before I can turn on Chase, say this is his fault—that we should have gone for the UTV when we had the chance—I notice the dead coyote in the driveway. Or more specifically, the crow twitching in its mouth.

Another spasms on the gravel nearby, coated with a fine layer of gray dust.

"What's wrong with all the birds?" Delaney says.

I glance up in time to watch a turkey vulture circle in the distance.

"The pilot was sick," I hear myself say.

Her brows lift as though to say, *So?*

I look from her to Chase. "The pilot was sick. The birds have been picking at the corpse's brains since the fire went out."

His eyes widen. "They're infected."

"And so is anything that eats them."

"Guys?" Delaney says, staring past us. She points to the farmhouse door.

It's marked with a red spray-painted *X* and a single dire message:

10 DEAD

7 A.M.

It takes an hour to secure the ranch. To track the path of the plane through the solar field before it crashed into the barn. Search for graves—and come up empty-handed. Find the gaping hole in a section of chain-link fence large enough to drive a small vehicle through. Dispatch Irwin and Preston to repair it, and debrief the others, who have more questions than we have answers for.

Was there any electricity? Did we get a cell signal?

Where did the others go? Was Noah with them? Why didn't he leave a note?

"We don't know," Micah says. "I'm hoping the security footage can give us some answers."

"Obviously Noah left because the pilot took out the solar field," Ivy says.

Chase shakes his head. "The crash had to happen after. No way Noah would've left an infected corpse right outside the silo entrance."

"Maybe the power lines just need repair and they're too short-staffed. There has to be power in the cities. It's been six months! And what about the vaccines?" Rudy says, looking for all the world like a disgruntled shopper at a customer service counter.

"We're running out of food, we don't know anything, and now you're saying the animals are infected?" Sabine says, sounding like she might be on the brink of a nervous breakdown. "What are we supposed to do? We can't stay here!"

"I'm going to town," I say.

"What are you going to do? Walk?" Ivy says.

"Yes," I say. "Gurley's a few miles from here. I should be able to get news, find out what our options are for supplies."

I feel Chase's gaze but don't turn to meet it.

"Until then, you have water, enough food. Assign guards, set up a patrol. Bury the dead."

"What if something happens to you and we're just here waiting?" Rudy says.

"The walkie-talkies have a thirty-mile range. You'll know as soon as I do what I find. Till then, I need food, fuel—anything I can trade."

"We'll get you set up," Irwin says.

Downstairs, I shove a change of clothes and a bottle of hand sanitizer into a backpack. Go out into the women's dorm and rifle through the bin of Julie's scant belongings. Pocket a few of the Excedrin from the bottle she keeps for migraines. Pause upon finding a photo of Ken standing on a sandy beach that I recognize as the Indiana Dunes, where they took me last fall when I was in the throes of obsessive panic, waiting for my meds to kick in.

I find her wallet. Feel a little guilty rifling through it even as I help myself to all of the cash inside—a stack of hundreds and a few twenties—as well as her credit cards.

It's a strange concept, money. Until eight months ago, I'd

never bought anything for myself. Never had any money of my own. Never even touched it except when selling packets of heirloom seeds and tomato seedlings at the New Earth farmers' market stall.

I waver on the stairs on my way to the infirmary. My feet ache, and I feel vaguely like I'm swimming as I realize it's been well over twenty-four hours since I last slept.

Nothing to do about that; I won't be getting any rest soon.

Rima rises from her desk at my arrival, moving so swiftly to intercept me that I think she's about to tell me something I don't want to hear. I stop, the heat leaving my limbs.

Instead, she raises a finger to her lips.

"The girls are still asleep," she whispers.

I nod, move toward her, knees like water. Ezra's asleep in a bay across the room, his foot bandaged and elevated.

"How is she?"

"The same. What did you find?" she asks. "Is Noah there? Is the electric—"

I shake my head. "No. There's nothing. I'm going to town for news and to get Julie the medicine she needs."

"Be careful," she says, her eyes, so large normally, widening.

"I will." I grab her hands. "But I need you to watch the girls until I get back."

"Of course," she says, squeezing my fingers.

"Thank you," I say, pulling away, feeling if I let her reassure me any more I'll break down right here.

I stride on silent feet to the bed where the girls are sleeping. Drink in the sight of them both. Smooth a tendril of hair from each of their faces before bending to kiss the top of Truly's head.

Stepping out, I quietly pull the curtain closed.

"What do you want me to tell them?" Rima asks.

"Tell them I went to town to get Julie's medicine. And that I'll be back as soon as I can."

I've just crossed to the stairwell door when a voice sounds from across the room.

"Wynter. Don't."

I turn. Lauren is standing barefoot outside the curtain.

She rushes toward me, throws her arms around my shoulders.

"Please don't go!" She starts sobbing.

"Lauren, I have to," I say, stroking her hair, baffled by this reaction. "Your mom is really sick."

"Let someone else go!" she says, clutching at me.

"I wish I could."

She pulls back and stares at me. "It won't matter."

"What do you mean?"

"She's dead anyway!" she sputters on tears and snot.

"Don't say that!"

"It's true. I've heard them talking. She isn't going to make it!"

I take her by the shoulders. "Yes. She. Will."

"How do you know?" she squeaks, her eyes begging for an answer I know I cannot give.

"Because she's tougher than you think."

"What if she isn't and you don't come back?" Her voice goes up an octave into a tight keen. "Who's going to take care of us?"

"Lauren." I hold her away from me so I can look her in the eye. "I'll be on a walkie-talkie. Someone will always be able to tell you what I'm doing and where I am and when I'm on my way back. I promise I *will* come back."

I hug her tightly to me. Hear myself tell her to take care of Truly and listen to Rima. And then I'm kissing her forehead and tearing myself away.

Only when I'm alone in the stairwell do I double over, my hands shaking. Sweat rolling down my ribs beneath my clothes.

8 A.M.

In the kitchen I help myself to as many MREs as will fit in my pack. Fill two bottles with water. Leave a note of what I took for Delaney, who, like Nelise, is crashed out in her bunk.

Irwin meets me in the atrium, where Chase is stashing a container of fuel in a rolling suitcase, effectively disguising it. As he zips it closed, I reach for the handle, but he doesn't hand it over.

And then I notice the bag over his shoulder. The black watch on his wrist. The headset over his ear.

"I'm going with you," he says.

"No," I say.

"I go with you or I can just stalk you. Either way, I'm going."

"These are fresh off the charger," Irwin says, hooking a walkie-talkie to my belt and handing me the headset to loop over my ear. "Should last eight hours at least. Twelve at the very most. After that, you'll have to find batteries."

If I don't find the medicine Julie needs in twelve hours, it won't matter anyway.

Karam comes to see us off, shadows beneath his eyes. "I wanted to come with you," he says, looking from Chase to me. "But it's going to take at least ten of us to patrol this place, and I can't leave my mother." He reaches in his back pocket, takes out a filtration straw, and hands it to me.

"Thanks," I say, stashing it in the side zipper of my pack.

He looks as though he'd like to say more but then, with a glance at Chase, simply nods. "Be safe."

Ten seconds later we're ascending the stairs to the door, where we're let out by Sha'Neal.

The sun's up, glinting off dew on the overgrown grass. Preston meets us at the hole in the fence. It's been mostly repaired, enough of a space left open to admit a person at a time.

"We haven't found the keys to the gate," he says, holding the chain link aside as we duck through, and then helping Chase with the suitcase. "Or any keys, for that matter."

Straightening, I take in the stretch of county road before us.

It's been six months since I stepped foot outside this ranch. Since my two-and-a-half-month visit to the outside world I'd been taught to regard as evil.

For a minute, the earth tilts beneath me.

"You okay?" Chase says, grabbing my arm. I jerk away.

"Fine," I say and start walking. A moment later I hear the wheels of the suitcase drag along the gravel behind me.

The sun is arcing up into the eastern sky on a cool June morning. The birds are singing. Just not the same song as before.

Nothing is the same.

"She dumped me for a doctor," Chase says.

I glance sidelong at him.

"My fiancée. Former fiancée. She dumped me for a doctor. She wanted a different life than what I could give her. She worked in pharmaceutical sales. He'd been trying to get with her for years. Held out hope that entire time. I thought he was an idiot for marrying someone obviously after his money."

I walk faster. Wonder how quickly I can cover six miles with this pack on. Can hear him dragging the suitcase faster, wheels tumbling over gravel.

"I ran into her a couple years later. She was pregnant, back home to have the baby. Said he'd sold his practice to join Doctors Without Borders—they'd spent the last year living in a hut in Nepal. Thing is, she was genuinely happy. I could see it. That guy wasn't an idiot. He'd seen something for them that he couldn't give up on."

"You know, just because you're coming with me doesn't mean we have to talk."

"Yes, we do. Because I need you to know that I would have told you eventually. I just didn't have a chance—"

I spin back, instantly incensed. "You didn't have a *chance*? When exactly did you not have a chance? When we were holed up in a barn for a night during a blizzard and—oh, that's right—you threatened to *leave me* and turn me over to the police if I didn't explain the samples in my possession? You hypocritical *bastard*!"

He lifts the suitcase and jogs to my side. Sets it back down to bump along behind him. "Wynter, you have to understand: I'd been told you'd stolen a bunch of medical samples! Except things didn't add up. *You* didn't add up. I just couldn't figure out if you were really that good a con, or—"

"Or what?"

"Or as naïve as you seemed. Or just that good, period. Which is what it was. What it is. You're a good person, Wynter. And when I think about that night in the bunkhouse—"

Someone clears their throat. "Uh, you folks know you're on comm, right?"

Irwin.

Heat rushes to my cheeks and I rip off the headset as Chase curses and does the same.

I walk the next mile in angry, humiliated silence, my headset in a sweaty fist. Gaze trained toward my left shoulder, away from him, vision threatening to blur.

"Hey, look," he says a few minutes later. I glance over to find him pointing at a farmhouse. There's a black *X* spray-painted on the door. But the markings are different, letters I can't decipher on the left quadrant. A zero in the bottom one.

The words beneath it are plain enough to understand.

3 DEAD

"It's like the markings on the doors in New Orleans after Hurricane Katrina," he says. "Except I can't tell who left it."

I don't know about that hurricane. But I feel the itch of panic at the back of my brain.

The door of the next house we pass isn't even closed. Three turkey vultures are gathered over a meal on the front porch and I realize this is where I saw them circling earlier. A sign in the front yard next to an old-fashioned well spigot reads: FREE WATER. The handle is up. Nothing's coming out.

Chase loops his headset back over his ear.

"Irwin? Yeah, sorry. Hey, doesn't look like the neighbors came through this that great."

The morning silence is eerie after the hum of generators and air systems we've lived with the last six months. The humidity feels sticky, the sun too harsh in the cloudy sky. Chase pulls a pair of sunglasses from his pocket, offers them to me. I ignore him and pull a worn baseball cap from my pack. It's the same one I wore with a fake beard when I disguised myself as a man after delivering the samples, the frayed bill shielding my eyes as I sped down I-80 hell-bent on the only thing that mattered:

Getting Truly out of the Enclave.

I tug the cap on, pick up my pace.

County Road 46 turns into First Street on the edge of a town that's far too quiet. We pass a trailer home, the empty door and window frames of which are shrouded in black soot. A white house that might be a hundred years old with a black X on its front door, a zero in the bottom quadrant. A Lutheran church, doors hanging open, a single word spray-painted across the white siding in front:

INFECTED

The town—which is really a village that once housed fewer people than the enclave of five hundred I grew up in—is utterly still.

Devoid of life.

My mind is churning. I'm looking for a medical clinic or, barring that, a vehicle. But for all the abandoned vehicles along the highway and back roads six months ago, for all of the campers I saw parked in driveways of the small towns we passed through last winter, I don't see a single vehicle now.

"Where is everyone?" I say, and realize I'm whispering. I can feel my pulse ratcheting against my eardrums.

And all I can think is: *What if it's true? What if we're all that's left?*

Magnus preached about the end of mankind. The few who would inherit the Earth and populate it anew.

Stop.

Even if Magnus was right, the earth would never pass to a known apostate like me.

There must be people alive out here somewhere.

"Maybe this is a good sign," Chase says, and I realize that he's unnerved, as well. "That there's shelters or supplies—maybe even vaccines—in the cities. We need to get to Sidney."

A flash of gray skirts across a yard and clamors up a tree trunk. Tumbles out of it a second later, feline claws flailing.

Clearly not right.

We walk past a bank of grain silos, straight for town—what there is of it, anyway. It's mostly just a street with a few storefronts. A bar and grill. A repair shop with a tall false front.

The crunch of our soles, the bump and scrape of the suitcase, is too loud in the silence. So much so that I put the headset on just to know Irwin's there.

The door to the post office has been broken in. The two newspaper dispensers out front stand empty.

The breeze stirs, carrying the smell of damp earth and decay. Something flutters along the concrete ramp to the door:

A piece of dirty paper with big block letters.

"Anything?" Irwin says.

"Place is a ghost town," Chase says as I go over and pick it up.

As I do, I note several more like it matted to the sidewalk.

I smooth out the weathered page.

STAY SAFE
STAY HOME

- Keep your doors closed.

- Do not leave your house.

- Quarantine sick family members to a separate part of the house, sterilize any surfaces they might have touched, and wear protective masks and gloves at home.

- If you must leave, wear protective masks and gloves.

Last updated 03/18 12:36

I read the flyer and then glance around. But none of the houses we've passed have shown evidence of occupants in weeks, if not months.

Where is everybody?

There's a similar notice stapled to the telephone pole on the corner, though as I get closer I can see it's slightly different:

STAY SAFE
STAY HOME

DO NOT leave your home seeking supplies or vaccinations!!

Do not believe rumors that vaccines are available!

Do not buy injections from those purporting to sell vaccines!

These injections are FAKE and may harm your health.

Do not trade food, water, fuel, or other vital supplies to anyone offering to sell a vaccine, cure, or other treatment for the disease commonly referred to as rapid early-onset dementia.

When a vaccine becomes available you will receive instructions from the Department of Homeland Security. Until then, stay safe—STAY HOME.

Stay alive.

Last updated 05/01 1:27

It's been stapled on top of the torn remnants of others like the one in my hand.

And then I notice the date at the bottom.

"This was six weeks ago," I say, glancing at Chase, who frowns.

Do not believe rumors that vaccines are available . . .

But they should be by now—shouldn't they? It's been six months since the National Guard sent a helicopter to retrieve Ashley and the samples from Fort Collins. Since I watched the best hope for our nation—and the world—roar overhead as I sped down I-80 toward Iowa in disguise to retrieve Truly.

Hiss of static. "What was six weeks ago?" Irwin.

I read the flyer aloud.

"Looks like people got impatient," Chase says. "We haven't seen a vehicle since we got here."

"Maybe there was another flyer. Info on where to go for the vaccine," Irwin says.

Chase lets go of the suitcase and circles the pole, glancing up and down. But I've already looked and there's nothing newer. I walk out to the intersection, glance down the unpaved cross street past a mobile home with a sidewalk that goes straight to its stoop. The front door hangs open, crooked on its hinges, a red X spray-painted on the siding to the right of it. A MAKE AMERICA GREAT AGAIN sign in the window.

"FEMA, or the National Guard, or whoever it is can't be everywhere at once. Especially a town as tiny as Gurley. I'm guessing folks would have to go to Sidney, at least. Better yet, North Platte or Kearney. Maybe even Denver . . ."

I turn in the middle of the intersection, shielding my eyes from the sun. Walk a little ways down the street past an old concrete building. It's been boarded up as though against a storm. I take in the junk heap beside it. The open lot at the end of the block.

The grass interspersed with rows of dirt mounds. Five mounds in each, the last row unfinished with only three.

As though waiting for two more.

And then I see it—a patch of earth darker than the others. Messier, where it's been disturbed.

A low growl sounds from the direction of the junk pile, the sound amplified by the old hood of a car.

"Back away," Chase murmurs, raising his pistol.

Too late.

A black dog darts from beneath the hood and I skirt back. But before it's gone four feet it wavers and falls sideways. Flails. Gets to its feet and starts for us, something not right in the way the front legs are churning as though independent of its back.

It falls again, worming against the grass.

A sound rises up in my throat, because even though the dog's the wrong color, it reminds me of Buddy. The size I imagine him to be now. How I pictured Truly playing with him in Wyoming, splashing through river shallows this summer. Curling up with him in front of the fireplace this fall.

But that idyllic dream is gone. Julie might not live till summer. How twisted everything has become.

"Cover your ears," Chase says.

I turn away as the shot rings out.

We have to move on. But without a car, nothing will be fast enough.

I glance at the sun. It's nearly midmorning, the hours passing too quickly. I fight down a surge of panic, wondering if we're too late. If Julie's slipped away already. I need to know what's happening at the silo. Lauren and Truly have to be awake by now.

"Irwin," I say, not needing to touch the button to speak. There's no one to overhear me. "Have you seen Truly or Lauren? Can you check on Julie?"

"Hold on."

I hear him a few seconds later in conversation with someone else.

Chase points to a double garage near the mobile home. I nod and draw my pistol. He grabs the suitcase handle, pistol in his other hand. And then we're crossing the yard and circling around to a small patio attached to the back, looking for a way in.

"Ivy's checking," Irwin says, too loud in my ear.

We come to a back door. Chase checks the knob and, when it doesn't turn, peers in through the window beside it—then drops back against the siding.

"What is it?" I ask.

He shakes his head.

"What?" I move to look and he takes my arm.

But not before I see the figure dangling inside.

I shove away, hands going to my knees as my stomach rebels. The image branded into memory by my sheer will to unsee it.

What is this world we have reemerged into?

Magnus's voice, once the voice of God Himself, comes unbidden to my inner ear.

Have I not told you what is to come?

Did I not say: not in an *age, but in* this *age? I tell you today: it is here. The end is happening even now.*

Shut up.

But from what I can tell, everything Magnus said has indeed come true.

I glance at Chase, who's looking through the window at an angle—not at the body, but at something along the wall.

He tries the door and, when the knob doesn't turn, steps back and takes in the patio. The black wire table and chairs that look about as comfortable as a cheese grater. The terra-cotta planters stuck with giant plastic candy canes and a Santa on a stick.

"What are you doing?" I say, wiping my mouth on my sleeve.

Static. Irwin in my ear: "The girls are fine . . ."

I straighten at his hesitation.

"But what?" I say.

Already bracing for the next months and years of wondering what more I could have done to save her. Just as I did with my own mother.

Chase pauses, hands on the edge of a planter, his eyes on me.

When Irwin doesn't answer, I say, "Irwin! What about Julie?"

"Sorry," Irwin says. "Ivy said she's awake, but not doing well. Hey, Micah's joining us."

"Uh, hi," Micah says, having apparently donned a headset.

"Micah," Chase says, tipping up a planter and looking beneath it. "Tell us something good."

"I was able to replay the security footage," Micah says.

"What'd you find?" Chase.

I walk back out to the street, look around the tiny intersection at the only stoplight in town.

Movement catches my eye from the building across the street. My head snaps up toward a second-story window crisscrossed with iron bars.

Where a gaunt figure is pressed against the glass.

Staring down at me.

10:30 A.M.

The hair rises on the nape of my neck—and then on my arms. I pull back but am standing in the middle of the street.

Nowhere to hide.

I raise my pistol.

The figure jerks out of view.

"Micah, hold on," Chase says. "Wynter?"

The mobile home behind me is set back from the street. I could be shot before even reaching the lawn.

So I bolt for the corner of the brick building. Flatten myself against its side.

"There's someone in the building across the street," I say, breathless.

"Where are you?" Chase. "Which building?"

"Brick. Second floor. I'm on the east side."

"Uh, what's going on?" Micah.

"Micah, I'm gonna need you to shut up." Chase.

I see him a second later, crouched against the end of the mobile home.

"See him?"

"Nope. Wait." A beat, and then: "What the—"

"What's he doing?"

"Holding a sign up against the glass."

"A sign?" I peer around the corner, but can't see anything from this angle. I glance across the street, see Chase squinting against the sun.

"'I don't have weapon. Am not sick,'" Chase reads, and then snorts. "Like he isn't the first person to say that in the last six months. Wynter, get to the next house over and drop north a block. He won't see you. I've got eyes on him. Go now."

I start to move and then hesitate.

The man upstairs is the first human we've encountered since leaving the silo. Which means he's the only one who can tell us what's happened.

And how to get to the closest medical facility.

"Wynter, go!"

"What if he's telling the truth?"

"We can't take that chance." He says it like I'm out of my mind. Like he can't believe he's having to even say this.

He glances back up to the window, squints again.

"What's he doing?"

"Writing on the window."

My heart drops. Just our luck that the first person we find is as deranged as the rest. But what did I expect from someone imprisoned behind barred windows?

"Writing backward so I can read it," Chase amends. "'Please help. Almost out of food. My name is Otto.'"

I glance around front, and then slowly step out.

"Wynter, what are you doing? Get back!"

I move out onto the sidewalk, and then into the street until I can see him. A young man, maybe only a few years older than myself.

His hair long enough to tuck behind his ears. His T-shirt hangs from his shoulders.

He pauses, a red marker in hand, behind the letters awkwardly scrawled on the dirty glass.

No sign of tremors. Lucidity in his eyes.

He lifts his other hand and gives a small wave. Smiles slightly. And then mouths a single unmistakable word:

Help.

I spread my hands as though to ask why he's there. Or how to help. Let him take it as he will as Chase jogs to my side, pistol ready.

Otto shrinks back until I just see his face peering around the frame. I reach over and put a hand on Chase's gun, lowering it.

Otto steps back into the window, points toward the first floor. Then crosses his hands to form an *x*.

My eyes go to the ground floor of what was obviously once a store. The broad windows have since been boarded up, the door painted only with OWNER ARMED. DON'T TRY.

Wild gesturing from above. I glance up, where Otto is waving his hands and shaking his head. He points around back.

"He says not to use the front door," I say.

Chase shakes his head. "I don't like this."

Above, Otto's got the marker out. Writes:

Front is trap. Back okay.

And then: *please.*

Chase looks down the street, shakes his head as though what he's thinking of doing goes against every fiber of his being.

I walk onto the sidewalk and around the building. He catches up to me a second later.

"You sure you want to do this?" he says.

"Yes," I say, reaching the back door. It's wooden and unremarkable except for the message painted on it:

COME IN AND YOU WILL NOT COME OUT

"Well that's encouraging," Chase mutters, stepping back far enough to take in the two small, first-story windows. They're too high to look into. Too small for someone to escape through, even if there weren't any bars across them.

Leaping, he grabs the sill of the nearest one. Pulls himself up to peer inside, toes digging into the brick wall. Getting up on his forearm, he grabs the flashlight from his back pocket, flicks it on, shines it inside.

He drops down a second later, flicks the flashlight off.

"Well, Otto didn't lie. There's a big hole in the floor right behind the front door."

"Anything else?"

"Other than the body on the sofa?" He considers the weathered wood of the door, turns on his heel, and then starts off across the street.

"Where are you going?" I ask. For a moment, the sight of his back sends a shard of panic into my stomach. Maybe because I've never considered the idea that he'd actually abandon me out here or because it brings back that night six months ago when, having failed to get real answers from me about the samples, he drove off, leaving me behind in a snowstorm—or so I thought.

The Chase I came to know would never abandon me, even when I told him to.

But that was a different man. Chase today isn't obligated to help me do anything.

I give a bitter laugh. "Figures. Great. Good-bye! It was nice knowing you," I say, throwing him a sarcastic salute.

"I'm getting something to open the door," he says through the headset in my ear.

"Oh," I say stupidly. I turn and stare down the block, seeing nothing. Feeling foolish. Relieved. Angry.

"Please tell me you aren't doing what it sounds like." Irwin.

"What does it sound like?" Chase asks, when I refuse to answer.

"Like you're trying to rescue someone who's probably sick and is going to come flying out of the house or down the stairs or wherever you are and probably kill you both."

"Yup," Chase says. I can hear his steps crunching back across the street, the wheels of the suitcase dragging behind him. "That's what we're doing."

I turn in time to see him round the corner, suitcase handle in one hand.

A sledgehammer hanging from the other.

"Where did you get that?" I say.

"The garage. Found the key beneath a pot." He leaves the suitcase on the sidewalk, walks over, and stands sideways near the door's hinges. I move toward the wall behind him. He raises the sledgehammer.

The bolt gives on the third strike and the door swings inward.

Chase pulls back against the building. Drops the sledgehammer. Draws his pistol.

I lay a hand on his arm.

"If there's a corpse in there it's probably infected. Let me do it."

"No."

"Chase—"

"We doing this or not?" he says, sounding angry.

I grab his flashlight, flick it on, grip it overhand. Pull the one from my back pocket and thumb it on. He nods, and we step through the frame all at once, Chase in front, me behind, flashlights shining overhead into the dark interior.

I take in the mass of empty clothing racks piled against the boarded-up storefront. The gaping hole in the wooden boards before the door. The radio set up on the squat coffee table, the soulless, old-fashioned TV. The corpse slumped back on the sofa, head lolled to the side.

Five steps in, Chase coughs, arm across his mouth.

Because even through our masks, we can smell it:

Decay. Death. Hanging in the air like soup. Stirred for the first time in what—weeks? Months?—by the breeze through the open door.

A soft knock sounds from somewhere above. Chase takes a flashlight from me, gestures me toward the front of the store, and then heads for what looks like a backroom.

I rip aside the fabric hanging in front of a dressing booth. Start at my own reflection in the mirror against the wall inside.

I step onto a lump of something. Lift my foot. Flash the light downward.

A dead mouse.

They're everywhere. On the bench in the booth. The coffee table.

The corpse on the sofa.

I cautiously move toward the hole in the floorboards, shine the flashlight into the earthen basement. Jerk back at the naked figure below before realizing it's a mannequin, arms at weird angles. Shelves line the wall crammed full of boxes, random objects, including a mantel clock and an old-fashioned cash register. I wonder if this was some kind of antiques store or pawnshop.

The knock sounds again. I pan the rest of the room. Finally force myself to take in the corpse splayed against the back cushion of the sofa. The worn jeans and dirty undershirt.

There's a note on the table—one of the flyers. It's splattered with blood. Someone—the corpse, I assume—has written on it:

If you find me and I am dead, please do not hurt my son.
Otto is different. He is not sick. Or at least he isn't as I
write this. It is May 2. My name was Michael Boone. I
loved my son.

And then I see the pistol on the sofa.

There's a scrap of paper beside it filled with a simple list. An inventory.

2 corned beef hash
1 canned carrots
3 canned spinach
1 carton steel-cut oats
2 gallons purified water
12 nut bars . . .

I glance around, but for all the dead mice, there are no wrappers or empty cans to be seen.

If this man was infected, he didn't die from the disease. He killed himself to conserve food.

Static. "All clear," Chase says through the headset.

The knock sounds again, followed by another and another until it becomes one incessant rap.

I move past an open restroom, the beam of my flashlight illuminating the vase of fake flowers in the corner. The garbage heaped around the trash can. The bucket I refuse to give more than a cursory glance.

The stench tells me plenty.

The sound continues, louder, more urgent, as I reach what turns out to be a small kitchenette, where Chase is unlatching a narrow door at the back. He throws it open and steps into the frame, pistol and flashlight raised. Glances up, and then at me.

"There's a second door. You sure about this?"

"Chase, I think that's his dad in there. He killed himself to conserve food for his son."

He looks away a moment and then lowers his head.

"Otto?" I call.

A soft rap.

"We're coming up."

Another rap.

"But you need to know if you make a single move to hurt one of us, we're armed, and we will shoot."

A moment of silence.

And then a double knock.

Chase shines the flashlight up the stairs, and then he's taking them two at a time, me on his heels.

The door at the top is sealed only with a chrome clothing rack section through a set of double handles.

"That's it?" Chase murmurs. "Why didn't this guy bust this down?"

"His dad said he's different," I murmur, four steps behind him.

"What?"

"He left a note."

Chase reaches the top landing. Tilts his head and slides the bar free. Pulls open the door.

Soft light filters down the stairs.

11 A.M.

Otto stands in the middle of the room, hands clasped together. He's skinny, his dirty white T-shirt hanging off his shoulders. I guess him to be in his late twenties. He's got fine bone structure, pale chin-length hair, and looks like he's just won some kind of award. His eyes shine as he bites his lips together, a tear streaking down his cheek.

We step up into a room with no furniture but a mattress. The walls are papered with pencil drawings of kids and old men, couples holding hands, a woman praying alone at a dinner table. A girl dancing in a tutu, a tiny tiara on her head.

The page Otto used to write his message to us lies across the bed, the red ink bleeding through the portrait of a grandma holding a plate of cookies. I can practically hear her self-conscious laugh, see her blush through the gray lead.

There's a row of buckets in the corner, food containers neatly stacked against the opposite wall, most of them open or empty. A neat pile of pop-top lids and another of wrappers. Yet another of broken-down granola bar boxes. There's a plate-sized hole high in the wall above the buckets—big enough to emit the faint breeze rifling through the drawings. Small enough to be plugged with a wadded-up sweatshirt.

"Otto?" I say.

He bounces a little on his heels.

But in that moment, for all that I can tell this is a gentle soul, that he is some kind of savant even, and my heart drops.

"Hey, man," Chase says. "Lift your hands for me. Slowly."

Otto glances at me, brows lifted. Like a scared kid.

"It's okay, Otto," I say.

He lifts his arms as Chase pats him down. When he steps back, Otto glances toward the stairs and covers his nose, clearly upset.

"My name's Wynter," I say. Because who's he going to tell? Who *is* there to tell? "That's Chase. Was that your dad?" I ask, tipping my head toward the stairs.

He lifts his free hand, thumb touching his forehead, his expression bereft. His hands shaking.

Chase looks around, scratching the back of his neck. It's the same thing he did the day I cornered him at a truck stop and asked to ride with him, not knowing what else to do. Not knowing he was hunting me the entire time. Except this time I know he's genuinely trying to figure out what to do.

"Otto, where did everyone go?" I ask.

He shakes his head, gestures to the room around him.

I try again. "Otto, is there a hospital nearby? A med center— someplace with a doctor? You know, doctor? My friend is very sick. I need to find medicine."

He looks intently at me, and for a moment I don't think he's understood. I'm about to rephrase the question when he suddenly glances around and then points at a wall. At first I wonder if there are actually medical supplies stashed in the wall behind his portraits.

I go over and touch one of them, feel the solid and seamless wall behind it.

Otto jabs his finger toward it again.

My forehead wrinkles. "Another house? Is there a clinic that way?"

"South," Chase says, looking at Otto. "South, where? Sidney?"

Otto nods. His stomach growls.

I glance down at his stained T-shirt.

"Hungry?" I ask.

A minute later, Otto's wolfing down an MRE and wrinkling his nose at the scent of the hand sanitizer lingering on his fingers as he tries to trade me the last remaining can from his stash: Dinty Moore baked beans.

I shake my head with a smile he can't see behind my mask. "You keep it."

Static in my ear. "Guys?" Irwin. "What's your status?"

"Looks like we're headed to Sidney," Chase says.

"Hand me that map," Irwin says to someone. And then: "Looks like fourteen, fifteen miles."

"Will the signal stretch that far?"

"Should be good to thirty."

"Guess we'll find out."

Chase draws me aside. "We can't leave him in the house with his dead dad downstairs," he murmurs.

"None of the buildings we've seen are safe," I say. "He tries to go somewhere else, he'll just get infected."

Otto finishes eating, points south again, and then at himself.

"Chase," I say.

He turns, and Otto points again.

"You want to go to Sidney," Chase says.

Otto points to us.

"With us."

He nods.

"Sorry, man. We don't even know how we're getting there. Unless . . . Otto, do you know where someone might be hiding a car?"

Otto nods.

"Can you show us?"

Otto starts toward the stairs. Stops. Visibly falters.

His hands go to his head and he lets out a yowl. It's the sound of an injured animal from a grown man's throat.

I try to reach for his hands and he pulls away. I let go, unsure what to do.

"Don't," Chase says. "Don't touch him." To Otto he says, "Hey, man, I have some bad news about your dad. But you already know that, don't you."

Otto glances down and nods.

Chase looks around, and then takes the dirty sheet from Otto's bed, bundles it under his arm, and goes downstairs.

Otto looks at me, wagging a finger. For a minute I think he's saying not to go. Or that Chase shouldn't have gone.

He points toward the stairs, where Chase reappears at the bottom a second later. "Otto, you want to say good-bye to your dad?"

He's so frail-looking as he gazes around the room that's been both sanctuary and prison for God only knows how long. I pick up the can of beans, a half gallon of water—all that's left in a row of empty gallon jugs. Add the beans to my backpack and strap the handle of the water jug to the side. Produce a spare surgical mask from the front pocket, hold it up, and point to my own.

"So you don't get sick," I say.

He silently puts it on. Slips his hands into the gloves I hand him next, his fingers as articulate as a pianist's. And then points to his ear and the headset attached to mine.

"Some friends," I say, unsure if he's seen walkie-talkies before. "You want to take any of the pictures?" I ask, gesturing to the wall.

He shakes his head and taps his brow. Retrieves a small sketchbook from the lineup against the wall and a carefully chosen pencil from an open case beside it. And then follows me toward the stairs, where he hesitates.

I hold out a hand, and after a moment's hesitation, he takes it, the gesture not childlike so much as innocent—except for the resignation in his eyes.

Downstairs, Otto pauses in the kitchenette. Walks slowly out from it toward the breeze stirring through the open door. Stops before the coffee table, tilts his head at the sheet-draped figure. I note Chase also hid the gun—as well as the dead man's last message.

Otto folds his hands, looks for a long moment at the figure, as a tear rolls down his cheek. And then he walks to the door, wincing at the sun.

We follow Otto down the block to an outbuilding behind a boarded-up house, only to find that the lock on the door has been broken. When Chase swings the double doors wide, the space is empty.

The car, if there was one, is gone.

Otto's expression is one of clear befuddlement. He wags his finger as he peers down the dirt lane behind the store before wandering out into the street, head cocked as though listening for something.

And then he's hurrying down the road, jogging stiff-legged, sketchbook swinging with his arm.

"Otto!" I say, hurrying after him, Chase dragging the suitcase behind us.

I slow as Otto turns down a street toward a fenced-in yard filled with a swing set and a bunch of kids' toys, the array of Big Wheels, tricycles, and other assorted junk so thick I wonder how many kids could possibly have lived in the tiny two-story house. Am afraid to see the number on the spray-painted X on the door.

Until we round the corner and I see the black and orange sign on the front of the chain-link fence:

FOR SALE

I stare at it, not parsing. Unable to imagine anyone wanting to buy a place filled with junk . . . until I see the row of bikes leaned up against the inside of the fence.

Otto's climbing delicately over the chain link when I realize he isn't even wearing any shoes.

"Hey," Chase says, letting go of the suitcase handle. But Otto's already over and tilting his head this way and that as though about to make the first major purchase of his life.

"Wait," I say. "Isn't there someplace with a car?"

"Do you see any cars?" Chase answers, vaulting the fence. He looks at the bikes and points. "I'll take that one."

Otto shakes his head, points to another and then at Chase.

"No," Chase says, pointing again. "That one."

Otto motions him toward another bike.

"Hey," I say, walking around the side of the house to take in the shed in back, the outbuilding of the next-door neighbor. "There's a lot of garages here we haven't looked in. Hello?"

When no one answers, I stride back in time to find the two men engaged in a heated, silent argument.

"Guys!" I say, as Otto gestures and then turns his back on Chase altogether.

"Oh, that's great," Chase says a moment later, shaking his

head as Otto walks a bike out and gestures to it like a game show hostess.

Even I, sheltered cult girl, know enough to tell it's a women's bike.

With a baby seat in back.

"I'm not riding that," Chase says, making a motion across his throat, at which Otto emphatically gestures to another. He makes a motion as though breaking a twig in two.

Static in my ear. "'Scuse me." Irwin. "I hate to barge in, but what the hell is going on?"

"Chase and Otto are arguing about which bike will offend Chase's delicate sense of masculinity the least," I say dryly. "Not realizing they're going to have to ride without me because I DON'T KNOW HOW TO RIDE A BIKE!"

Otto and Chase glance at me as one. A second later Otto holds up a finger, marches off, and returns with a new bicycle.

It's got training wheels.

For a minute, no one moves.

Chase bursts out laughing first, Otto joining in with a guttural sound that reminds me vaguely of a donkey.

"Oh, very funny," I say, showing them both some one-fingered sign language of my own. Which only makes them laugh harder.

I nearly do, too. Can only imagine what the three of us must look like: the only people alive in this patch of the Midwest, arguing about who gets to ride the coolest bike as though anyone's going to judge.

I feel myself start to smile. Can sense Chase gazing at me as I glance away, fighting back a chuckle.

Until I remember that we were supposed to be on our way to Green River, Wyoming.

Instead, Julie's dying. And here I am, miles away from Truly, chasing medicine I don't even know if I'll be able to find. About to travel even farther away from where I left her and Lauren surrounded by diseased animals and squatters who might want their house back, and closed in by a door that will not lock, lest it shut them in forever.

Sweat breaks out across my neck. I lean forward, hands on my knees, feeling like I might throw up when the breath that nearly became a laugh gushes out as a gasp.

"Hey," Chase says, instantly at my side. I don't bother to push him away. He fumbles at my pack, and I hear him unscrew my water bottle. Sliding an arm around me, he lifts it to my lips.

"I'm fine," I murmur, and then gulp down water so fast I sputter.

"We're going to have to sleep at some point," Chase says. "Can't keep this up forever."

"I'll sleep when I get back," I say, straightening and taking the bottle. "Now. Show me how to do this."

12 NOON

Nebraska Highway 385 is a flat stretch of two-lane road bound on one side with inert power lines until they cross overhead and continue on east, as though they have better places to be than here.

I pedal steadily down the right lane, the air devoid of all sound but the squeak of a wheel beneath me, the tread of Chase's tires in front of me as he pedals standing up. The whir as he coasts, the gas can strapped to the baby seat behind him.

I glance back at Otto just long enough to see him, face lifted to the sun, something sublime in his expression. I even think his eyes are closed, until he points ahead and I straighten in time to realize I've drifted toward the left shoulder. My handlebars jitter and I briefly panic. It took me fifteen precious minutes, one wipeout, and a near collision with a curb (and then a mailbox) to tame this yellow, old-fashioned-looking Schwinn with a basket in front like something from *The Wizard of Oz*. But no one snickered as I shimmied the front wheel down the street, overcorrecting my first turn.

I curve back into the right lane, even though we have yet to see another vehicle. Search the sky with quick, furtive glances. Looking for life.

Or barring that, buzzards.

Static. "We've got Micah back," Irwin says. He sounds tired. So does Micah, when he comes on, both their voices so subdued as to sound like the public radio Ken used to like listening to in the morning.

"Either of you get any sleep yet?" Chase says.

"I admit I dozed off while you were picking up your friend," Micah says.

"You were saying something about the security footage," I say, hoping talking will take my attention off my wobbling handlebars.

"Yeah, so the drive is designed to hold up to three months of footage—depending, obviously on the number of cameras, etcetera. It doesn't record continuously. It's triggered by motion. People coming and going, maybe birds or other animals. When the drive gets full, it starts recording over the oldest stuff."

"Okay," I say.

"But someone disabled all the cameras except the one on the front porch," Micah says, "and reconfigured the drive to quit recording as soon as it was full so the recording at the beginning wouldn't be erased. Which happens to be the only one with any people in it, including Noah."

"What were they doing?" Chase asks, sitting down on the bike's seat and glancing back to check that we're behind him.

"Leaving. There's three people carrying bags and boxes out of the house, Noah last of all. It's weird, he looks right up at the camera as he passes beneath it, and then reaches up with his free hand and adjusts it so it points out toward the driveway where a truck is waiting—Mel's, I think. The other three load up the truck and get in while Noah unlocks the gate. The truck drives out, Noah closes the gate and locks it behind them. And then he walks out to the truck, gets in, and drives away." I practically hear Micah rub the scruff on his cheek.

"So he wanted whoever found the drive to know he left," Chase says.

"Not just him, everyone. The entire front yard was empty. It's a message, except it doesn't tell us why they left, or where they went."

"What day was that recording?" I ask, my mind pedaling as doggedly as my legs. "Can you tell?"

"It's time-stamped March twenty-first."

The date on the tear-off calendar.

"There's nothing else after that but footage triggered by animals, the occasional moth, a few storms. Until May first, when a billow of smoke rolls across the yard from the direction of the barn."

"The plane crash," I say. I wonder if the pilot was dropping flyers over towns like Gurley.

"It burns for a couple days, uses up the rest of the drive space. And that's it."

I think of the *X* on the front of the house. Try to imagine what anyone else would think on seeing Noah so purposefully film his departure.

I wish I could see the footage myself.

"Did he look sad? Angry?" I ask. Not that Noah was one to show much emotion.

"Hard to tell." Micah pauses, and then adds: "He was wearing a mask."

But Noah didn't wear masks. Whether out of faith or bravado I never knew. The night he welcomed Chase and me before sending us off with two of his vehicles to breach the Colorado border, he'd only had on gloves.

"Everyone admitted to the ranch was tested for the flu just like us," Chase says.

I falter, foot missing the pedal so that I nearly wipe out again as I say, "You saw the *X* on the door."

"But we never found any graves," Chase says.

"I suppose it's possible they could have burned or removed the bodies to protect themselves or even the water supply," Micah says.

"Then why move?" Chase says.

"I don't know."

It doesn't make sense. Why would Noah just take everyone and leave? Especially knowing we were there!

"Which direction did they go?"

"East, toward the road. They could have gone anywhere from there. Oh, he had your dog, Buddy, under his arm in the video."

I'm relieved, at least, that I don't need to wonder if Chase shot Buddy early this morning. If he limped off, alone, to die. It's the first sliver of decent news we've had since the door opened.

But it's more than that. Carrying Buddy wasn't a coincidence. Noah did it so we'd know that Buddy is with him. That he's safe.

Something scratches at the back of my mind, bothering me, but by now I'm so tired I can barely move, each rotation of my pedals done with leaden limbs, my brain sluggish in the climbing heat.

Static in my ear. "Guys, I'm about to turn in for a couple hours," Irwin says. "Delaney's offered to relieve me."

"Sleep well, Irwin," I say. "And thanks."

"Yup. Signing off for a bit."

My forearms by now are pink, my skin fairer than I ever remember it being, after six months belowground. Otto, who's even paler, is going to look like a lobster tomorrow.

We stop by the side of the road a short time later, walk the bikes off to the shadow of a copse of trees. Otto retrieves the partial gallon of water from my front basket, where his sketchbook and pencil are stashed, as Chase and I sit heavily on the ground and drag the water bottles from our packs. I take off my cap, hold it out to Otto.

He touches his chest, head cocked.

"You need it more than me," I say.

He takes and examines it, points to the *B* on the front.

I shrug.

"Boston Red Sox," Chase says. "Baseball."

Otto hands it back.

"Dude, your face is getting sunburnt," Chase says.

Otto wrinkles his nose, brushes it with a finger.

"What, you don't like baseball?" Chase says. "Who doesn't like baseball?"

Otto raises a brow.

"Fine. The *B* stands for *Boss.* It means you're the boss. Better?"

Otto puts the cap on as I dig the Excedrin from my pack. I offer a couple to Chase.

"What's this?"

"Caffeine."

He takes them, washes them down. Studies me as I do the same.

"How're you feeling?" he says.

It takes me a minute to realize what he's asking. That the question is code for where my anxiety levels are after months without the medication I was on before. Without sleep, and under stress.

As I watch the only family I have fall apart.

My first impulse is to say I'm not that fragile.

But the last time I said that to Chase, I ended up in his arms.

I return the water bottle to my pack. "Fine. I started new medication three months ago."

Chase blinks and looks away, guilt etched around his eyes. "Because of m—"

"Because of me. Let's get going."

I get up and shoulder my backpack. As I do, a dove flies down from the tree in front of me, runs a short ways, and flutters on the ground.

I back a step, startled, as Chase scans the horizon. Looking, I know, for the nearest farmhouse or anywhere else we might find a car.

And then I note the bird's wing, out at an angle as it skitters farther away. The same way I'd seen others like it do anytime we came near their hatchlings in the Enclave's fruit trees.

"This bird isn't sick," I say, turning to look up into the tree behind us. Otto does, too, leaning in toward the trunk and then gesturing me over. He points through the branches.

"Yup," I say. "It's faking. Drawing attention away from its nest."

I walk to my bike, knock the kickstand up with a toe.

Stop. Kick it back down.

"Micah?" I say, glancing at the bird on the ground.

Silence.

For a minute I panic, thinking my battery has run out.

"Micah!" I say, louder.

A snort issues through the headset, a snore cut short.

"Here," Micah says, voice rough.

I release a breath. "The light on the control panel in Noah's office. Was that the ark door?"

"The light on the—yeah. Why?"

"The label had been peeled off."

"What?"

Otto steps his way, barefoot, to the pebbly highway shoulder. I make a mental note to find him some shoes.

"There was a sticky mark, like when you peel off a label but it doesn't come all the way off," I say.

Rosella, New Earth's kitchen manager, had been manic about

labeling jars and bins of produce, dried herbs and fruit—leaving others like me to scrub off the sometimes years-old sticky remnants with our fingernails anytime a container got emptied.

Chase pauses beside his bike, where he's just fitted a spare T-shirt over the baby seat and gas can, both. Which only does so much to disguise the spout.

"You're saying someone peeled it off on purpose so no one would know what it is," Micah says as Otto waves a hand in my field of vision. I turn away.

"I think Noah did."

"Okay . . . why?"

Otto slaps the seat of his bike. A guttural sound issues from his throat.

"Because some of them were sick."

"Then why move everyone?" Chase asks.

I hesitate. Because it sounds absurd at least, egotistical at most, to suggest that he was trying to protect those of us in the silo.

But that's what Noah did. What he would do. Why he'd built the silo in the first place. In his mind, his own salvation depended on it.

Otto comes around, grabs the sketchbook from the basket of my bike. Flips through pages until he finds the one he wants.

He turns the pad toward me.

Noah's face stares back.

1 P.M.

I slowly take the sketchbook from Otto.

I'd know the gray hair curling against that dark scalp, the amused whimsy of that smile, that kind and haunted gaze anywhere.

"Micah, hold on," I say, and then instinctively cover the microphone with my hand, though I'm not sure why. "Otto, you know Noah?"

He nods.

"How?"

He gestures with both hands, a finger sweeping in front of his chest.

"You . . . used to live there?"

Otto shakes his head. Holds his hands up facing each other, and then steeples them.

"You went to the same church," Chase says.

Otto closes his eyes, shakes his head.

I think of the bars across his windows, and his father's inventory list, though his stockpile was obviously far too limited. "Was your dad a prepper, too?" I ask, dubious.

Otto looks away as though searching for patience to deal with village idiots. A minute later, he digs the pencil from my basket, flips to a blank page in the sketchbook, and bracing it against his middle, writes:

Small town. Every 1 know Noah.

Chase leans in to read. So close I can smell his skin. Sense the lean strength of him, lethal in the right conditions. So gentle in others.

"Then you know about . . ." I hesitate, and after a moment, he adds:

U from silo?

He looks from me to Chase.

"Yes," I say. "The others are still there."

Otto's brows draw together as though he's trying to put something together. He writes again:

Rumor sick person sneak in, close silo, kill 50+ with her.
Noah and others leave before silo open n corpses infest.

"*What?*" I say. "But that's not true. We're proof of that." And then: "Do you know where Noah went?"

Otto shakes his head.

"You said 'her,'" Chase says slowly. "Did you ever hear who this sick person was?"

Otto writes:

Winter.

A chill claws its way down my spine as Otto lowers the pencil to the page.

And then slowly points at me.

A dozen scenarios flash before my mind at once. Of Otto, fists flying. Cowering, that raw yowl scraping from his throat. Running in the other direction or fleeing on his bike, back the way we came. Of Chase, having no choice but to run him down, unable to risk anyone else knowing that the silo is open, safe, and filled with vulnerable others.

Until I realize he's known all along. He was scared when we found him—I thought because of Chase, a man who never needed to announce his history as a Marine for others to know, instinctively, he wasn't someone to mess with.

But it was because of me.

An urge to protect this gentle soul rises up inside me all at once, the swell of it practically unbearable.

"Why didn't you run when I told you my name?" I whisper.

He lifts his shoulders in a small shrug. Writes:

If sick, U be dead.
If murderer, U not ask medicine 4 friend or give food.

"Can't argue with that," Chase says, walking off to study the road as he relays the conversation to Micah.

I'm about to thank Otto, strangely touched by his direct and simple logic, when he tilts his head, his expression sad and far too old for his years as he writes:

I know kind eyes. Worried eyes. I see hurt heart.

My vision blurs as he writes something else, but I can't take any more. Not right now. I turn away, feeling more vulnerable in his silent and guileless presence than I did even when I was on trial in the silo, humbled and broken by it at once. So that I feel like something inside me might have cracked like the first fissure in a dam.

"If Wynter's right, then Noah started the rumor himself," Micah says.

"And as far as anyone knows, Wynter Roth the homicidal maniac has been dead for months," Chase says, coming back. "At least until the others leave the silo."

"I'll talk to them," Micah says.

I swipe at my eyes, in serious danger of losing it. Especially now that I realize what Noah did—not just for me, but for Truly. I've lost track of the conversations Julie and I had those early weeks in December about how dangerous it might be for anyone to know whose daughter she is.

"Desperate people do crazy things," Julie had said. "Governments have no conscience when it comes to protecting their own people or getting a leg up on someone else, and they'd have absolutely no compunction about kidnapping her for leverage on Ashley, to get a vaccination illegally, or exclusively, or just to screw over the rest of the world."

And I knew what she said was true based on Magnus's willingness to put Truly, whom he believed was his daughter, in jeopardy.

"I mean, just look at that Syrian guy who gassed his own people that Rima tells all the stories about," Julie had said. She got worked up whenever she got on the topic of people she considered crazy—or worse, idiots. But she'd stopped herself, knowing my triggers, finishing only with "No one can know who Truly is."

And now, thanks to Noah, no one will.

As I pull onto the road behind Otto and watch him lift his face to the afternoon sun, I know once again that Magnus was wrong.

There is beauty in the world still. Even now.

And it's worth saving for that reason alone.

Static in my ear. "Hey, guys," a female voice says. "Micah's gone to get some sleep. So this is DJ Delaney coming at you live from the maintenance room at KSILO radio."

"Got any music?" Chase says.

"Actually . . . just give me a second," she says. "I take it that means you want to skip hearing about today's lunch special."

Seconds later, I'm pedaling down the road to a song I've heard Delaney play often while prepping in the kitchen.

Just a small town girl, livin' in a lonely world
She took the midnight train goin' anywhere

When the chorus comes, Chase sings along. He's got a nice voice. I wish he didn't. Otto bobs his head without benefit of a headset as he rides off to my left.

"You know this song?" I ask, figuring he's had as sheltered a life as I have.

He looks as me as though to say, *You don't?*

Smart ass, I mouth. But I smile as the song ends, the silence somehow more bearable, less menacing than before.

"Don't DJs get docked or something for dead airtime?" Chase asks.

"Sorry, guys," Delaney says. "Much as I'd love to regale you with my entire eighties playlist, gotta conserve batteries. So that's it for—whoa."

"What?" I ask.

"That's weird. Air system just shut off."

"It shouldn't." Chase. "We still have fuel."

"Chase, there's a red light on in the big electrical cabinet—"

"The disconnect panel?"

When she doesn't answer right away, he says, "Laney?"

"The lights just went out," she says.

"There's a flashlight on the wall next to the panel."

A few seconds later, she says: "Got it."

"What does it say next to the red light?"

A moment, and then: "Battery."

"*Battery?*" he says weirdly. "The generators should have switched back on if it was running low."

"What do I do now?"

"Get Irwin."

"What's happening?" I ask, pulling alongside Chase.

He shakes his head. "Place is shutting down."

2 P.M.

"Who's with the girls?" I say after Delaney's woken Irwin. "Delaney! Who's—"

"I'm headed down, hold your horses. It's not like the place is gonna explode." A beat, and then: "Is it?"

I blink and glance at Chase.

"No," he says dryly. "You'll just be living like the rest of the country, without ovens, washing machines, or flushing toilets."

A few minutes later, Truly's voice comes through the headset.

"Winnie?"

"Hi, Truly. How are you? Is it dark there? Are you okay?"

Otto points: Smoke on the horizon. Soot, staining the sky.

We're headed straight for the haze.

"Yes," Truly says. "We have a flashlight."

"Good. You hold on to that. Is Rima down there with—"

"Did you find it?" Lauren.

"Not yet," I say.

When she doesn't respond, I say, "Lauren? I'm coming back. With your mom's medicine. I promise."

"Hurry." It's all she says before Delaney's back on the headset.

EAST OF SIDNEY, the highway broadens into four lanes at the junction of Interstate 80. Beneath the bypass, a train sits like a slumbering thing on the tracks near a grain elevator. From here we can see three individual plumes of smoke rising from the edge of town.

Chase points to a blue *H* sign, and it takes me a minute to realize what it means.

Hospital.

My heart accelerates, and my pedals with it. Never mind that my legs feel like Jell-O.

Static. "Looks like the system was set to run on solar if the ark door was open," Irwin says. "Except there's been no solar ever since the plane took out the inverter. So it's been running on the battery, trickle-charged by the generators, the last twelve hours until it ran out just now."

"Can you switch it back to the generators?" I ask.

"Yeah, but we'll run out of fuel."

"How much do we have left?" Chase asks.

"Ahh . . ." Irwin blows out a ragged sigh. "I'd say enough to last two, three days, tops."

We veer into town on Highway 30 past a seed company on one side, mobile homes on the other. Garbage in the street.

And then I see something up ahead that makes my heart skip: a woman sitting on a stoop. No mask, no gloves. Never mind that there's something shell-shocked about her expression. That she's wearing a sweatshirt and it's well over eighty degrees.

There's a kid playing at her feet, rolling a green tractor through the dirt, a bandanna over the lower part of his face. Even from here I can tell he's far too thin. There's something unsettling about the way they stare as we go by.

But they're alive. The place isn't a ghost town.

I slow to a stop at the edge of the property, pull my pack around. Farther down the street Chase and Otto make wide turns and start back.

I've just grabbed the zipper to the main compartment containing the MREs. And then I hear it:

The unmistakable cock of a pistol.

I look up to find the barrel aimed right at me where the woman sits, weapon in her hand. The lifeless expression in her eyes hasn't changed.

"Hey, whoa," Chase says, coming to a stop beside me, palm lifted.

The barrel doesn't move; only her eyes swing in his direction.

"I've got food," I say. "For your little boy. I'm happy to share."

"Keep going," she rasps.

I hesitate, glance at the kid staring at me from the dirt, tractor forgotten in his hands.

"You sure? They're sealed," I say.

"One . . . two . . ."

"Wynter," Chase says, warning in his voice.

"Okay." I slowly sling the pack over my shoulders.

My back prickles as I imagine the barrel following me down the block.

When I glance back, both the woman and the boy are gone.

Lauren's last word echoes in my mind.

Hurry.

I stand up and pedal. It's the closest thing to running.

And then I see it. The hospital campus with its parking garage and portico over the concrete drive, the SIDNEY REGIONAL MEDICAL CENTER sign across the brick, the logo like a three-petaled flower— no, a wind turbine—beside it.

Then I notice the windows, which should reflect the June sun.

Half of them are broken, dark soot around the second-story sills.

4 P.M.

The drive is piled with garbage bags and littered with trash: food wrappers and Git 'N Split cups, a stained pillow and a dirty-faced doll. A red car is crumpled against a pillar at the entrance, the driver's side door open, shattered glass on the concrete like crystal confetti.

I ride past the car to the front entrance, climb off the bike, let it drop to the pavement. The open door is plastered with notices like those in Gurley, the most recent of which reads only:

WE DO <u>NOT</u> HAVE VACCINES!

"Otto, stay with the bikes. Wynter, wait!" Chase says, running to catch up to me as I step inside.

No one sits at the front desk. A yellowed article calling Sidney "One of America's Top 100 Rural Communities" hangs on the wall, the glass in the frame shattered. The staircase and second-story walkway beyond it are littered with debris, the ceiling charred black.

I hurry past a row of open rooms with desks but there's only offices down here. I whirl around, start for the stairs.

"You're not going to find anything left up there," Chase says, catching up to me.

"You don't know that," I say.

"Nothing could have made it through that fire."

I ignore him.

"Hey," he says, grabbing my arm. "You could fall through the floor!"

I turn on him, jerk my arm free. "I don't have time to wait for the building inspector!"

"You're not going to be any help to Julie or the girls if you're dead," he says flatly.

I hesitate then, if only because that thought is the one I've been trying to ignore since we left. Not that I could die, but that if anything happens to me, Truly and Lauren will be at the mercy of whoever will take them in.

"If I die, get back to the silo and take care of the girls. Please," I say. "You owe me that much."

It's not true; he doesn't owe me anything. But I have no doubt that he'd defend them, help them find a safe place. Might even look after them himself for a time. He and Truly genuinely took to each other—another reason I'm angry with him, for my having to break her heart as I explained that we wouldn't be living in Green River with Chase. He might have lied to me, but I've never doubted his feelings for her.

He stares at me with an unreadable expression for a moment.

"No," he says finally.

"Excuse me?" I say angrily.

"Truly would never forgive me. And I could never look at her without seeing you and wishing I could do it all over again. Better. The way you deserve."

I look away.

"Chase—"

"Which is why I'm making sure you get back. Alive." He pushes past me, pistol drawn, and heads upstairs.

Something inside me boils up.

"No."

He pauses, and when he turns and looks back at me, I rip off my headset and stalk to the foot of the stairs.

"No. You do not get to play hero, go off and get captured again, or shot—or whatever it is that fuels your addiction!"

"Wynter, my only addiction is you!" he shouts, tearing off his own headset. "Don't you see that? I could've left by now! I promised you I would. So I guess in that regard I'm a liar all over again. But I can't. Because I can't fathom not being around you. Not being with you. Or worse yet, the thought of you being with someone else. And you're right. I would take care of Truly. I love that little girl, like—" He wheels away with a curse, cords standing out on his neck as I stare. Trying to parse what he's just said.

He rounds back. "But you know what? I don't think you want to be away from me, either. I think something inside you is saying, *Prove it. Make me believe you the way you made me believe we met by accident.* And has been saying that since the night of that witch trial in the storage room. So I am. Because I might not have told you the truth about who I was, but I'm not usually wrong—and I've never been wrong about you."

I take a step back at the onslaught of those words. The emotion behind them tightening his jaw and the set of those lips.

I don't know what to say about his obvious egotism. His vehemence.

The fact that he's right.

Coming down the stairs, he takes my hand, brushes my knuckles with his thumb. Stares into my eyes. "So I won't let anything happen to you—not because I have to be a hero. But because I couldn't live with myself otherwise. Because I don't want to live without you."

I take in those turbulent blue eyes, the strong lines of his brows. The hair curling behind his ears. It was military short the day we met.

"Give me a chance," he whispers.

His gaze falls as my hand drops from his—then abruptly lifts as I close the distance between us, his eyes going to my mouth as my fingers slide into his hair.

It takes me a second to register the sound of an incessant bell ringing from the direction of the entrance.

We fall away from each other, startled, pistols raised toward the front desk.

Where Otto stands, palm hovering above an old-fashioned desk bell.

He glances around. Raises his hands.

Chase lowers the gun. "Otto . . ."

With two fingers, Otto points to his eyes and then down the hall adjacent to the desk that leads in the other direction.

"Something down there?" Chase asks. "And what happened to waiting outside?"

Otto shrugs.

"Come on," I say, hooking the headset over my ear.

Otto slides the bell from the desk, cradling it as Chase moves ahead, pistol raised.

I gesture Otto to stay close, find him studying me sidelong.

"What?" I whisper.

He slides a gaze to Chase and back to me. Wiggles his brows.

"Shut up, Otto," I say as his lips part in a toothy smile.

The hall leads to a separate wing closed off by a set of double doors. There's a window in each. Through the glass, I see what looks like a waiting area. Or, rather, what might have once been. Today, a tarp draped between two chairs separates the area into two rooms. Clothing, shoes, and a bedpan litter the floor of the nearest, where a backpack and several shirts hang on a wall covered with graffiti.

A pair of dirty feet protrude from the second.

"Otto, I think you better stay here. Or better yet, outside. Keep an eye on the bikes," I say, though what I mean is *Guard the fuel*. "Don't touch anything you don't have to."

He clutches the bell in one hand and nods, Adam's apple bobbing in his throat, and then turns and hurries toward the entrance, arms straight at his sides.

Chase steps back, weapon ready.

I holster the pistol. Push the bar on the right door. Locked. There's no handle on the left.

I bang on it.

"Hey!" I shout.

The feet protruding from the tarp twitch. I pound on the door again until a face appears at the window so abruptly that I jerk back.

He's maybe eighteen, unruly curls held off his forehead by a sweatband, a dirty surgical mask over his nose and mouth.

"Yo. What do you want?"

"I need to find medicine," I say through the door. "Please. Someone's dying."

He rolls his eyes. "We're all dying, yo. Ain't you read the Good Book?"

More times than I can count.

"Is there someone there I can talk to? Please. We won't stay. We're not asking for food or anything else."

"You got food?" he says, brows lifting.

I pause, curse myself. "Yeah. Some. And money."

"Money don't matter," he says like I'm an idiot. "Only food. Water. Fuel."

I can't give up the fuel; we're going to need a car.

"I have food. Some water. But I need medicine."

The kid looks away, rubs his cheek.

"Lemme see," he says, nodding toward my backpack.

I take it off and lower it to the floor, the kid craning to see as I pull out two MREs.

I hold them up.

"How many you got?"

"Six."

It's a lie. But we may need the remaining two to trade for something else. Or to eat, if only for the strength to pedal back home.

I swear I can see him salivating.

"Okay, listen. Just you. He stays outside. You come in armed, I shoot you, simple as that. You got me?"

"No," Chase says.

"Yeah," I say.

"You bring the food, I take you to the man in charge."

I shake my head. "No. Food stays out here till I get the medicine. No medicine, no food."

The kid shakes his head, bobs it once as though angry. "No, no good! I got people to defend, man! You see that? You see them? How do I know you ain't sick?"

"I ain't—I'm not. Sick. Would we be bargaining if I were?"

He looks around, obviously unsure what to do.

"Stay here," he says at last, and walks out of sight. I crane against the window, an MRE in each hand. When he doesn't return a few seconds later, Chase grabs the backpack.

"Get those back in here in case we have to make a quick—"

Movement beyond the window. An East Indian man in a dingy white coat walks over. His hair is rumpled, and even with his glasses on I can see the circles under his eyes.

I don't even bother trying to tamp down the surge of hope inside me. It feels disconcertingly like panic.

"What can I do for you?" he says through his surgical mask.

I read the name on his coat: Dr. Banerjee.

I grab the slip of paper in my back pocket. Unfold it and hold it up to the glass.

He leans in, squints, and then shakes his head.

"You won't find any of that here," he says, sounding defeated.

"But this is a hospital! I don't need them all. Even just one." I turn the page around. "Maybe just the piperacillin-tazo-tazo bactim. Bactam. Or the vanco-mycin. Or just the az-aztreo—"

He stops me as though it's too painful to listen to me fumbling over their names.

"We haven't seen vancomycin or any IV antibiotics for months. Not since the place was overrun. Whatever was left got destroyed in the fire."

"Isn't there a locked cabinet or anything that might have—"

He shakes his head. "Even if we had any antibiotics, we'd have run through them months ago."

Chase leans into the frame. "Can you tell us where we could find some?"

The doctor sighs, and then stills as the kid leans toward him, whispering something behind a cupped hand.

The doctor glances at us. "You have food?"

"Yes," I say uncertainly.

"How much?"

"Six MREs."

"Are you armed?"

"Yes," I say.

The doctor glances from me to Chase. Chews the inside of his cheek a moment before saying, "Okay. But just you. I open the door, you bring the MREs and leave your gun outside with him."

"No," Chase says, shaking his head. "I'm not letting her come in alone. We'll put the guns away—"

Dr. Banerjee shakes his head. "We have a no-gun policy."

"We'll leave them out here," Chase says, gesturing to the hallway behind us.

Soft static. "Guys." Delaney. "I don't like it."

The doctor shakes his head. "You want to know where to find the medicine? Those are my terms."

"Fine," I say, unslinging my backpack.

"Wynter, don't," Chase says tightly.

"Chase, don't let her." Delaney.

"We have no choice!" I dig out three packs of MRE pizza, three of bean stew. Hold them up. Transferring them to the crook of one arm, I pull the pistol from my holster. Hold it up, and then hand it to Chase.

"He waits at the entrance," Dr. Banerjee says.

I nod as Chase picks up the backpack, mouth set in a hard line. He backs up several steps, chin lifted to see through the door's window. Looking, I know, for any threat. Finally, he gives me a last glance and turns on his heel. Strides out of sight.

Static in my ear. "Anything happens . . . " Chase says.

"Hightail it out of there?" I murmur. It's meant to be a joke; the last time he said that he was the one stepping into a shady situation, and I went in after him.

"No. Say the word. I'll find a way through that door."

I don't doubt him.

Dr. Banerjee unlocks the door, pulls it open. I step through.

The kid comes to take the MREs as the doctor bolts the door behind me.

4:30 P.M.

"Hey, these are the ones with the Wet-Naps and little candies inside," the kid says like it's Christmas.

"Come with me," the doctor says. I follow him past the waiting room, bracing for the stench, the sight of a corpse beyond that tarp. Not at all prepared to find the two feet attached to a teenager in a purple medical mask lying with his head on a bundle of clothing, a book propped on his chest. His eyes lift as we pass.

"Yo, Gabe, check it," the kid carrying the MREs says, holding one up.

The nurses' station is graffitied as well, doors missing from cabinets crammed full of clothing, the counters piled with junk.

Thin mattresses line the hallway, some of them canopied by sheets secured to the wall and draped over chairs, others housed in improvised lean-tos and squat, corrugated booths. Through the open end of one, I glimpse several picture frames propped on a milk crate next to an old-fashioned alarm clock, a couple of mugs stacked in a bowl. The woman inside doesn't even glance at me as I pass.

Farther down the hall, someone shouts and shuts a door. Music drifts from one of the rooms—a guitar. It reminds me of Jackie, who learned to play when we came to the New Earth Enclave. Until we committed to join—an act that required giving up every influence of the outside world, including our hair ribbons and Mom's makeup— and Jackie's opportunities to practice became fewer and fewer. We had important work to do preparing for the coming apocalypse, canning food with holy zeal.

The hospital rooms are filled with people sitting on mats and sleeping bags. Women holding children, older adults gathered around small end tables or stretched out on the floor side by side next to kids and teenagers like multigeneration families crammed into a one-room apartment.

Static. "Everything okay?" Chase.

"Lot of people here," I say. "Are they waiting for vaccines?" They can't all be patients; they look relatively healthy, all things considered.

"There are no vaccines," the doctor says, sounding weary as he stops at the nurses' station and pulls out a rolling chair. "Won't be for a while. It takes too long to produce antigens for a new disease that we don't even know where it came from, let alone to mass-produce it."

I hesitate. How can that be? It's been six months since the National Guard delivered Ashley and the samples to Omaha. "I heard they were working on it at the University of Nebraska Medical Center."

"You heard wrong," he says simply, reaching for a prescription pad.

But I know for a fact I'm right.

I just can't say so.

His certainty, though, is disconcerting. "Are you sure?" I ask.

He nods. "Guy in town is a ham radio operator. They're the only people who know anything. Some of them post written updates on telephone poles, but so far no news on a dementia flu vaccine or the aid Germany and Korea and a bunch of other countries pledged in food and supplies—which is probably rotting in our own ports while we wait for fuel to distribute it.

"Last time I saw anything come this way was when a train of Humvees passed through on the way to Cheyenne last February and dropped off a batch of flu vaccines from last year. We administered them anyway, thinking they'd offer some protection. The problem is, they told anyone who asked that the hospitals had vaccines. We ran out in a day.

"But people continued to show up for weeks, some of them having walked for days to get here. And then they had nowhere to go and no energy or food to get there. So they camped out on the sidewalks and in the parking lot, waiting for the next batch to come. Finally, things got so bad they rioted, took over the north wing, looted everything. Fire broke out, forty patients died."

"I'm sorry," I say, still wondering what's happening with the vaccine. "What about the police? The National Guard?"

"Do you see any police around here?" Dr. Banerjee says with a mirthless laugh. "They're all gone. The National Guard pulled out of most major cities when martial law failed."

"Pulled out to where?"

"To protect the ports," he says, and then studies me. "Which is also why the first vaccines won't be coming here, but going to the military, government, and whatever first responders we've got left. Where'd you come from?"

"Uh, Wyoming," I say. "Near Green River. Have been holed up for months."

"What kind of shape is Cheyenne in?"

I shake my head. "Don't know. We steered clear. We did come through a small town with no one in it. I just assumed everyone had gone to bigger cities for food and vaccines."

"A lot of people did. And never came back. You don't want to be in a city. If the street gangs don't get you, starvation will. If you're lucky, you'll die of dysentery. Most people these days are fleeing to Canada. Especially now that Mexico's got their wall up."

"What?"

"Oh, yeah, they built a wall—to keep us out. Have started shooting anyone who gets through. Coyotes are making a killing smuggling people out of the country. But I guess Mexico City's really bad now, a lot of people dying. Colombia's shut its borders, so the ones who can afford it are fleeing at night by boat to Venezuela. But anyone who's smart and has the skills to do it will stay rural and live off the land. Worst things anyone has to worry about out here are sick people, starvation, and the witch hunts."

"Witch hunts?"

"Anyone acting a little off. Or just not completely normal."

I think back to the note Otto's father penned before shooting himself. Wonder how many people might, with a cursory glance, mistake his difference for sickness. Miss the purity of his humor and empathic eye.

"What do they do to them?" I ask.

"Shoot them. Or lock them up. Take them to a crazy colony."

"Crazy colony?"

"I guess it makes people feel better, since they're not killing them directly." He shakes his head. "Okay, show me what you're looking for again."

I unfurl the paper I've been clutching all this time, spread it out on the desk in front of him. He glances at it, then lifts his glasses and rubs the bridge of his nose. "So explain to me why you want these.

Because maybe you don't need IV antibiotics but something else. What's it for?"

"A friend. She cut herself. And it, uh, got bad, and she took some antibiotics that she had, but they didn't help. And now she's sick, and feverish, and . . ." *And she only has hours to live.*

He holds up the paper. "Who wrote these down for you?"

I can't tell him we have our own doctor. "Her husband was an MD before he died. I looked her symptoms up in one of his books. I think it's cellulitis. This was what it said."

Hiss of static. "You know, you're scaring me," Chase says. "You used to be a horrible liar."

"Is there green pus from the wound site?" the doctor says, setting his glasses back.

I nod.

"How long has it been?"

I shake my head faintly, the days running together. Hardly able to think from lack of sleep, my arms leaden, legs heavy as cement blocks.

"Five days. Maybe six?"

He rolls back from the desk. "My advice: go back to Green River. If you had a place with vegetation and water in Wyoming, you never should have left. There's a good chance your friend is already dead, and even if she's not, she will be by the time you get back. It's not worth risking your life to get these," he says, tapping the page.

"My sister's holding down the place," I say quickly. "My boyfriend and I brought my friend in, she's nearby. We just need to know where to find what she needs."

He blows out a sigh. Slowly shakes his head.

"You need a city big enough to have a hospital. But the bigger the city, the more dangerous it is and the more likely that everything's gone. That rules out Denver."

Denver? Even if the medicine was there, Julie doesn't have that kind of time!

I look around, trying to think. Through the break in the counter I see an older man crawl out of a crate the size of a large doghouse.

"What about a veterinarian?" I say suddenly. "There's farms everywhere out here. Would animal antibiotics work?"

The doctor throws up his hands. "Don't you think we tried that ourselves? There's nothing left. The veterinarians have all traded what they had for food or been outright robbed. I know of at least one animal doctor who was killed for the medicine in his vehicle." He pauses. "I assume you have a car?"

"A car? No." I shake my head.

Static. "I'm working on it," Chase says.

"How did you get here?" Dr. Banerjee asks, looking at me strangely.

"We biked. Pulling our friend on a trailer."

His brows draw together and he shakes his head. "It's impossible."

"What is?" I say.

"You cannot get anywhere that will have what you need in time. I'm sorry."

Something within me sinks. But another part of me refuses to accept what he's saying.

I lean over the desk until I'm inches from his face. He jerks back.

"I didn't ask if it was possible," I say evenly. "I asked where to get the medicine I need. I've given you the food. Now tell me where to go." I straighten. "Please."

He gives a curt nod. "All right. Then you need to get to North Platte."

"How far is that?"

"About a hundred and twenty miles."

My heart stops.

"It's the closest city with a hospital."

"North Platte hospital."

"No. Stay away from the hospital; if it's functioning at all it'll be overrun with sick, the pharmacy under guard if it isn't depleted."

"Then why do I need a city with a hospital?" I say, impatience—or desperation—lacing my words.

"Because it means there should be a VNA office."

"VNA . . . ?"

"Visiting Nurse Association. An organization of nurses who treat patients at home—including IV therapy. Because it's a business office and not a clinic or pharmacy, most people wouldn't think to loot it except other medical professionals. It's where I'd go if I were desperate."

He slides to the desk. Pulls a pen from his pocket and writes:

Trimethoprim
Sulfamethoxazole

He points to the pad. "If you can't get the ones on your list, look for these two, which are basically the ingredients of Bactrim. Or, if all else fails . . ." He writes:

Dicloxacillin

"It won't work on drug-resistant staph, so if that's what your friend has, it won't help. But if it's all you can find, you'll have a fifty-fifty chance."

It's more than Julie has now.

"Thank you," I say, as he tears off the page. He sets it beside the rumpled one Rima gave me and then frowns.

I follow his gaze, searching for the thing that's snagged his attention.

And then notice the line printed across the bottom of Rima's note.

BOONE STEEL WORKS, ROAD 38, GURLEY, NE

He turns, seems to take me in as though really looking at me for the first time—from my cheeks to my sunburned arms, which are far too pink for someone who's biked all the way from Wyoming, where she's been living off the land the last six months.

His eyes narrow.

"He said they'd all be dead by now."

It sounds like the non sequitur of a lunatic, except that he's been lucid this entire time.

"Who?" I ask, my pulse ratcheting a notch.

"The people in the silo."

Otto's scribbled words flash before my mind's eye:

Every 1 know Noah.

The doctor rises. I take a step back.

"Do they still have food? More MREs like these? Medicine! What medicines do they have?" he demands, his eyes suddenly alive and glinting like shards of onyx.

Static. "Wynter, what's going on in there?" Chase.

"I don't know what you're talking about." I grab the pages on the desk.

Chase, in my ear: "Wynter, get out."

"What's your name?" he says, moving toward me, as though unable to help himself.

I skim around the counter as the doctor shouts: "Vin! Gabe! Stop her. Don't let her leave!"

I'm running full tilt for the door when they both step out of the waiting area before it.

I wheel around. Bolt back the other way. Veer left this time—

And then realize that the corridors form a square, and this one rejoins the main hallway.

"Chase, I need another way out!" I say, doubling back as Vin and Gabe come around the nurses' station.

"Wynter? What's going on?" Delaney.

I grab the counter, cut past the long desk to where Dr. Banerjee is waiting to intercept me.

I run right at him. Knock his arm aside. He grabs me by the shirt with the other hand. Threads pop, the collar choking. I swing toward him, wrap my arm around his as my free hand flies toward his neck. Hook his leg and send him falling backward.

And then Vin and Gabe are on us, Vin leaping over the doctor as I sprint down the hall.

5 P.M.

"He knows," I pant.

"Knows what?" Delaney says.

"That we came from the silo."

"*What?* How?"

"There's an exit to the garage on the north side," Chase says.

North. I glance at the window as I run past a room. See the set of doors at the end of the hall. Seize the edge of a rolling tray serving as part of a tarp shelter and knock it to the floor behind me. Same thing with a metal chair. One of the guys goes down. Someone screams. I don't know who, am too busy tearing off a tarp, throwing a crate of knickknacks—anything I can reach—down in my wake.

I get to the doors, fumble with the lock as one of the guys grabs my hair.

My head snaps back.

"You ain't leavin' yet," Vin says.

I step back to keep from falling. Pivot round, nearly going to a knee.

Ram my fist into his groin.

Vin drops.

A second later, I'm running past an elevator.

A metallic thud sounds down the corridor like someone banging an aluminum bat against a wall.

"Is that you?" I say, breathing hard.

"Yes. Keep coming," Chase says, striking faster.

I reach a set of double doors. See Chase through one of the small windows, Otto behind him, sketchbook under his arm. I unlatch the door to the right and shove it open.

Chase slams it closed behind me and rams a lug wrench through the handles.

"Where'd you get that?" I say. He nods toward a nearby car— an old silver Honda with a broken driver's side window. It's one of at least twenty cars on this level. Our packs and the gas can sit beside it.

Movement through the window. Vin and the doctor running toward the doors.

"Come on," Chase says.

He goes to the Honda, loads the gas can in the trunk. The doors of the medical center rattle behind us.

Otto points to himself and then the front seat.

"Sure," I say, grabbing our packs and climbing in back. The upholstery smells like mold and fast food. And sure enough, there's a shriveled french fry on the floor.

Only then do I notice there's a screwdriver protruding from the ignition. Chase turns the handle. The car starts.

"North Platte?" he says.

"Yeah."

We head to the garage exits, one of which is blocked by a truck with its hood up. As we pass through the second, I notice a figure bent over the engine. A man.

He lifts his head as we drive past. Blood running down his chin, a hose in his mouth.

"Was he—" I stop.

"Eating car parts?" Chase says weirdly.

"So, guys," Delaney says. "Preston's calling a meeting to decide what to do."

"What to do?" I say.

"We can't stay here. Not if people think we have supplies. Better to take them with us than get killed for them."

"I'm sorry," I say, pulling off my gloves and rubbing my eyes. "This is my fault."

"No, it's not," she says, sounding tired. "No one wants to see Julie die. But you're going to have to figure out what to do when you get back. How you're going to move her, where you'll go."

"We can't," I say. "Not till she's better."

But even as I say it I realize she won't be better for days. Maybe longer.

"I don't think you'll have a choice," she says. "A few of them are talking about heading out tonight."

"*Tonight?* Where are they going to go? There's no cars in Gurley, at least that we saw."

"Karam's organizing a search party to some nearby farms. To look for vehicles since we still have fuel. A few others are planning to walk to Dalton."

But if Karam goes . . . "Rima isn't leaving, though—is she? She can't!"

"No. I don't think so."

"Tell them not to do anything till we get back," I say. "The doctor at the med center only now figured it out. There's no way any of them are going to get there until—" I try to calculate, but my brain isn't working right. "At least five hours—six. Assuming they know where the Peterson place is. You've got enough people to patrol it and weapons to defend it. Even without electricity there's no reason to leave yet."

"There's something else," she says.

"What?" I snap.

"Ezra's sick."

I look blankly around me in the backseat. "Sick . . . "

"He has it. Sha'Neal's beside herself."

"How's that even possible?" Chase says.

But then I know. The crash site. The pilot's blood was all over it at one point.

My hands go cold.

Ezra was in the infirmary.

"Where is he now?" I ask. "Where are the girls? You have to move them. You have to tell them not to touch—"

"Rima quarantined his bay and moved Julie to the women's dorm. The girls are with her upstairs. They're moving all the medical supplies upstairs." Delaney hesitates a moment and says, "They're talking about leaving him."

"How? Locked in the infirmary?" Chase says.

"With a gun."

I pinch the bridge of my nose. "Tell them not to do anything until—actually, let me talk to Preston."

"Hold on."

A hundred and twenty miles. Nearly two hours to get to North Platte. That's four hours total, assuming we find the VNA quickly. A half hour to find and get to the VNA, then. Four and a half hours—and that's with a car.

"What kind of gas mileage does a car like this get?" I ask.

"Thirty, thirty-five miles per gallon, maybe?" Chase says.

I run through the math, head spinning. It's a five-gallon can. It looked full when we left. A hundred and twenty miles at thirty-five miles per gallon is 3.4 gallons—call it 3.5, margin of error.

"That leaves us a gallon and a half for the trip back." Which won't get us even halfway back to Sidney—not to mention the fourteen miles from there to the silo.

I fight down a wave of panic. Where are we going to find two more gallons of gas? It was hard enough to find fuel six months ago. Anything with gas in it will have been scavenged by now.

"Hey," Preston says.

"Preston, tell everyone to hang tight till we get back. Okay?"

"That's going to be hard. People are afraid of getting sick. None of us locked ourselves underground for six months just to catch the disease the day after the door opened."

"Where are they going to go?"

"A few of them are talking about setting up camp on the river, where they can at least put out throw lines for fish, or Lake McConaughy. Others want to go north, to Canada."

"They have a much better chance of getting sick anywhere there's people," I say. "And of getting shot by Canadian border patrol."

"I'm just telling you what's being said."

"Well tell them what *I* said!"

"I will. But I can't guarantee none of them will leave after we finish burying Piper and Jax. You want us to put your name on one of the markers? I don't know if it would help, but we can. Chase, too. After all, there's two bodies, male and female."

I shudder.

"What I want is to know who's going to stay with the girls till we get back!" I yell. "It can't be Rima. She's been around Ezra." I feel bad saying it but can't afford to be diplomatic.

"Rima quarantined herself just in case. They're with Sabine right now, keeping Evie occupied so she can pack."

"What if Sabine leaves before I'm back?" I say, on the verge of hysteria.

"How long do you think you'll be?"

Four and a half hours. An hour to find gas. We have no other option. "We should be back tonight. By morning at the latest."

"Worst-case scenario we don't find any fuel and have to get creative," Chase says.

"So, what—two days, tops?" Preston says.

If we're not back in two days Julie will be dead and this will have all been pointless.

"Two days, tops."

"Okay, I'm sorry to ask this, but if you're not back by then and everyone's leaving . . . do you want the girls to stay behind and wait for you? Because Nelise and Irwin said they'd be willing to take them."

My first reaction is to say no. No way.

But what if something does happen to us?

Truly's six and Lauren doesn't know how to defend herself, let alone another person. Nelise knows how to handle a weapon and make anything grow, and Irwin can make anything run.

I feel ill.

I would've wanted them to be with Rima and Karam, but she won't even know in two days if she's infected or not.

"Where are they going?" I ask, throat dry.

"They were talking about heading south. That's all I know."

They could disappear with the girls and I might never see either one of them again.

I cover my face. Draw a shaky breath.

"If we're not back by this time in two days . . . tell them to take the girls and go."

"Okay," Preston says. "I'll relay the—"

Static on the other end.

"Hello? Preston?"

No answer.

"Delaney?" I wonder if she leaned up against something and pressed her button, inadvertently taking over the channel. I reach back to check the unit on my belt, in case it's me.

"Chase, can you check that you're not pushing your button?"

"It's not the button," he says, reaching back to unhook the unit. He lays it on the weathered console followed by his headset.

"Delaney! Preston. Hello?"

"Wynter, we're out of range."

I panic. "I didn't get to say good-bye! Chase, turn around. I didn't say good-bye to Truly or Lauren."

He pulls into the next crossover and makes a U-turn. And then we're accelerating back toward Sidney. The wrong way.

"Hello?" I say. I wait a few seconds. There—I recognize those grain bins in the distance, had been staring at them as Preston said he'd relay the message.

"Preston. Delaney."

Chase glances at me in the rearview mirror.

"What?"

"We can't afford to burn any more gas if we want to get there. Or time if we want to get back."

I close my eyes.

"If you can hear me," I say softly, touching the button. "Tell the girls I love them."

I DOZE OFF recalculating gas mileage. For thirty-one miles per gallon. Thirty-eight. Forty. Until the numbers run together, the answer is always the same:

Not enough.

7 P.M.

I wake to Otto jabbing a finger into my knee.

"What?" I say. It takes physical effort to form the word. Hurts to be conscious.

"We're ten miles out," Chase says. He rubs his face, his fingers scratching against stubble. He looks rough, and I feel guilty for sleeping. Especially as I recall Otto shattering the silence with one of his strange cries earlier, and Chase thanking him. Otto patting him on the shoulder.

I glance out the window, eyes burning from fatigue. Count five vehicles askew on the median, three on the shoulder. More on the horizon, one of them sprawled across the right lane against the haze of distant fires. It's how I remember this stretch of highway, except the cars no longer look abandoned so much as returned to the earth, debris on their hoods and roofs, a shrub growing up through the open engine compartment of a faded blue Mercedes.

"Did we go by Lake McConaughy?" I ask. I've heard Sha'Neal and Rudy talk about it enough that I'd hoped to see it, if only because they said its white sand and blue water looked like the ocean—a thing I've longed to see my whole life but have only viewed in pictures. But also because I was curious to know if people were living there in houseboats as they thought, grilling fish and drinking water out of filtration straws like the one Karam gave me.

"Yes," Chase says. "You can't see it from the highway. But, Wynter?"

"Yeah?" I take the headset from my ear, having kept it on just in case someone managed to get through. I unclip the unit and tuck it into my backpack.

"Let's do that one day."

"What, go to Lake McConaughy?"

"No. See the ocean."

I pause and then glance up to find him studying me in the rearview mirror. Waiting for an answer.

"We're going to have to find a lot more fuel," I say at last.

"I'll make it my mission," he says, his expression as soft as I've seen it in months, gaze lingering on mine.

Otto leans between the seats, right into my line of sight. He looks excited, like someone one letter away from winning Bingo. He points to himself.

"Of course you can come with," I say with a smile.

"Hold up," Chase says. "Who said you were invited?"

Otto pokes him in the shoulder. Points to Chase's eyes and then the road.

"So bossy," Chase mutters, but he's smiling.

We pass a Burger King billboard advertising free Wi-Fi. The billboard beside it is collapsed on top of a jackknifed tractor-trailer, the back end crumpled like a box, the grass grown up around it.

"Which exit?" Chase says, glancing at the fuel gauge. The needle's in the red.

"We can't be out of fuel already!" I cry.

"I didn't have time to dump it all in," Chase says.

I fall back against the seat in relief.

Otto points to an approaching blue sign:

HOSPITAL
EXIT 177

"Have you been here before, Otto?" I ask.

He nods, points to the sign.

I want to know if it was for the thing that caused his muteness. Or if it had to do with his mother, wherever she is. I make a mental note to pack the bin of pencils when we get back to the silo. To ask him, when Julie's healthy and we're someplace safe, if he'll write out his story. It only seems fair that someone who sees others so well be seen—and heard—himself.

I glance at the clock. Forty-six hours.

Chase takes the exit and slows to navigate a gauntlet of cars strewn along the curve. Their windowless, burned-out shells so mottled and so many that it looks like we've mistakenly pulled into a junkyard, or wherever it is that cars go to die.

"What happened here?" Chase says, pulling onto the shoulder around a rusted-out minivan perfectly angled across the road. "It's almost like someone purposely—"

He hits the brake, and I catch myself against the back of Otto's seat.

And then I see them:

Five figures emerging from a blockade of trucks ahead. Obscured from the highway by the rise of the bypass.

And carrying assault rifles.

"This isn't good," Chase murmurs.

My first thought is that Dr. Banerjee reported me. That he figured out who I was and these men are here to bring in a fugitive.

Until I observe the T-shirts and camouflage. "I take it that's not the military," I say.

My next thought is that they're here for a bounty on my head.

"Get down," Chase says, throwing the car in reverse.

I shove Otto's head down in front of me as Chase backs onto the shoulder, accelerating around the minivan. Glance back just in time to see a truck pull onto the road behind us, blocking the narrow corridor through the maze of cars.

Chase slams on the brake with a curse.

I slide my pistol from the holster. Thumb the safety off.

"No," Chase says, hands gripping the steering wheel. "Put it away."

We loop our masks on as the men come toward the car, weapons raised, and fan out around it. And all I can think is: *It can't end like this. Not with Truly and Lauren thinking I abandoned them. With their not knowing what happened to me.*

In a flash it occurs to me that all those months in the silo I spent waiting for our lives to start over, I should have been living—right then—with the people I love.

But that moment is gone. And this is the only one that exists. Staring down the barrel of a rifle pointed at my head.

I wonder if it hurts. If you feel anything at all.

"Don't make any sudden moves," Chase says low.

The man closest to the driver's side door shouts: "You! Get out of the car!" He's wearing sunglasses and a dust mask, a plastic exhalation valve over his mouth like a poor man's Darth Vader. An American flag on his hat.

Chase reaches slowly for the door.

And all I can think is we haven't seen the ocean yet.

Chase opens the door and steps out, hands in the air.

"We're just trying to get to town," he says.

The man beside him slings his rifle over his shoulder and shoves Chase against the hood.

"You two, hands where I can see them!" the first man says as his companion removes Chase's pistol.

I grasp the back of the passenger headrest as Otto's hands go to the front of his head, shaking so hard they flutter against his brow.

"You got any other weapons in the vehicle?" the second man says, patting Chase down.

"My girlfriend does," he says.

I see Otto turn his head slightly, glance at me from the corner of his eye. And I can practically hear the wry comment being shelved for later.

The first man up-nods over the hood of the Honda and a rifle taps my window. Its owner crooks a finger at me to get out.

I do, slowly. Not looking directly at his face or camouflage bandanna, the helmet-clad skull tattooed on his arm. The name tag on his vest that says BUCKEYE.

"Hands on the hood," he says.

He slips the pistol from my holster as he pats me down. I close my eyes when his hands loiter at my breasts. Tamp down the knee-jerk reaction to whip my head back and break his nose.

"You military?" I hear the first man say and open my eyes to find him regarding Chase. It isn't the first time I've heard someone ask him that, though with his hair grown out I'm a little surprised.

"He's good," the man behind Chase says, stepping back.

"Yes, sir," Chase says, straightening, his hands up by his shoulders.

"Lemme guess," the first man says, looking him up and down. "Navy."

"Good eye," Chase says, looking impressed.

The one who patted him down peers inside the car.

"Tank's on E."

"Buckeye" slaps my butt as though to signal that he's finished. Jerks me back from the car.

"Over there, by your man," he says before turning to Otto. "You. Out."

I move around the back of the car, aware of the rifle tracking me from the man stationed twenty feet behind the car. Of the sixth man watching from inside the truck.

"Hey, darlin'," the first man says, pulling me toward him when Buckeye's finished. A ring of keys jangles at his belt as he drapes an arm around my shoulders. The patch on his chest has no name. It reads only: THE WARDEN.

He smells like BO and alcohol.

"So tell me, what's your business in town?" he says, looking from me to Chase, as though we're all good friends.

"We don't want trouble," Chase says.

"Now, see?" the Warden says. "We both don't want the same thing. But what I asked was what your business here was. How 'bout we let the lady answer this one."

"Our friend's sick. Blood poisoning. She needs medicine," I say, eyes fixed on the ground.

"I'm real sorry to hear that," he says somberly, shaking his head. "Where are you fine folks from?"

"We've been holed up in a friend's bug-out cabin north of Lake McConaughy," I say, trying to avoid a repeat of what happened with Dr. Banerjee.

"The Ogallala hospital didn't have what you need." It isn't really a question.

I didn't know Ogallala had a hospital. "We didn't even try. Were hoping if we got to a big enough city you might have vaccines—or at least know where to get them." They had to have had hundreds, if not thousands, of people through here already looking for the same thing.

"Well, it just so happens we've got all those things," he says. "Right on Leota Street across the highway. There's a fine emergency room you can walk right into and they'll get you all fixed up."

"Thank you," I say, knowing that can't possibly be true.

Can it?

"This one's good," Buckeye says, stepping back from Otto. "But he smells like rotten meat."

Otto clasps his hands in front of him, gaze fixed on the ground as Buckeye shoves him around the front of the car.

"Well then," Chase says, "if we're all done here—"

"Thing is, amenities like ours take resources in already short supply away from local residents," the Warden says, looking at Chase. "So me and the boys volunteer our time to serve in part as welcoming committee and tour guides, but also to make sure those from out of town don't take advantage of all that our fair city has to offer by collecting donations."

I glance tensely from the Warden to the others, who almost look bored, their postures relaxed. I wonder how many people they've done this to.

I take a mental inventory of everything with us. But only one thing matters: the gas can in the trunk. Everything else, I will gladly hand over.

"Fair enough," Chase says, rubbing his chin.

The man with Chase's gun pulls our packs from the backseat. Unzips Chase's, and upends it, sending ammo, tools, two flashlights, two water bottles, some clothes, and MREs tumbling to the ground.

"And that's just it. I wanna be fair. Thing is, vaccines and medicine don't come free," the Warden says as my backpack gets opened next.

The man sorts the MREs into a pile, opens and then peers down the water filtration straw, checks the flashlight, dumps out my extra clothes, and then twirls a pair of my underwear around his finger, shimmying his shoulders and fondling his own chest till the Warden drops his head and shakes it with a chuckle.

"You'll have to excuse him," he says. "Jenner's a virgin and . . . easily excited."

My cheeks go hot as the others laugh. I can see Chase's mask ticking with his jaw as Otto's gaze flits around like a nervous sparrow.

Jenner digs Otto's pencil from the bottom of my pack before checking the pockets, pulling out the cash and Julie's credit cards, and then untangling the headset plugged into the walkie-talkie.

"Aw, isn't that sweet," the Warden says, after Jenner retrieves Chase's from the front console, along with Otto's bell. "His and her walkie-talkies. Though they do say communication is key to a good relationship. Hey, man," he says to Otto, arm still draped over my shoulder. "Where's yours?"

Otto gives a small shrug, his eyes darting to Jenner as he pulls his sketchbook from the backseat and flips through it. Tosses it back in the car.

The Warden finally lets me go to amble over and peer at the inventory, hands on his hips, and then glances up at Buckeye and Jenner. "Are we forgetting something?"

Not the trunk.

Buckeye starts, and then comes around the back of the car and hands over my pistol as Jenner quickly pulls Chase's from his waistband and does the same. The Warden studies mine for a moment, so intently that I wonder if he recognizes it—after all, we took it off a dead man.

"That's a nice piece," he says, as though to himself. "I might just have a hard time letting go of this one." He releases the magazine from Chase's pistol, pockets it, and hands the gun to Jenner.

He turns, standing in front of our things. "So, I'm thinking that we might need to take your packs. We've all got mouths to feed."

Chase works his jaw a moment before saying, "All right."

"I think we've got some needy folks who could use your water and clothes, too." He pauses. "Anyone check the trunk?"

No.

The others look around at one another and the Warden shakes his head. "Have I taught you nothing? There are plenty of people who'd gladly volunteer to serve their community, no matter how long the hours. Do I need to get someone else?"

Buckeye slings his rifle over his shoulder and goes around to the trunk. Fumbles for a latch until Jenner looks inside the car and finds the release button. The Warden shakes his head.

The trunk pops. Buckeye pulls out the gas can and gives it a shake, the liquid sloshing inside.

"Aren't you three full of surprises," the Warden says, glancing at each of us in turn. "Now I just don't know what to do. I can think of five kids who'd really like to eat dinner this week and at least one lady in dire need of some clean undershorts."

I take a quick breath but Chase shakes his head. Watch nervously as the Warden considers the contents of our packs and then the gas can, hand on his hip.

Take the packs. Take the guns. Anything but the gas.

"Aw hell," the Warden says, sweeping an arm out. "We'll just take the whole lot. You three go enjoy yourself as much as you want, and we'll call it a wash."

Panic surges inside me.

Without gasoline, I stand to lose not just Julie, but the girls.

"Sir?" Chase says as Jenner stuffs things back into the packs. "Is there any way we can hold on to that gas?"

"Please," I say, raising my palms. "Our friend doesn't have long. You take that gas, and we'll never make it back in time to save her."

"Am I hearing you right?" the Warden says strangely, rounding on me. "Are you—are you *trying* to say that your friend's life is more valuable than one of ours?"

"No," I say quietly, trying to remember how long it took us to get from Gurley to Sidney on bikes. To calculate how many hours it takes to ride 134 miles. Ten? Fifteen? But I just don't know.

"You don't think we have sick people here?" He waves my pistol toward his men. "People who might need to go somewhere else to find the medicine they need? Just who do you think you are?"

"No one special," I say, looking him right in the eye at last.

"Trust me, little girl, I'm doing you a favor. It'd be irresponsible of me as a fellow citizen to let you go into town carrying that gas can. You know what would happen to you?" He gives a low whistle. "It'd be like walking into a bear den in a meat dress. Like oh . . . who was that who had that meat dress? Jenner." He snaps his fingers.

Jenner shrugs.

"Katy Perry?" Buckeye says.

The man stationed at the front of the car nods. "Yeah, her," he says.

"Katy Perry," the Warden says, as though that settles it.

I'm starting to shake. Am this close to losing it. Trying to come up with anything else to say. But I can't think over the clock ticking down with each hammer of my pulse.

"All right. If we're all settled, we'll get going," Chase says. He takes Otto by the shoulder, his eyes telling me to start moving.

The Warden drops his head with a sigh. Curses.

"Okay, look, I'm willing to let you keep the car just because, I'll be honest, I think I might have got the better deal taking this heirloom off your hands. How's this thing shoot, anyway?" he asks, holding the pistol up.

But what good is the car when it's on empty?

"Fine," I say.

He nods. "We'll have to take it to a vote. Buckeye?"

He shrugs. "Sure."

"Jenner."

"Yup."

He points to the others in turn. I start for the car.

"Whoa, hold your horses," the Warden says. "It might be a formality, but let it never be said I didn't do things according to procedure. You get to vote, too."

I force myself to look at him.

"Yes," I say tightly.

"Yeah," Chase says, so tense he looks ready to snap.

Otto nods.

The Warden cocks his head.

"Speak up, boy!"

Otto nods again.

The Warden glances around at us. "Something wrong with him?"

"He doesn't talk," Chase says.

"That's a shame, given that this is a verbal vote."

"You know what?" I say. "Keep the car. We'll go."

The Warden shakes his head. "No, you can't do that. Because I fully intend to make this right, and I'm nothing if not a man of my word."

Otto glances around, eyes wide. Takes a breath. With a grimace, he forces out a wheeze like the bray of a donkey.

The Warden cocks his head. "Well, I can't make heads nor tails of that, can you?"

"We said we don't want the car!" Chase says, a vein bulging near his temple. "Keep it. Call it a gift!"

It happens in slow motion, like a car accident. Like the time my sister and I were riding in Mom's old Buick, down some road in Chicago. I don't remember where we were going. Just the curvy red sports car that pulled out in front of us. Jackie throwing her arms out in the front seat. She must have screamed, but if she did, I didn't hear it, too fixated on that red car getting bigger. Mom turning the steering wheel for what felt like forever before everything sped up and the seat belt cut across my chest.

Like the time on Dad's birthday she'd poured steak sauce on the side of his plate before coming to set it in front of him with shaking fingers. Jackie and me watching from opposite sides of the table as though everything depended on that single piece of meat. Watching in horror as her thumb slipped on the saucy rim, the plate taking so long to fall I'd already heard the screams from the fight to come, seen the fresh bruises by the time it hit the floor.

The Warden turns. Almost casually raises the pistol.

I scream as Chase throws his arms up.

Am already running as the shot cracks the air.

They were standing so close to each other I don't even know which one he was aiming at until Otto looks down . . .

At the dark stain blooming down the front of his T-shirt.

8 P.M.

Otto sags in Chase's arms, his own sprawled like broken wings.

I skid to my knees, cupping Otto's head as Chase lowers him to the ground. Otto looks between us, eyes wide.

"I got you. I got you, buddy," Chase says, pulling his shirt over his head. Balling it up on top of the wound.

It's the second time he's had to do that in the space of months.

"Now, it's unanimous," the Warden says behind me. "Even saved you an extra mouth to feed."

My head snaps up. Vision red. And I can *feel* my lips pulling back from my teeth as I plant my foot beneath me.

Chase grabs me by the wrist so hard I jerk in his grasp, pain like white light behind my eyes so that I barely register the hard shake of his head.

The Warden claps Jenner across the shoulders as they start back up the hill. "Open the barricade, boys. Let's let these fine folks through."

Otto writhes on the ground between us, blinking at the sky.

There's so much blood.

"What do we do?" I cry. "He said there's a hospital. We have to get to the hospital!"

Chase blows out a breath, squeezes his eyes shut. Reopens them, blinking several times before leaning up into Otto's line of vision.

"Hey, buddy," he says softly.

Otto's gaze meets his.

"You wanna get out of here?" Chase says.

Otto nods, expression strained.

"Okay. Wynter, hold this." He nods toward the T-shirt. "Lots of pressure." He gets up, goes to the car. Returns a few seconds later and kneels down. "All right. Let's go."

Otto's brows lift, bemused—and then clamp down in pain as Chase scoops him up, my hand pressing against the wound, the other beneath Otto's head.

We rush to the car, where Chase has laid the front passenger seat back. Get him in, Chase holding the sodden T-shirt in place as I climb in back and reach over the console. Press it down again as Chase closes the door.

All this time the car has been running.

I glance up the hill where the exit merges onto the bypass just in time to watch the trucks move out of the way, one of them pulling out completely before rumbling down the road away from town.

Chase gets in and two seconds later we're emerging from the maze of cars and pulling onto the bypass.

I glance in the rearview mirror, catch a brief glimpse of the truck turning just past the Days Inn.

Otto clasps my wrist, breath shallow. A wheeze coming from his chest.

"I'm so sorry, Otto," I say softly. "I'm so sorry! Hang in there, okay? We're going to get you help."

I lower my head, free hand reaching for his.

It's been a long time since I've prayed. Obsessing is far easier. Checking, reviewing with a matching compulsion in the search for assurance and control.

All an illusion.

There's no compulsion for this. For what to do next when all your options are gone.

So I pray. Remembering that the ground has always met my foot when I couldn't see beyond my next step. Believing that the world is too in need of beauty to give up a person like Otto. Who isn't an extra mouth at all. Only a gift.

We follow the blue *H* signs toward the hospital. The roads are clear, the sun gilding the street.

But when we get there, the lot is a jungle of cars, of fallen-down tents and garbage everywhere. Flyers mashed into the concrete. The windows of the hospital broken, like a thousand eyes, put out.

Chase pulls around back. Gets out and runs to the ER entrance.

"I can't wait for you to meet Truly, my niece," I say to Otto, squeezing his hand. "She's never seen the ocean, either. Maybe we'll just want to stay. What do you think of that?"

He gives a faint, pained smile.

"We'll have to get you sunscreen. Lots of sunscreen," I say. "A big, floppy hat. You won't even need shoes."

Chase comes walking back to the car.

"Okay, here we go," I say, reaching over Otto to get the door.

I stop as Chase comes back to the driver's side, something in his hand.

"What?" I say, as he gets back in.

"Place is one of those colonies," he says, holding up the crumpled paper.

INFECTED

NO SERVICES. NO VACCINES.

UNSANITARY CONDITIONS.

THIS IS A QUARANTINE AREA.
***DO NOT* ENTER UNLESS YOU**
ARE ALREADY ILL
WITH R.E.O.D. OR DROPPING OFF
SOMEONE WHO IS.
DOOR <u>WILL LOCK</u> BEHIND YOU!

I read without comprehending.

"Guard said there hasn't been any hospital staff since May. They're all gone."

Otto's breath is rattling in his chest, his lips tinged blue.

Chase looks at me, as though to ask: *Where?*

We pull out of the parking lot, past the line of trees, the sky aglow in purple and red. Otto lets go of my hand and reaches as though to touch that palette of color, fingers splayed against the window.

I glance at Chase.

He turns down the main street, accelerating toward the edge of town. Past stores without windows and neighborhoods lit only by burn barrels, abandoned schools and empty grain elevators. Running on fumes. Chasing the sunset.

We end up on a gravel road, drive for a mile. Past fields that should have been planted, sprouting by now. Green and lush with weeds.

There's a creek ahead; I can tell by the meandering line of trees. Otto points and we head for it.

The car slows and then stops, having taken us as far as it will go.

Chase comes round, the dash blinking. Lifts Otto from the passenger side and carries him toward the creek, Otto's head against his chest.

I let go of the sodden T-shirt in my hand.

We prop Otto against the trunk of a locust tree, his face tilted to the sun, the way it was as he pedaled down the highway. Curl up on the earth beside him as color fades over the horizon.

"It's beautiful, Otto," I say, looking up at him. He nods, faintly.

Frogs sing from the creek bed against a choir of cicadas.

Sometime later, Otto gasps.

"What is it?" I say, eyes going to the wound, which has not stopped bleeding. But when I look up his face is filled with wonder.

His hand lifts, so slowly. Touches his forehead with his thumb. The same way he did when I asked him about his father.

"Your dad?" Chase says.

Otto nods.

I turn my head against his chest, tears soaking his bloody shirt. Sputter an uneven exhale. A minute later I feel him pat my shoulder.

By the time I've collected myself the field has come alive, fireflies sparking the air like Christmas as twilight descends.

I pray, disconsolate, and wait for a miracle.

Sometime later, I open my eyes.

The moon's up, so bright the trees cast nocturnal shadows. A lone cicada sings a sleepy chorus.

"Otto?" I whisper and lift my head.

His eyes are closed. He might be sleeping.

As I sit up, his hand falls open.

A last firefly takes to the air.

"Otto?" I say, his name breaking on my lips. Diaphragm hitching with sobs as I shake his shoulders.

His head lolls and he slumps to the side. His thin frame an abandoned thing.

Chase shoves to his feet and walks off, arms clasped over his head. A minute later he bends, grabs something off the ground. Throws it with a savage yell and rages at the sky.

DAY 182

We lay Otto in the creek bed, having no way to bury him. Cover him with stones.

Sleep the last hour till dawn in the Honda.

6 A.M.

L ashes brush against bare skin. Sticky against my cheek. Chase's
chest rising and falling beneath me.

I twitch at the sensation of something crawling on my arm. Push
up, head pounding. Mouth like cotton.

Needing to pee.

I clumsily extricate myself from Chase's arms. He's sleeping so
hard he doesn't even move as his hand slaps back to his chest.

It's smeared with dried blood.

I slide out of the backseat. We never bothered to shut the door.
Glance down at myself as I unbutton my jeans.

Hands caked with blood like the murderer I'm supposed to be.

Squatting behind the Honda's back bumper, I can't help but wonder
if somehow I am. If Otto would be alive right now if I'd stayed silent. Or
if Chase had. Or I'd pointed to another exit. Or chosen a different car.

If we'd just all walked away.

Stop.

I notice something on the floor of the backseat as I come around
the car.

Otto's sketchbook.

I drop to sit on the ground beside the open backseat. Slide the sketchbook from the floor.

There's blood spattered on the front of it.

I scratch it with a fingernail, brush a few bits away. After a moment, I open the book. Find myself looking at an older woman holding a casserole. Even though it's a pencil sketch, I know her hair is gray. She's laughing, in that bashful and self-conscious way people do when you compliment them. And I swear I can see the vivacious girl she once was in those wrinkled eyes.

I page through a few more until I come to the portrait of Noah. Wonder where he is now. If he had a contingency plan of some kind—a backup bug-out compound.

Surely he did.

I wonder if he planned to come back for Open Day.

And then realize it's officially tomorrow. The same day the others are leaving. He could come back to find everyone gone.

Just Ezra, locked in the infirmary, raging with dementia.

Or dead of a self-inflicted gunshot wound.

I flip through the rest of the pages, knowing we have to get going. That we've already lost far too much time.

But feeling like it's only right that these drawings be seen, admired in Otto's presence one last time.

I pause on the page he scribbled on. Was it really just yesterday?

I know kind eyes. Worried eyes. I see hurt heart.

There's a line I didn't see before at the bottom:

He loves U. U know. Dad loved Mom same look. His north always where she was.

I catch my breath and stare. How did I miss this?

And then I remember how I turned away when he started writing again, unable to take any more.

I become aware of Chase behind me.

"It's true," he says, his voice raw. "I love you, Wynter."

I glance up at him, closing the sketchbook.

It's always been this way between us since he learned about the night Magnus tried to rape me: that I come to Chase. The arm around me invites, but never pulls. His mouth opens in response to mine.

This time as I slide into the backseat after him, I hesitate, my mouth the span of a whisper from his lips. Close enough to feel their warmth like an electric charge, to taste the breath shuddering between them until his arm tightens around me, closing the distance between us at last.

I ALLOW MYSELF to drowse only a few moments. Because I can almost pretend we've stepped out of time to a place where only we exist. Needing the world to fall away.

And because it physically hurts to move.

But every minute skipping by costs more than the one before; we can't afford to loiter.

Haven't even discussed a plan.

I have one.

A bad one.

The cicadas are singing again.

I force myself out of the car. Shield my eyes against the sun as I try to get my bearings, the edge of the city to the east.

Something isn't right.

"Chase."

"Yeah," he says, with forced alertness. He leans through the seats to peer at the dash. "Oh, my God."

I pivot and squint directly at the sun shining a minute ago on my back. Search out the gravel road pointing directly toward it.

The color drains from my face.

5 P.M.

I whirl around in a panic. Grab Otto's sketchbook, heart jackhammering to life.

"Holy—" Chase looks around as though for something he forgot—including his mind. But other than Otto's book, we literally have nothing except a car we cannot drive.

"How could we do this?" I cry as we jog toward the road. "How could we sleep through the day?"

What's happening at the silo? How many are preparing to leave—have already gone?

Is Julie one of them, having shed her body as Otto did last night?

I won't forgive myself. I can't. I accepted that Julie might die out of our sheer inability to find the medicine she needs.

But not my own negligence.

"We'd been awake for two days straight," Chase says. "That's how."

But that's no excuse, even as a part of my mind says: *Is that all?*

It seems like a week ago that the silo door unexpectedly opened. Days since we scouted the ranch. Since my literal crash course in bike riding after meeting Otto in Gurley.

Impossible that he was in our lives for mere hours.

He deserved better. He deserved laughter. An audience for his snarky wit. To be filled with wonder at all that those around him took for granted. To be loved as he loved others.

And what did he get?

Not even a pair of shoes.

This last thought breaks me.

Chase takes my hand, but the tears won't stop. The memory of his grief, so raw as he roared at the moon, shatters me all over again.

I'm a mess by the time we pass an old farmhouse with an X on it. Have seen so many by now that I don't need to look twice to decipher the number in the lower quadrant:

Two dead.

There's another mark beside it, too: an E.

"Evacuated?" I hazard. "Empty?"

The trash bags piled around the bin have been scavenged many times over by animals, their contents scattered across the yard. Whatever's in them has been out so long it no longer even smells.

When we go around back, we find what we're looking for: an old-fashioned water pump. The same rusty red, even, as the two in the Enclave.

I set the sketchbook out of the way as Chase takes the handle, works it up and down, the hinges squeaking. The pipe gurgles, and a few seconds later water rushes from the spigot.

It's cold and clean—the best water I've ever tasted.

We splash our faces and hands, and I take over the pump as Chase rubs the dried blood from his torso until we're both shivering in the afternoon heat, wet pants sticking to our legs.

"Ready?" I say, and then stop. Take in the man standing there, half naked, hair wild, his jeans stained with Otto's blood.

Anyone, at first glance, would assume he was deranged.

I know I don't look much better.

I scan the house. Consider the flimsy door on the old screened-in porch.

And then I'm crossing the yard and running up the stairs.

"What are you doing?" Chase calls after me.

I try the door and, finding it latched, put a foot through the screen. Cross to the glass storm door and try the handle. Glance around me when it doesn't give and grab a large terra-cotta pot.

Bash it through the glass. Kick in the shards.

Chase comes through the screened-in porch, takes me by the shoulder. "Wynter, stop. It's not safe!"

"Not for you," I say, gently pulling away. "Stay here."

"Wynter—"

I step through the door into the kitchen and am instantly transported back to my grandma's house where Jackie and I used to spend a week every summer before we joined New Earth. Pictures and business cards on the refrigerator. Yellow Formica counter. A one-thousand-piece puzzle on the dining room table with its edges completed.

Everything but the smell.

It comes from the La-Z-Boy recliners in the living room, each one draped with a blanket.

The cabinet doors hang open, plates dashed to the floor. The pantry empty.

The place has been looted.

I make my way down the hall, take the stairs two at a time past at least three decades' worth of wedding, baby, school, and graduation photos.

Up to the master bedroom, where the drawers have already been pulled from both dressers. I rifle through the clothing on the floor. Grab a navy top, a pair of women's overalls from one end of the bedroom. A black Dodge RAM T-shirt, torn work jeans from the other.

"Guns?" Chase says when I reemerge.

I go back and search the house, including the earth-floor base-ment lit by half windows near the ceiling. I find the gun safe—open. Everything gone, an empty shell box lying on the floor.

Upstairs, I scan the living room, eyes averted from the draped figures. See something glint from the carpet beneath one of the recliners.

A bullet casing.

I move to the La-Z-Boy and steel myself.

Julie. Lauren. Truly.

I twitch the edge of the blanket away just enough to look at the corpse's arm—his hand, more specifically.

The last two fingers are crooked, as though holding something. The first two bent back at an impossible angle.

I drop the blanket back into place.

"Gone," I say, reemerging onto the porch.

6 P.M.

We stop at the nearest gas station, which was looted so long ago there's dirt on the shelves.

Including a fine layer on the phone book beneath the counter.

It's a thing I remember having in Chicago but have never used—except to sit on when I got too big for a booster seat at the dining room table.

Chase flips past the white pages to the yellow ones in back.

"Visiting Nurse Association," he says, and reads off an address on Jeffers Street—before flipping to a local map in the back.

"This book's amazing," I say.

"Yes, it is."

I slide it back beneath the counter—along with Otto's sketchbook.

Just for now.

We spend the next twenty minutes walking down A Street, past shattered storefronts and peering through residential neighborhoods, *X*s and *E*s on half the doors. I note more than one business called Cornhusker something-or-other. An abandoned car with a Go Big Red license plate holder and a front yard with a Huskers football helmet painted on a decorative flagstone.

We see exactly three people. One, watching us through the window of a house. When I stare back, she gives me the finger. The second, guarding a garden patch from a lawn chair, camouflage hat on his head, shotgun across his lap. The earth around his tomato plants smells like feces.

The third, walking past a Kentucky Fried Chicken with WE HAVE NO FOOD in its front window, holding a cell phone that can't possibly work to his ear, in a heated conversation with no one.

We stop before the two-story brick building with the brown awning at 210 Jeffers Street. Stare at the recessed entrance set between the doors to the accounting and law offices on either side, their front windows broken, the ones upstairs barred and intact.

I tell myself not to take it as a sign. Don't dare to hope.

And then do, anyway.

It's also right next door to the Lincoln County Sheriff's Office and Detention Center—a location I assume might have discouraged early looting. Even if the corner windows of the sheriff's office are broken.

There's a guard posted outside.

Movement in the distance; a black truck coming over the viaduct from the direction of the bypass.

Chase tugs me into the recessed cove, presses me to the wall.

"Was that—"

I feel him nod against me.

We wait, but the truck never passes.

"Where'd he go?"

"Must've turned."

Now I notice where a wide decal has been scraped from the metal door, as though whatever business was here before has closed. There's no VNA sign at all.

No.

It has to be here. We have nowhere else to go, and no time to get there.

I try the door, but of course it doesn't move.

"Where's a sledgehammer when you need one?" I say, trying to remember which of the houses we passed had outbuildings. Wondering what we were thinking coming here empty-handed, expecting to just walk in.

"There's more than one way into a building," Chase says.

He steps out and goes to the end of the building. Peers around the corner. Holds his arm out for me to stay put. Comes back and grabs me by the hand.

"They pulled into the sheriff's department," he says as we hurry the other direction past the front of the adjoining print shop.

We skirt the side of the building to the back. From here, we have a clear view of the detention center, the service bays in back.

Voices from out front. The slam of a truck door.

"Which way did he go?" I ask—and then hear the truck's engine revving down the street beside us.

We step around the corner out of sight—crouch behind a half wall meant to obscure a garbage bin as the truck turns up the street behind us.

"I'm really curious what he's got in there," Chase says as the truck rumbles back toward the bypass.

Meanwhile, he's staring at a stack of wood pallets on top of a green commercial Dumpster.

He tilts his head and now I see why: the Dumpster's been moved against the back of the office building, which is only one story and looks like it'd make a neat patio area for the second story rising up from it as long as someone was willing to climb through the window.

Which they could do, because the ones in back have no bars.

Chase looks around us. Goes toward the curb out front. Bends and retrieves something from it.

Comes back with a chunk of concrete.

"Ready?" he says.

He gives me a foot up onto the Dumpster. I take the concrete rock from him. Toss it up onto the roof.

If anyone would have told me ten months ago that I'd be searching for guns in dead people's homes and trying to steal drugs by bashing in windows, I'd never have even been able to picture it, let alone believe it. Didn't know what drugs were. Would never willingly have touched a gun.

Of course, I'd never have imagined myself as an accessory to Magnus's death, either.

I climb onto the pallets, haul myself up onto the roof. Retrieve the piece of concrete as Chase comes up.

My heart skips a beat as I peer through the window. I see a desk and what looks like a locked closet at the end of the room.

And then I see the blue logo on the back wall.

VNA.

"This is it," I say, hushed.

Not only that, but the door and windows are intact.

Which means the medicine should be, too.

I'm wondering how much we can transport home. Am already imagining the food and fuel we'll be able to buy.

"You want to do the honors?" he says.

I grab the thicker end of the concrete chunk with both hands and go stand beside the window. Swing around hard, the concrete connecting with a dull crack.

The glass spiderwebs all the way to the frame, only a tiny hole in the middle.

Chase turns away, spewing a laugh. Comes back and abruptly walks off as he cracks up again.

"That's not how I saw that happening," I mutter, before kicking the glass in as Chase leans his hands on his knees, his torso shaking.

He comes over and offers me his hand.

"Sorry, I just—" He bites his lips together and looks away. I take his hand with a scowl. Step up onto the windowsill, and leap down to the floor.

As I move toward the closet, a metallic click and slide sounds from the other end of the room. A distinct sound I've come to know well.

Of a round being chambered.

7 P.M.

The woman holding the gun is the kind of thin fashion models eat nothing but lettuce and egg whites to achieve—or too many laxatives, in the case of Lauren's friends. She's pretty, or would be, if not for the acne on her face and the drawn-on brows that look like sideways commas.

She's also sweating.

But what I'm most concerned about at the moment isn't the gun.

It's the fact that her hands are shaking as she swings toward Chase, who has just dropped down beside me.

"Hey," I say, lifting my palms. The office smells like smoke and air freshener with a portable toilet thrown in.

"Sorry," Chase says, laughter gone. "We didn't know anyone was in here."

"You weren't supposed to," she spits. "That's the point. I got 'em!" she shouts over her shoulder toward the hallway.

Crap.

A male peers around the doorjamb. He's got a short beard, and in his plaid shirt and glasses, he looks like someone's science teacher.

"Now what're we gonna do?" she says, glancing at him. "Huh? They're gonna notice that the window's broken. They'll know we're here!"

"We'll have to move," the man says, coming in to stand behind her.

"I don't wanna move! I like it here!" she says, and even though I put her at maybe thirty, she sounds like an angry teenager.

"Sorry about the window," I say. "We're just desperate—"

"There's nothing here!" she says.

The man tilts his head. "What are you looking for?"

"Our friend has blood poisoning," Chase says. "She needs IV antibiotics or she won't make it. That's all we're here for. Nothing else."

"Please," I say, and don't even have to pretend to beg. "We're just trying to save a life."

The woman shakes her head like there's a fly buzzing around inside it and then curses. "What do we do now?"

They have it.

The pistol visibly trembles in the woman's grip. I shift my weight away from the closet, toward Chase and the window. The pistol dips a fraction of an inch.

"So are we," the man says, gesturing to the hall behind him. "We've got a friend who's sick, too."

"You got anything?" the woman says, hurling her words like darts.

I shake my head, stomach sinking. Because we literally have nothing to trade, let alone medication.

"There's supposed to be stuff here," Chase says. "If you want, we could look together. Both get what we need."

"Nah," the man says, chewing the inside of his lip. "What we need is all gone. Someone must've took it. But I—I think what you're looking for might be here."

"Oh, man, thank you," Chase says, hand going to his chest. "You don't know how—"

"But we need something, too. Sorry. That's just how this has to work."

"Like I said, we don't have any drugs," Chase says.

"We know where they are," the man says as the woman glances at him. "We just need someone to go get them."

"Okay," Chase says, stuffing his hands in his front pockets. "Sounds easy enough."

We don't have time. We need the antibiotics I am certain are in the closet behind me—now.

And knowing they're locked just eight feet away is making me nearly as jittery as the chick at the other end of the room.

"Can we, uh, sit down and talk about it?" I say. "You can write out the details?"

If she'd come closer, Chase could disarm her. I could disarm her. But right now I'm seriously worried about one of us getting shot just by accident.

"We have it. Hold on," he says, and walks out into the hallway. A few seconds later I hear him in conversation with someone else.

How many people are in here?

"Where is it?" I hear Plaid Man say. The reply is mumbled, followed by a door closing farther down the hall.

"So those guys," Chase says. "The ones at the bypass. What's uh—what's their story? I saw one of them pull into the sheriff's office a few minutes ago. Is the Warden . . . a sheriff?"

The woman snorts.

"There's no sheriff. No 'law enforcement,'" she says, with a sharp laugh. "No Easter Bunny neither! Just James Elcannon and his friends doing what he's always wanted to do ever since he got a job in the Municipal Department and tried to run for City Council and got laughed off the ballot. No one wanted the guy from sewer services."

Sewer services?

"Though it probably had more to do with him getting kicked out of some militia. Too psycho for the three percent." She snorts, and then flicks a nervous glance toward the window as though worried who heard it.

"What do you mean doing what he always wanted to do?" Chase asks.

"Take over the city. Duh." She wags her head as she says it: *duh.* My sister used to do that.

When she was ten.

"He and his 'orderlies' "—she air quotes—"hijacked the last fuel tanker to go through here from the Love's truck stop almost six months ago. Moved it over to the self-storage place they operate out of on the north side of town. Probably dance around it at night. When the hospital generators started running out of fuel, they had to go to him and he became real important real fast. Especially cuz he provided security. When he got tired of supplying fuel, he closed the hospital down."

I'm still trying to comprehend something she just said. "He killed our friend over a gallon and a half of fuel—and you're telling me they have an entire *tanker?*" I say, my hands starting to shake.

She lifts her brows till they become apostrophes. "Rumor has it it's running low. Not that it matters. Everything goes through him now."

"What's he doing in there?" Chase nods toward the sheriff's office.

"They been stocking stuff there ever since they ran out of room at the Store-More. He stops by every day when he's making his rounds. Has a habit of paying surprise visits to his orderlies at the city entrances and hospital and wells where people line up for water every day at eight and five."

"The *E*s on the houses," I say with slow revelation. "They're for Elcannon. His men have gone through them."

"Ye-eah," she says, waving the gun. "He runs. The city. Like I said."

"How'd you know about this place?" I ask.

She looks away like she's not sure whether to answer that question. Lifts a shoulder toward her ear as though it itches.

"My sister used to work here," she finally says. "Her and another nurse. When they got sick, I took down the sign, told everyone the office closed down. That they shipped everything off to the one in Kearney."

I stare, trying to reconcile the idea of a closet full of meds going to waste in the middle of a crisis.

She lifts her chin. "Oh, spare me. You should be thanking me!"

"For what?" I ask, wondering if she's insane.

"Havin' the medicine you need to save your friend. You're *welcome*," she says sarcastically.

"We appreciate it," Chase says. "Do you know anywhere in town we could also find some gas?"

She laughs. "Sure. Just go up to the Store-More and ask nicely. I'm sure Elcannon would be *glad* to give you some."

I narrow my eyes.

Plaid Man comes back, something in his hand. A laminated card of some kind.

"This is what you need," he says, and tosses it to Chase, who catches it.

It's some kind of ID badge for a Josh Lowell.

The top reads GREAT PLAINS HEALTH.

The hospital.

"I don't understand," Chase says. "The hospital doesn't have any medicine anymore."

Plaid Man sniffs and wipes his nose. "It's there."

Chase turns it over. The handwriting is barely legible.

"At the hospital," I say slowly.

Plaid Man nods toward the ID badge. "We took care of him for a while. When we started running low, he said not to worry, he had access to all this stuff. Things were getting so bad, no one was paying attention like they used to. Until he got caught."

"If he got caught they would have cleaned out his locker."

"It's not in his locker. It's in the base of a lamp in the staff room." He pauses. "Or in a sofa cushion or above a ceiling tile. He wasn't right before he died."

I stare. "Seriously?"

"Do we look like we're joking?" the woman snaps.

"Sorry," Chase says, and tosses the name tag on the desk. "This isn't gonna happen."

"What do you mean?" she says.

"The place is a crazy colony!"

She jerks her head to the door. "Show 'em!"

"What antibiotic are you looking for?" Plaid Man says.

"Piperacillin-something or vancomycin," I say.

Plaid Man pulls something from his pocket. Two small glass jars with metal tops.

My heart stutters as he studies the labels and then holds one out, toward me. He takes a couple steps closer. Just enough so that I can read the label.

VANCOMYCIN

"That's it, isn't it?" Chase murmurs.

It's all I can do not to launch myself at Plaid Man, the room having shrunk to that single glass jar.

"How many of those do you have?" I ask.

"More than this," he says.

"Prove it."

He hesitates, and then walks back out.

I look toward the window as though judging the time. But I'm straining to listen.

Again, murmured voices. A door shuts farther down the hall.

Plaid Man comes back with a box and three bottles in one hand. He tosses the box on the desk.

Surgical masks. A few pairs of gloves.

He turns the bottles in his hands. Holds them up, two in one hand, one in the other, for me to see. Shakes them slightly so I can see the white powder inside.

"We have IV equipment for it, too," he says.

I bet they do.

I glance at Chase as though asking if we can get a puppy. Not for my benefit, but for theirs. Because (a) I have every intention of possessing those bottles one way or another in the next hour, and (b) as desperate as I am, they are, too.

"That's all you see till we get ours," the woman says and waves the gun toward the window.

"What if we can't find it?" I ask.

"Then your friend dies."

7:30 P.M.

Chase paces behind a professional building two blocks away, the box of masks on the ground between us.

"No," he says. "No way."

The cicadas are out again and the smell of smoke and garbage—or burning garbage—is thicker than it was before, irritating my eyes and throat.

"I have to," I say. "There's no other choice."

"There's infinite other choices than you going into a hospital looking for something that isn't there just because a bunch of addicts want you to produce white magic pills from out of nowhere! I'm telling you, that stash doesn't even exist. 'Oh, it's in the lamp. I mean the ceiling. Or the sofa . . .'"

"What if it is? I go, get the pills, we trade for the antibiotics."

And then there's the small technical issue of getting a working car and fuel.

"Wynter, addicts will say anything to get what they want. They were keeping him supplied! I promise you, if we don't show up in the next twenty-four hours, one of them *will* go to the hospital looking for it themselves, knowing just as well as we do that it probably doesn't exist. Because that's what junkies do."

"How do you know so much about addicts?" I demand.

His brows draw together. "Because my sister's one."

I blink. "I'm sorry."

He shrugs. "She couldn't cope with our sister Natalie's death. I lived with her for a while before I moved to Ohio. Saw what was going on. The family finally gave her an ultimatum, she went to rehab, got clean. Decided to move to France to start over."

So that's why his parents were visiting her when the pandemic started.

"I had no idea," I say.

His eyes plead with me. "Please don't think I kept this from you. It's just never come up."

"I know," I say, and mean it.

"Thank you," he says, looking relieved. "So what do we do?"

"If there's any chance the pills are in the hospital, it's worth a shot."

"No, it isn't. A house with two corpses who can't sneeze on you is one thing. A hospital full of live infected is another. And even if you *are* immune, you're talking about locking yourself in a building full of crazy people. You could get mauled. Bludgeoned to death. Raped. Strang—"

"I get the picture."

"The only way you go in is with me."

"No. Out of the question."

"Then that plan is out."

But all I can think about is those three glass bottles that have cost us so much—too much—already.

We have less than twenty-four hours to get back and no guaranteed transportation but our own feet.

"So what, then?" I demand.

He glances around. "We find it in one of these houses."

I stare at him.

"Didn't you hear back there? They've already been systematically cleaned out by Elcannon!"

He shakes his head. "Unless his guys are addicts, they probably didn't find half the pills stashed in those homes."

"Some of them probably are. I may be naïve, but I'm pretty sure those are not the only addicts in town," I say, pointing back to the VNA office. "Besides, why would an addict leave anything behind?"

"Because they got so sick they forgot where they stashed their stuff."

"You mean like the guy with the drugs at the hospital."

"No! That guy was *lying*."

"How do you know?" I raise my palms. "It doesn't matter. We could spend days looking for hidden drugs in houses and not find any."

"Okay. Then I wait till tonight and go back to the VNA."

"You think they won't be prepared for that? Did you *see* how paranoid she was? Besides, they had a gun!"

"I think I can disarm an addict in withdrawal."

"You don't know how many guns they have," I say.

"*What do you want me to do?*" he shouts, throwing his arms wide. "I know you love Julie! I know you can't bear the thought of wondering your entire life if you could have done something to save her like you do about your mom. But I love you. And some things *just cannot* be controlled by an act on your part. Including the fact that she might already be dead."

"I am not treating this like a compulsion!" I say angrily.

Am I?

"I'm not saying you are. What I am saying is no one person can save the world!"

He reaches for me. Seems to choose his words carefully as he holds my hands between his own. "Look. Would I stand by and watch you risk your life for Truly or Lauren? Yes. Absolutely. I'd do it with you. Would do it *for* you, if you'd let me. But Julie wouldn't want or ask this of you. Not at the risk of you losing both her and the girls. At some point you have to realize that the thing you may need to do for her is be there for her daughter."

Staring into his eyes, I know he's right.

But what he doesn't know is that it isn't just Julie.

I can't face Lauren knowing I promised to keep her mother alive. I couldn't face her then, knowing she'd already given up.

And if I don't get back in time, I might not get to face her at all.

"I say we give it an hour," he says. "If we don't find anything, we figure out how to get back. The longer we take, the less it's going to matter whether we get those antibiotics or not."

I nod, but an hour is exactly sixty minutes too long.

8 P.M.

I flip one cabinet open after another as Chase pushes aside the pantry's folding door in the fourth house we've come to since he found a crowbar in a toolshed.

We've searched under dresser drawers, floorboards, and mattresses, inside furniture cushions, behind sofas, attic access panels, and even the crevices in floors for anything resembling a pill.

We've come up with a stash of pornos, a kid's time capsule, a set of unsigned divorce papers, and a can of mushroom pieces sitting right on the shelf that even looters didn't want. Also, a set of his and hers battery-operated stick-on lights pried out of a bookshelf that work just fine as flashlights.

No drugs. No guns—just a gun lockbox with its door pried off the hinges and a fire safe with chisel marks and blowtorch burns.

Chase goes to the mudroom as I start yanking open drawers, pausing briefly to rummage through one filled with junk and pens. I pull out a plastic Hello Kitty watch that still works. Buckle it on as a punch—no, kick—slams into what sounds like the washer. Again, and again.

I know the feeling. Have had to tamp down desperation just enough over the last half hour to keep from choking on it.

Chase comes out, hands in his hair. "Safe's been drilled. It's like someone systematically . . ."

He goes still. Looks at me.

"That girl said Elcannon kept a bunch of stuff at the sheriff's office for his guards. The one at the hospital was armed. I thought he was just a gang leader. But if they've taken over the city . . ." He shakes his head like he's an idiot. "I've got to get into the sheriff's office."

"No," I say.

"Wynter, I can't. Do. Anything," he says, "without a gun. I can't get the medicine. I can't get a vehicle."

"What's this 'I' stuff?"

"Okay, *we* need at least one gun. And *we* know where they are."

"*We* don't know how many guys are in there," I say. "And even if we get in, you think he's going to have the stuff just sitting by the front door? It's a *jail*. He's got the stuff locked in the *cells*! Or— wherever they keep evidence or whatever. I guarantee you, he doesn't leave the keys with anyone there. He goes there every day because he's the *only one who has them*."

I have no way of knowing if this is actually true, though it makes enough sense, at least, for Chase to turn away with a curse.

"You're right," I say. "They have to have missed something some- where. I remember Julie talking about how, when they moved into their house in Naperville, they found a plastic bag full of sex toys in the crawl space under the garage."

Chase gives me a weird look, pulls the stick-on light from his pocket, and heads down to the basement.

The instant I hear him open a door somewhere below, I grab a Sharpie from the drawer and swiftly write on the white tile counter:

C,
Went to hospital. I'm sorry.
Do NOT come inside after me.
I need you to let me out.
Will be at door—

I glance at the watch.

—at 8:37.
W.

I pocket the pen, slip out the back door and through the neighbor's yard.

And then I'm running down the street.

8:07 P.M.

I turn west at the Runza restaurant to get off Jeffers, the main
street through town, which I've realized becomes the bypass. Jog
past homes I would have liked to admire in another life, with their
gables and big front porches, having wanted nothing else for Mom,
Jackie, and me when I was a kid.

Over half of their doors are spray-painted with *X*s like dead cartoon eyes. The *E* painted on the brick or siding beside it. Sometimes
the garage. They look like nothing so much as giant caskets to me
now. The smaller brick ones too much like the little houses in grave-
yards with dead bodies inside them.

It feels good to run, to unleash the fear I've been trying to ignore
for hours, to burn panic like jet fuel, sneakers pounding the pavement.

I've always been prone to earworms. I heard one of Jackie's
friends play a classical song on the piano once when I was six and
have carried the rhythm around with me for years. Tapping it out on
my desk at school, walking to it toward Percepta Hall in the Enclave,
falling asleep to it at night.

But it's Julie's words that play on a loop in my head as I tug my mask down to my neck, breathing the warm June air while I sprint down Vine Street.

Desperate people do crazy things.

I beat them out on the pavement a syllable at a time.

Des-per-ate-peo-ple-do-cra-zy-things

I know I'm being watched. I see the curtain move in more than one window.

I hear the truck before I see it, rumbling down the cross street behind me. I dart over the curb to the old oak slowly dislodging the sidewalk and press myself behind it, breathing hard. Step around the trunk as the vehicle rumbles on, catching sight of the American flag on the fender.

Must be a slow night at Exit 177.

I move toward the street corner. Peer around the front porch of a house.

"He ain't a good person," a voice says both above and behind me.

I whirl around to face a figure sitting in the shadows. An old man, I think at first—no, a woman—slumped into a wicker chair as though her body was melded to it.

"Pardon?" I say.

"He's like a radioactive spill that turns people into monsters. Makes one almost want to get all this over with."

"All what over with?"

"The end of the world. When everything dies after all the good is gone. So it can start over pure."

I wait for the sick twist of my stomach. For the old anxiety to send my pulse racing—faster than it was when I was sprinting down the street.

"This isn't the end of the world," I say as the truck finally turns.

I jog to the end of the block. Turn right and cut through several yards to come out on Willow.

A sound echoes down the street behind me.

No, a voice.

"Wynter!"

I glance back and find Chase a block away, his face white as he bolts right for me.

I put my head down and run. Turn at the corner, breathless, following the signs to the ER entrance past ambulance bays and windows retrofitted with boards and bars, drum barrels lining the roof. Navigate garbage bags and torn tents, cars like animals ridden to the ground. I pull my mask up over my nose and mouth.

There—the yellow plastic wind block outside the entrance, the guard standing outside it to the left. He's got the same ventilator dust mask and automatic rifle as Elcannon. I slow at the last second and start to walk. He turns when he sees me, weapon raised. And it occurs to me that when I told Chase to let me out in thirty minutes I never considered how he'd get me past the guard.

"Don't come any closer," the guard says. The entire entrance is plastered with weathered warnings like the one Chase brought to the car the other night.

"I need to get in," I say, out of breath.

His brows draw together.

"You got an order?"

"What?"

"A note ordering you to report to the hospital."

"No," I say, shaking my head. "There's no time."

"Okay. This"—he gestures to the entrance behind him—"is for sick people," he says, as though I obviously don't understand. "Not regular sick people. The crazies."

"I know."

He glances at my forehead, my cheeks.

I'm sweating, flushed from running.

He looks away, like he's about to say something against his better judgment. "Don't you want to get checked out first or something?" he finally says, voice low, "Isn't this your job?" I say. "To let me in?"

"Are you armed?" he says.

"No."

He looks at my overalls. Motions for me to turn around and put my hands out.

I comply, bracing myself, but he's quick, efficient, and obviously baffled.

"Look, are you from here?" he asks when I turn back around.

I hesitate. "Does that matter?"

"You might be more comfortable in the privacy of your own home, is all I'm saying."

"I don't have one."

He gestures toward the direction I just came from. "There's houses all up and down the street! Pick one with an *X* on it!"

"No, thanks."

"Lady, once you go in there, that door locks behind you. No one will let you out, including me, no matter how much you scream. No matter what happens. There is no food, and barely any water. You *will* die inside there. If there's any chance you don't have the disease now, you will within hours."

"Got it."

"But you'll probably die at the hands of an inmate first."

"Yup. Can I go in?" I point to the entrance.

"Do you understand what I'm saying?"

"I don't mean to be rude, but can we speed this up?"

He blinks at me and then suddenly raises his gun.

If he orders me away, I won't get a second chance—I'm positive Chase will physically restrain me from even trying.

"You really are nuts!" he says.

"You have no idea."

I hear running footsteps coming up the drive. Chase shouting "Stop!" as the guard moves out several steps and orders:

"Proceed to the door. Upon reaching the door, press the lever until it opens and proceed through. Failure to fully—"

I stride to the door and shove it open.

Inside, I turn just as Chase reaches the entrance. His stricken face is the last thing I see before the door falls shut, locking me in.

8:12 P.M.

I take in what was once the waiting area. The ugly pattern of the green and blue seats, which look a lot like the ones in the Naperville ER and my shrink's waiting room, as though they all ordered from the same catalog. The cushions are torn, two of the seats upended. The TV on the wall hangs at an angle, as though it could fall at any time. And like everyone here, it's cracked.

Ambient lighting shines near the top of the room, and I realize that the windows have only been boarded up most of the way, leaving a few inches of light to drift inside.

The laminate floor is streaked—I don't want to know with what, but based on the smell, I could take a guess.

I move toward the door near the check-in desk—and then falter when a woman drifts over in a rolling chair and smiles.

"Can I help you?" she says. Her skin is ashen, her hair matted to her head as though she's slept on it for days, the corners of her mouth cracked and bloody. She's wearing a My Little Pony sweatshirt.

"Uhh . . . yes," I say. "Can I come in?"

"I'm sorry, that's for patients and authorized personnel only." She smiles.

She's missing most of her teeth.

I glance at the open door to the emergency room bays and try again.

"I'm trying to find the staff lounge."

"I'm sorry, that lounge is off-limits to patients," she says slowly and carefully, as though she just learned that line.

"Uh-huh," I murmur, looking around.

This isn't the first time I've had to deal with a crazy, though it's admittedly been a while. The last one was six months ago—a guy waving around a gun at a truck stop that was convinced everyone else there was a lizard.

A scream issues from down the hall. A man's shout. The scream again.

I lick my lips, unnerved. Make a mental note to avoid that wing.

I smile slightly, back up, and then stride for the doorway.

"No, no no!" the woman cries, leaping out of her chair. She's barely five feet tall, but comes at me like an attack Chihuahua.

I back away, hands up.

"I have pizza?" I say.

"Sorry, you'll have to go around back," she says, straightening her stance a few feet from me.

I glance at her shirt. "I have ponies!"

She stops.

"You do?"

The question is so innocent, I wonder what her name is, who she was before this. She's got to be forty—is she someone's mom, wife, sister? Was she a postal worker, a preschool teacher?

She clasps her hands, beside herself.

"Three of them. But I need to see where the lounge is so I can bring them in. Okay?"

I sidle past her and she watches me go as though she's just met Britney Spears.

"Which way was it, by the way?" I ask.

She shrugs happily.

I move swiftly past several examination rooms, purposefully not looking inside them. Covering my mask with my hand against the smell. There's no lounge here, and definitely not one with lockers. It's got to be in the main building.

I move through the permanently open electric doors toward the hallway—and then stop.

It's crowded with people. Some of them milling, some sitting against the wall. Others sleeping—or dead—in the middle of the floor.

I search for a different route to the main building, but there isn't one.

I go back, stare down the corridor, hoping some of them have moved.

What am I doing?

What if I'm not immune? If I get sick, I stand to infect Chase, the girls.

I wonder if it hurts, going insane. If you know that it's happening.

I've thought several times in my life that I was, as I spiraled into obsessive rumination. I wonder if it's like that.

Because if it is, if everyone's crazy is their own brand of daily madness just a thousand times worse . . . I wouldn't live through it. Wouldn't want to. And I wonder if that's why they're here, without food, water, or sanitation. Because languishing with your demons for too long is inhumane, too.

For the first time since pushing my way through that door, I'm scared. Am having trouble catching my breath. Want to take off my mask so I can breathe, but don't dare. I swallow convulsively as I walk off, trying to get it together.

I glance at my watch. 8:21.

I start toward the hall and balk. Walk off again, and come back.

They're not that different from you on your worst days.

Technically, you have the same virus in your blood, just in a different order.

Or however that works.

Julie.

Lauren.

Truly.

I push my way into the hall. Weave past people in scrubs, jeans, a suit, as a few of them pick at my hair and clothes. Step carefully over one person and then another, hoping no one grabs me by the ankle.

"Hi," a young man says, looking at me.

I nod as though we were passing on a street.

"Wanna be my girlfriend?" he asks.

I keep walking.

"Hey," he shouts, and then he screams the bloodcurdling cry I heard earlier, at which I push through the people in front of me and trip over someone on the floor and go sprawling on top of them.

"Sorry," I say, until I realize the body's cold.

And then I'm up and hurtling myself out of the hallway toward the waiting area of the next wing. Dashing to the closest thing to a nurses' station I can find. Scanning the room numbers in the dim light and following the rail along the wall.

Someone's shouting. No fewer than four naked people are fighting on the floor.

At least I think they're fighting.

There, across the hall: STAFF LOUNGE.

I bolt for it, grasp the door handle, but before I can turn it some-one grabs me from behind.

"That's my room!" he says, tossing me into the opposite wall.

My vision speckles as I try to suck in a breath. Panicking as I wait for my lungs to obey.

I roll over and look up at one of the tallest men I've ever met and know I won't survive a beating from him—that anything I do even in self-defense is gonna hurt. Especially given that his face looks like it's taken twenty punches today alone without a pain receptor ever registering a complaint.

"You get away from *MY ROOM!*" he roars.

"Okay," I say, scooching back on the floor, hand out in front of me. *"MY ROOM!"*

"Did you hear there's pizza at reception?"

He looks at me like I'm nuts.

It was worth a try.

I push up, slowly, noting the weird angle of his leg. Wonder if it's broken and he's so far gone he has no idea.

Getting to my feet, I start the other direction. Glance back. "If you don't catch me, I'm taking your room!"

He stares at me for an instant, and then he's lumbering after me.

I bolt back down the hall past a long sink that looks like a trough. A hose rigged above it drips water frcm the valve.

I slow a little around the corner when I realize how much trouble he's having keeping up until he's on the other end of the square track. And then cut across the nurses' station straight toward the lounge.

This time when I grab the door handle, I just pray it turns. It does, and I slip inside as he comes after me shouting profanities. I push the button and lock it. Take a swift look around.

It's not terrible. No bodies, no obvious excrement.

Pounding on the door behind me.

I pull the stick-on light from my pocket, punch it on, hold it up. Take in the ceiling tiles, the locker area, the sitting area. There's a ceramic lamp on the little table. I grab it in one hand and dash it to the tile floor.

The bottom breaks, but when I shine the light inside it, it's empty.

I pull out the chair cushions, unzip them, stick my hand inside the casing. Squeeze the foam between my fingers. Check the bottoms of the drawers beneath the counter, the cabinets. Get up on top of the counter and check the soffits. Nothing there but dead bugs.

I glance at the time. 8:27.

The lockers all stand open, only garbage inside them. I feel underneath, gloved fingers skimming the metal surface with rising despair that Chase is right—the guy said what he had to—even as I look around for a broom handle or anything I can use to push up the ceiling tiles.

My fingers stumble over a bump too big to be a wad of chewing gum. Crinkly when I touch it. I get down on my knees, fingers tugging at the edges of what feels like a baggie. It comes away with a rip of masking tape.

I look down at the packet in my hand, thumb the blue and white tablets inside.

There've got to be forty pills in here.

I stuff it in my front pocket as I notice the banging on the door has stopped.

I snag what's left of the lamp. Move to the door. Take two quick breaths, and then yank it open.

Chewbacca comes raging into the room, stops. Sees me as I skirt out. I throw the lamp at him. He fumbles to catch it as the shade goes flying.

I start toward the nurses' station, but the screaming boyfriend is coming toward me, something stork-like and weird about his move-ments, locked arms flung in the air as though they don't have joints.

I take off running—the other way, having no choice as Chew-bacca emerges in time to yell at the boyfriend, who screams in his face. A thud sounds behind me. The screaming stops.

Chase was right: I'm going to die.

I crash into the corner and barrel into the turn, taking out some poor crazy drawing on the wall.

"Sorry," I say, as his pencil skitters across the floor. Feeling guilty for knocking down the one guy just minding his lunatic business.

I stoop, grab the pencil, put it back in his hand . . . and then stare at the landscape on the wall.

It's a thatch-roofed village on a river, palm trees in the distance. Reeds grow by the side of the water as kids fish off a skinny wooden bridge. There's a girl standing before the open door of a hut in a conical hat. It's exquisite, and I wonder where it is. China, maybe, by the look of the girl and her outfit.

"Thank you," the man says in a voice I know.

Which is how I also know this isn't China, but Vietnam.

I turn to the artist and find myself face-to-face with Noah.

8:29 P.M.

Two thoughts slice through my mind at once, and all the emotions with them:

Noah!

And: *No.*

A white beard softens the angles of his cheeks, his eyes overlarge in a face gone gaunt, giving them a more soulful stare than ever. The sight of him is wonderful and terrible at once.

"Noah, what are you doing here?" I say softly, taking in his ashen skin, the thinness of his arms.

When he doesn't respond but turns back to his drawing, I reach an arm around his shoulders, give him a gentle hug.

He pauses. "Do I know you?" he says, looking puzzled.

"Yes. It's Wynter," I say, pulling down my mask so he can see my face.

"Oh, no," he says with a chuckle. "You can't fool old Noah. It's June."

"You're right," I say, as a tear slips down my cheek. "Almost summer."

He looks at me sidelong and points to the picture. "I was

here," he says. He licks the corner of his mouth. It's chapped and cracked.

And his eyes somehow still manage to twinkle.

"Vietnam," I say, nodding.

"How did you know?" he says, looking at me with surprise. "Have you"—he points to the village with a finger more wrinkled than I remember it—"been there?"

I give a quiet smile. "You told me."

It's a place where, by his own admission, he'd done things he wished he had not. Things that inspired his life work of saving others—and himself, in the process.

But this is not being saved.

I look away and swallow. Crane to see down the hall, this time not for Chewie, but for Mel or Noah's other trusted hand, Zach.

"Noah, what happened? Where are the others?"

"Well," he says gently. "I haven't drawn them yet. Just be patient, you'll soon see them all." About twelve feet away I spot another landscape, of a farm I know very well. A young woman sits on the dirty floor gazing at it, her hair ratted, her face serene as a muddy angel's.

A shout sounds from down the hall in the ER.

Chase. Shouting my name.

I glance at the watch. 8:37. I open my mouth to say I'm coming, but the boyfriend goes screeching down the hall like a pterodactyl.

I can't leave Noah here like this. I take him gently by the arm.

"Noah, we need to go," I say.

"You go on," he says, patting my hand. "I'll stay here till everyone's safe."

I lower my head, tears falling to the floor.

"Please, Noah," I say, my voice breaking.

"There, don't cry," he says, turning back to the wall. "Old Noah's right where he needs to be."

I fish in my pocket and slip the Sharpie from it, set it down beside him. Take three pills from the baggie in my pocket and slip them into the pocket on Noah's T-shirt.

He pulls it open to look at them.

Chase shouts again, voice tinged with fear, desperation.

Desperate people do crazy things. One more minute, and I have no doubt he'll come in after me.

"I love you, Noah," I say.

I get up to leave and then hesitate.

"Noah," I say, turning back. "I met Otto."

Noah glances up at me, puzzled.

"Otto?" he says. And then he smiles. It's the same smile that welcomed Chase and me into his home six months ago. Full of knowing and reassurance. "Otto." He nods. "Such a gift, that boy. How is he?"

His eyes shine.

I swallow. "He's good," I say with a small smile. "He's perfect."

I wait a beat longer for a hint of recognition. Any sign that he knows me.

It doesn't come.

I stagger down the hallway toward the main building, forgetting not to see those in the emergency room bays.

A naked man facing the wall in shame.

A woman shaking in the corner.

A figure crumpled on the floor.

Chase stands in the doorway, the late spring evening streaming in behind him.

"Wynter," he says. "Run!"

I glance behind me as the boyfriend lets out a scream and grabs me by the collar, ten more behind him clamoring for the light. I twist free and sprint, arms pumping, for the door.

We shove it closed behind me. It shudders with the impact of the mob as I collapse, sobbing, to the pavement.

9:15 P.M.

Rage and grief are twins you birth at once. With gnashed teeth and high, tight keens.

Until there's nothing to feel but pain and stupor.

I open puffy eyes inside a shed illuminated by a single pop-up light. Chase practically dragged me here after I sank to my knees outside the hospital, frantic as he searched me for injury.

He crouches on the concrete, heels of his hands pressed to his eyes.

There's a rifle slung over his shoulder.

He's wearing a fresh mask and gloves, the old ones on the floor where I stripped off my own before slathering myself with hand sanitizer from the bottle he found in the guard's pocket.

The shed is a veritable man cave, complete with a TV and the stuffed chair I'm sitting in. It's got a drink holder built into the arm, currently occupied by the packet of pills.

The guard is bound on the floor, his mask on top of the worktable along with a walkie-talkie handset.

"What're you doing?" he said when Chase brought me here as he tried to inchworm behind a recycling bin filled with beer bottles.

"Don't touch her! She's sick—she was in the asylum! You touch her and you'll get sick, too! Oh, God, please let me go."

He's turned now toward the wall, nostrils and vulnerable mucous membranes averted from my contaminating presence, my outburst proof of madness and my infectious state.

And he might be right. Because I'm entertaining some very unhinged thoughts.

The words of that old lady cycle through my head.

Everything dies after all the good is gone.

The earth doesn't have to go up in flames for it to be over. A world without people like Noah or Otto is already dead.

Chase turns his head, takes the hem of his sleeve, and wipes his eyes. And then he straightens and clears his throat.

He kicks the guard's feet, which are bound together. "Hey. I'm going to ask you something very simple. And I need you to answer."

The guard nods.

"Where can we find gas? Elcannon's got to have some stashed around the city."

The guard shakes his head. In fact, all of him's shaking, the back of his T-shirt darkened with sweat.

"You won't," he says.

"My love?" he says, turning toward me. "Maybe you should go breathe on him."

"I'm telling the truth!" the guard says with a fearful glance over his shoulder. "He's gotten really weird about the fuel. Won't let anyone but Buckeye or Sidewinder even touch the tanker." He squeezes his eyes shut. "Please don't breathe on me."

I cut a glance to Chase, thinking of what that chick said about Elcannon's fuel running low. And how the guard tried to turn me away, wanting to spare me the horrors of the asylum.

"I believe him," I say. I get to my feet, grab the packet of pills, and glance down at the guard. "You're not going to get sick. At least not from me."

"We should get going," Chase says.

"What about him?" I say.

"Put a bonus pill in his pocket and tell them they can have it when they let him go." He snorts. "Don't worry," Chase says, stepping past the guard. "They're dedicated addicts. You won't be here more than a few days."

I move to the door, feeling guilty about leaving him here like this. But the last thing we need is Elcannon on the hunt for us as we try to leave the city.

"Wait!" the guard says, back arching. "Wait. I'll have access to a vehicle."

We stop.

Chase tilts his head. "You just said—"

"At ten o'clock. If you let me go, you can siphon out as much gas as you want."

"What happens at ten o'clock?" Chase asks, looking at me.

"My relief shows up. I go home for the night after I return the vehicle to the compound. My daughter and I live in the Days Inn."

Chase steps back and studies the man. They're nearly the same height. "It'll be dark. I could wear his mask," he says to me. "Think I could pass?"

"What? No!" the man says, as though just realizing his mistake. "You can't just take it."

"Your relief won't know."

"Elcannon will know!" he cries. "He'll know when I don't show up to return my ride!"

He doesn't sound scared.

He sounds terrified.

"He knows where my daughter is. Oh, no. Oh, God. Please, she's all I have left." He turns his face against the floor and begins to sob, his entire body shaking.

My eyes well at the sound of those sobs as Chase leans back against the wall and sighs.

"Tell me the entire routine," he says.

"That's it," the guard says, words sputtering. "I take the vehicle. I stop by the Store-More, pick up my pay—"

"He pays you daily?"

"Yes."

"In what?" I ask.

"Food, mostly. Maybe something for Keira, like a dress if he's got it. Toothpaste. But always food. It's how I keep her fed. She's seven, and already smaller than the kids her age. The ones that are still here, anyway."

"Then what?"

"I go to the Store-More, drop off the vehicle, fill out a report, and walk home. Get Keira from the lady next door. Make her dinner."

"I don't get it," Chase says. "If you're afraid Elcannon will hurt your daughter, why do you work for him?"

"I've got no choice!"

"Everyone has a choice," he says. It's the echo of a conversation Chase and I had once, the night we were stranded in the snowstorm and he learned everything—about the samples, about me.

There's always a choice, I'd said.

Not if you want to do the right thing, he'd responded.

His saying so now, to this man, is a test.

"No," the guard says. "I don't. Keira needs insulin. I don't know if you noticed, but there's no pharmacies around here, and the hospital's been 'repurposed.' I know how to live off the land, but what I don't know is how to make insulin. So even if I stole a truck after my shift, drove off, and kept on going as far as the tank would take us—and don't think I haven't thought about it every single day—where would we go? Insulin starts to go bad after a month without refrigeration! I could find a way to keep it cool, but there's nowhere to get it. Do *you* know of any places that still have insulin? I'm asking. If you do, please tell me!"

"And Elcannon does," I say.

"It's the reason he shut down the hospital!" he says. "People think he was tired of spending fuel and manpower to keep the place running when it had become nothing more than a quarantine. That security team wasn't there to protect the patients or even the fuel. It was to protect the meds! Meds he stockpiled."

He shakes his head. "The Warden's power over people isn't fuel, or even guns or booze, though there's plenty of that at the jail. No. It's food and the fact that almost all his orderlies have a family member who needs some kind of medicine."

I feel Chase's eyes on me as I weigh the package in my palm.

"What'd you mean when you said I wouldn't get sick from you?" he asks.

"Trust me, if I thought there was a chance you could, I'd tell you not to get your kid tonight," I say. But I'm not going to touch or cough on him, either.

"What were you doing in there anyway?" the guard asks, twisting enough to look at me.

I hold up the package. "Looking for this."

He blinks. "Are there more meds inside there? They said they were all gone. That—"

"No. Not the kind you're looking for." I lift my chin. "What's your name?"

"Simon Mattias," he says, sounding defeated. "If you don't believe me, my wallet's in my back pocket."

Chase fishes it out, glances through the guard's driver's license and credit cards. A YMCA card and Children's Museum membership.

"I used to manage a Bill's Sporting Goods," Simon says hollowly. "Hated it. There isn't a day I don't wish I could have that life back."

Chase pulls out a picture, holds it toward the stick-on light: Simon, with a dark-haired woman in her thirties and a little girl at a park. Chase turns it over. It's dated two years ago.

Keira, age 5.

I know for a fact the silo has insulin—and that none of the Denizens are diabetic.

"If you have no intention of letting me go, please," he says. "Put a bullet in my head now."

Chase closes the wallet back up and takes a look around the shed.

I glance at the Hello Kitty watch. 9:31.

"Simon, if you help us, we can get you the insulin Keira needs," I say.

Simon slowly rolls onto his back to stare up at me, as though unsure whether to hope I'm serious or believe someone could be so cruel.

When I don't move, he shakes his head slightly.

"Tell me what to do."

10:02 P.M.

My eyes sting in the darkness, from a combination of grief and the smoke that lingers, like a low-grade fever, in the air.

We're not where we said we'd be; have taken position behind a solid wooden fence two lots down from the corner on Oak in front of a house so long and with enough angles and porches to create a veritable maze.

Ten minutes ago, I was propelled by the certainty that we'd be back at the silo by 12:30, possibly by midnight. Already anticipating kissing Truly's sleeping forehead, Lauren's relief. A crash course in IV administration if necessary.

Confident that we might save not just one, but two more lives in the process.

But now, utterly still for the first time since waking this evening, I'm bombarded by doubt.

Maybe Simon was acting. Some people are that good.

Maybe he and his relief are coming right now to shoot us. Which might be hard for Simon, given that Chase has his magazine.

Maybe he's having second thoughts.

Chase stares up at the sky, head resting against the fence, holding a cardboard box of stuff he found in the shed, including a length of garden hose, a screwdriver, a box cutter, and a roll of duct tape—a veritable apocalyptic car repair and contingency kit. The crowbar's in there, too, along with a couple bottles for storing water.

"Did we do the right thing?" I ask.

"We had no choice," he says, turning to smile with the echo of that earlier conversation so many months ago.

My pulse accelerates at the sound of a vehicle coming up the road. Chase turns to peer through a gap between the boards.

"You gotta be kidding me," he says with a grimace.

"What?"

I hear the vehicle slow to a stop at the corner.

"Wait here."

He's gone the next instant, running low against the fence and leaping over the chain link dividing it from the neighbor's yard.

I close my eyes. Play a game my mom taught me the first and only time I had to get a cavity filled and played every time I was bored at morning service or stuck for the thousandth time in Penitence: I tell myself it isn't really now. It's midnight and we're almost to the silo and I'm just remembering this moment, like the dentist and those hours spent in service and those nights in Pen—

A soft, fluttering whistle sounds from the corner.

I feel along the wooden fence boards, find the handle of the gate, and step out to the curb. Stare at the blue subcompact that backs up to meet me.

Compared to the big trucks I've seen around town, it practically looks like a golf cart.

I fold myself into the backseat of the Versa, and five seconds later we're headed north.

Simon cuts the headlights.

"I radioed in that I had a flat," Simon says. "Said I had to change the tire."

"So what, uh, happened to the trucks?" I ask.

"Only the Warden's inner circle drive trucks," Simon says. He's got his mask back on.

"How's the fuel situation?"

"Under half a tank," he says. "About five gallons."

That's it?

"Which will get us how far?"

"A hundred seventy-five, ninety-five miles?"

I exhale. Far enough.

The plan is simple: he lets us off a couple blocks from the VNA. We exchange the pills for the antibiotics. Skip the Store-More for rations and go directly to the Days Inn for Keira instead.

And then head west and cut south through the golf course to avoid the checkpoints.

That's assuming this car can off-road. If we have to get out and push, we're doomed.

Something in the rearview mirror catches my eye: a bright glow on the southern horizon

"What is that?" I ask.

"Portable light tower," Simon says. "Elcannon keeps the compound lit up at night. Show of power. Also keeps people from thinking they can sneak in and steal stuff, and no one living there can smuggle stuff out."

"How many people live there?" I ask.

"About eighteen. Used to be more, but the Warden's gotten paranoid and tightened his inner circle. I guess some towns east of here have started posting warnings about this place—the orderlies have to ride out and take them down. You're the first people I've heard of arriving in nearly a week."

"What happened to the last ones?"

"They had a crazy with them. Tallest guy I've ever seen. The

Warden ordered him into the asylum and the other two with him just to be safe. Took three guys just to get the one in, practically clubbed him to death first."

Chewie.

"There was a man in there," I say, and pause to make sure I can get the question out without breaking down. "An older black man—do you remember him? Sixties. Has that look like . . ." But how do you describe purpose and serenity? The assurance so few people have about their chosen path?

I think of the horror of where he is now and feel my chin start to quiver.

"No, sorry," Simon says, glancing in the rearview mirror. "I just got moved from the well to the hospital a week ago. The Warden makes sure people don't get too comfortable in the same place for too long."

He pauses.

"There was a group that came through here nearly a month ago. Camped out in Cody Park near the river, where they could watch their lines, make sure no one took the fish off them. No one wanted them there, thought for sure they must be sick."

"What happened to them? The people by the river."

"Eight of them turned themselves in for evaluation. Craziest thing—heard the orderlies talking about it that night when I went for rations. Never heard of anyone willingly doing that—until you came along. Most people go kicking and screaming."

"And the others?" I ask, wondering if they're still here, if Mel or Zach might be less than a mile away even now.

Or if they walked into the asylum with Noah.

"They were gone by morning. I was on well duty near there early the next day and they never showed up."

There's a glow off to our right as well, though not quite as stark.

The sheriff's office. Where Simon's told us two guards patrol the outside.

We stop by the gas station, retrieve Otto's sketchbook.

Three minutes later, Simon pulls into an alley between a pizza place and a Mexican restaurant two blocks down from the VNA, cuts the engine.

"I'm gonna need that flashlight," Chase says, nodding toward Simon's vest.

"Make sure the guards don't see it through the window," Simon says as he hands it to Chase. "I know you know what you're doing. But this is my daughter's life on the line."

He looks scared.

"We've got kids on the line, too," Chase says before we get out.

We skirt down the middle of the block to the back of the print shop attached to the VNA office building, the south side and roof of which are aglow in the light of two lamps shining on the sheriff's office beside it—one in front, one behind. Each powered by a portable generator.

Chase peers around the corner, rifle ready.

"Go."

I slip around the corner. Run low, to the near side of the trash bin—and then nearly break an ankle as my foot finds and slips through a wooden pallet on the ground. I fall, hands slapping the wooden slats. Grimace, unmoving, as Chase crosses to me in the silence.

"Was that there before?" he says, reaching for me.

"I don't remember," I say, stepping carefully up on the pallet, testing my ankle.

"Ready?"

I nod.

Static breaks the silence maybe twenty yards away. A mumbled voice on a walkie-talkie giving a status update unintelligible to my ear, except for the "over."

We crouch, unmoving, as someone else answers on the channel.

I can smell it, wafting on the stale night air: smoke. Not of the garbage-burning variety, but the Marlboro kind.

I wonder how many of those are left, if they get rationed out like food.

Or in lieu of it.

The sound fades, and the smoke with it. Chase leans out and then straightens, slings the rifle over his shoulder, lacing his fingers together to give me a foot up onto the bin.

I land with a soft thud, step onto the pallets, and pull up onto the roof—which I swear was easier before.

I wait, flat, as Chase joins me, hands planted on either side of my chest. From here, I can see the guard in the camouflage pants and black vest at the far end of the sheriff's building staring off down the street, hand on his rifle.

"Where's the other one?" I whisper.

Chase points toward the delivery bays around back. And then we wait, to see which direction the guard in front will go.

After a few seconds and a quick glance around, he reaches into a vest pocket, pulls out what looks like a comic book. Flips it open and, holding it covertly against his far side, ducks his head to read.

We push to our feet, run low for the broken window, where I crouch beneath the sill as Chase steps up on it to land with a soft thud in the office below.

A floorboard squeaks as he moves toward the door. I'm waiting for voices, for sarcastic, hissed comments. A gunshot from a paranoid addict.

When I hear none of those, I glance up over the sill in time to see Chase silhouetted in the doorway as he shines the flashlight down the hall.

A garbled voice—a woman's—issues from somewhere inside, and he disappears around the corner.

Something's not right. I know it as I vault over the sill into the office and stride out to the hall, where Chase is crouched over the sprawled form of the woman who'd had the gun.

Plaid Man lies beside her, in the doorway to another room.

And then I see it:

The spray-painted *E* on the wall.

10:13 P.M.

"They took everything," she says, glancing from Chase to me. Her nose is bloody and there's a black shadow beneath her eye. "Even your stupid antibiotics."

There are three other people huddled in what looks like a conference room, a fourth curled beneath a long table.

I glance at Plaid Man, facedown on the commercial carpet, note the stain beneath him.

And all I can think is: *Now what?*

"They shot him when he tried to protect me. I told you they'd figure out we were here after you broke that window!" she says, blood spraying with her words. Her expression twists and she looks away, lifting her fist to bite her fingers.

Chase walks off a few steps, hands laced behind his neck. Staring up at the ceiling.

"Who was he?" I ask. Not that it probably matters.

"Attorney from downstairs," she says, not looking at me.

"Hey," someone says from inside the room: a scruffy guy who looks like he hasn't eaten in a week—or seen the sun in years.

"You that girl? Is that her?" he asks, looking around. When no one answers, he says, "Did you get the stuff?"

I look down a moment.

"Yes," I say at last.

The woman's head snaps up, and she looks at the guy in the room as though they've just seen a miracle.

"Did you bring it?" she says.

"Yes," I say.

She struggles to get to her feet. Chase puts his hand on the rifle.

She pauses. Pushes unsteadily to her feet and looks wildly around.

"They took the stuff you were looking for. But we—" She stumbles into the conference room, starts rifling through some dirty clothes on the floor. "We've got—Riley, where's that radio, and that chewing gum?"

The sight of her looking desperately through belongings that wouldn't even be considered good enough for a thrift store hurts. For an instant, she's standing not in a conference room at all, but in an ER bay, between the woman shaking in the corner and the man facing the wall in shame.

"I don't want that," I say.

"Well, what, then?" she says, voice tinged with desperation. "I got a necklace my sister gave me. It's a butterfly, real pretty—" She gestures to Riley for help like a game show contestant seeking answers from the audience.

I pull out the baggie of pills from my front pocket. Step over and hand it to her.

She takes the silver package that's been freshly sealed with duct tape from the shed. I've divided the tablets into two bags: one to trade for the antibiotics . . .

One to keep as currency.

"Is—is that all?" she asks, comma brows knitting together, excitement mitigated by disappointment. The fear of pending pain.

"Yeah, sorry."

I don't know if I'm doing the right thing giving anything to her at all. If it's wrong, maybe it's only half a sin.

SIMON VISIBLY JUMPS when we reach the car, having come from the other direction after the woman let us out the front door.

"Did you get it?" he asks, looking at us. "Did they have it?" But as he looks from the grim set of Chase's jaw to my empty hands, it's as though I'm watching his daughter's life fade from his eyes.

"Oh, my God," he says, hands starting to shake. "I have to get her. Take her someplace. But she has to have insulin. I'll turn myself in—"

"Stop that," I say. "Pull yourself together."

"What are we going to do?" he cries.

"It's time for another plan."

10:25 P.M.

E ven in sweaty hands, the rifle feels cold.

Please don't make me shoot you.

Movement at last.

I open my eyes in the darkness of the trunk but they might as well still be closed.

When we stop, I brace myself. A few seconds later, I hear a muffled voice from outside the car.

"I was," I hear Simon say. "Till Josie's crew brought in a haul off a minivan near Maloney half hour ago. Five cases of moonshine. Warden doesn't want it sitting around overnight. Said he'd be by before end of shift to put it up."

The other man says something and then a car door opens.

Three seconds later the trunk lid lifts. The guard I saw reading the comic book earlier blinks down at me, uncomprehending.

But he understands the muzzle pointed at his chest just fine.

"I will shoot," I say.

He slowly raises his hands.

BY THE TIME we arrive on the east side of the building, Chase has the second guard pinned on his back ten feet from his rifle, arms locked around his neck and under an arm. The guard kicks like a half-squashed bug, tries to buck and roll. Chase just pivots with him.

"Man, just stop," Chase says. "I told you, I can do this all night."

I retrieve the rifle, Comic Book's weapon slung over my shoulder, his walkie-talkie clipped to my pocket, switched to a different channel.

"Hey," I say, peering through the rifle's sight.

The guard turns his head and freezes.

"I'd get up real slow if I were you," Chase says, as Simon pulls around in the car.

10:37 P.M.

We follow Simon past a body scanner into the lobby and stop at the front desk. Double doors to my left, hallway to the right.

"Which way?" I ask, going over to shine my stick-on light through the glass doors. Workstations and conference rooms, their neat order destroyed, chairs and papers strewn in the aisles, cubicle walls toppled, light fixtures dangling from the ceiling.

"I've never actually been in here," Simon says. "But there's a lot less windows on this side of the building."

The door at the end of the hallway is locked. We move aside, and Chase goes to work with the crowbar, his light stuck to the front of his shirt like Iron Man.

"So you two . . ." Simon says, glancing between us.

I raise my brows.

"You, uh, obviously did this kind of thing before."

"What, break into jail?" Chase says.

"No, I mean . . ." He shifts his weight, as though thinking better about what he's about to say, unable to help himself from saying it anyway. "Breaking into places. Dealing drugs. Throwing people tied up with duct tape in trunks. I mean, no judgment. Obviously, it comes in handy, having *certain skills*."

Chase pauses to look askance at him.

I blink, and then realize: he thinks we're criminals.

With an insulted chuff I say, *"Excuse me?"* What makes you think—"

And then stop.

Eight and a half months ago, the mere thought of seeing, let alone touching, a gun would have been my worst nightmare—second only to reentering a world on the brink of the apocalypse I'd been taught would destroy and renew the Earth for the faithful.

While heretics like me and unbelievers burned in Hell.

Eight and a half months ago, I hadn't taken so much as an aspirin, worn pants, been alone with a man in private, or eaten meat in fifteen years.

But since then, I have stolen—cars mostly—traded drugs for information, learned how to fire a gun, fight if I have to, swear, evade capture, and lie. I've held others at gunpoint, threatened to kill, and blown up a building . . .

And lived out one of my intrusive OCD thoughts and run over someone.

On purpose.

"No," I say, realizing just how desperate Simon must be to throw his lot in with us, despite all appearances.

The lock cracks, and five seconds later we're hurrying past a series of open offices—also trashed, if not as severely as the ones in the front—and stepping through a broken glass door to emerge in some kind of intake area, the walls lined with concrete blocks. Painted booger yellow.

I step over a toppled computer station. Glance inside a bare, windowed room. The one across from it is full of bins labeled

S, M, L, XL, 2XL, sandals, blankets. A few of them still have orange clothing in them.

"Here," Chase says, rapping on the window of a metal security door just past the work bay. Simon shines the flashlight through it. The room's full of tables with attached stools like kids have in kindergarten and surrounded by cells with narrow windows in the doors like I remember from my single year of public school.

The far tables are loaded with totes and boxes, the barrels and muzzles of weapons sticking out from one of them. Boxes of what I assume to be ammo in another. Bottles crowd the surface of the table below the stairs, a case that says BACARDI LIMÓN perched on the closest stool. I crane to see into one of the cells but can't.

"Arms, ammo, and alcohol," Simon says, echoing what he told us earlier when we asked what Elcannon kept here.

Chase stands back and studies the door. There's a singed hole where the handle used to be, another in the cinder-block wall beside it. A length of chain threaded through them both is held in front with a padlock.

"Not much security," Chase says, unslinging his rifle.

"Doesn't need it," Simon says. "His deterrent is a group of order-lies who all need something from him. For whom failing Elcannon means failing someone they love. That lock's just a symbol. None of them are going to let someone break it—"

Chase bashes it once, twice with the butt of the rifle. Plucks the broken lock from the chain and tosses it away.

". . . if they can help it," Simon murmurs.

Inside, we move from cell to cell, trying doors . . .

And throwing them wide.

"Electronic locks," Chase says, touching the button inside one, glancing out toward the bay like a nurses' station.

The first one has more booze than spring break.

The rest are stockpiled with arms and ammo.

The place is a veritable armory.

Ten seconds later Simon's shoving boxes of cartridges in his pockets and slinging a hunting rifle around his neck as Chase helps himself to a handgun and a handful of ammo.

I double-check the cells, tugging down bins to peer into rubber totes stacked beneath, tearing open boxes and checking under bunks.

No meds.

"They're not here," I say, even though Simon said they wouldn't be, saying there was no way Elcannon would keep something that important out of his sight for long or anywhere but in the hands of his most loyal orderlies.

Still, I'm disappointed. Had dared to hope we might be speeding down some gravel road out of town five minutes from now.

"Let's go," Chase says, handing me a pistol, which I slip into the front pocket of my overalls.

At the end of the hall, Chase turns and lifts his rifle. Shots punch through the air. Bottles of booze explode on the table.

And then we're running for the entrance.

We break out the windows in the entrance, Simon and I shoving orange rubber sandals beneath the doors, propping them open as Chase runs around back.

And then we look at each other over the John Deere green generator hooked up to the bank of lights.

Knowing that when they go out, we'll have only minutes.

"Just tell me you'll be there," Simon says. "If not for me, then for my daughter."

"We'll be there," I say, grabbing one end of the generator by the frame. "And, Simon?"

"Yeah?"

"We're not criminals." Though these days the line between survival and crime is so thin I'm no longer sure if that's true.

"I never did get either of your names," he says, grabbing the other side.

"Sylvia," I say, giving him my mother's. Because I'm pretty sure knowing mine might send him over the edge. "And Buck."

Simon puts the flashlight in his mouth and we lift the generator between us—thing has to weigh a hundred pounds.

And then I pull the plug.

The light goes out.

We rush into the building carrying the generator between us, down the hall to the detention center. Set it heavily on the floor. Push it onto its side. Return to the open office to find Chase lugging the generator from out back to the middle of the room. He drops it with a thud and kicks it over.

And then we're piling papers, chairs, artwork around it. Sweating as we dump bins of towels and orange prison outfits from intake into the detention block—followed by seat cushions and armloads of files from a cabinet in the bay.

Simon comes barreling down the hall with a cart full of books. Rams into the pile of broken booze bottles, books falling to the floor.

"You better get going," Chase says to Simon.

A second later he's jogging down the hallway.

Chase glances at me as though to say, *Ready?*

I nod, and he leans over and unscrews the gas cap on the generator, then comes back to stand next to me as I pull out the matches we took off the back guard.

I strike one and send it flying.

10:58 P.M.

S ixty seconds later, we're across the street watching the second fire illuminate the office windows.

Chase lifts his walkie-talkie, still on the original channel. Pushes the button.

"We got a fire at the sheriff's department—we need some help here!" he shouts.

Static, and then: "What the—"

Chase switches it off, slides the unit in his pocket as a window shatters in the fire, spewing glass onto the concrete. A *pop . . . pop-pop-pop* sounds from inside, and by the time we turn up Third Street, it's crackling like the Fourth of July.

11:25 P.M.

We cross the river west of the bypass, on Buffalo Bill Avenue. Cut east up South River Road, slowing if only because it's impossible to run anymore, gravel crunching beneath our soles. I can see the light from here, a glaring glow over the horizon turning a line of trees into a stark silhouette.

Static on the walkie-talkie. "I just saw three pickups take off for town," Simon says, low.

I grab my handset and lift it, finger on the button. "Got your daughter?" I ask, breathing heavily. My lungs feel like they're on fire, my feet so sore from the last two days that pain shoots up my legs with every jarring step.

"Got her. We're headed to the rendezvous point."

"Good," I say, as we cut through a field toward I-80. "We'll be there soon as we can."

We dash across the interstate in time to see two more trucks speed across the bypass, into town. Cross the frontage road of the exit. I can see the sign hulking across the single lane in the darkness. Don't need light to know what it says.

83 NORTH, DOWNTOWN

We run down the embankment and I stumble, go sprawling in the overgrown grass, butt of the rifle knocking my cheek. I roll over, seeing stars, hand to my face. My throat so dry I can't swallow.

"You okay?" Chase says, taking me by the arm, dragging me upright to my knees. And then bending down to rest his hands on his, head dropped between his shoulders.

No. I am not okay.

But I've got 134 miles yet to go tonight.

I nod in the darkness and shove up to my feet. Stagger a step, adjust the rifle, and check for the walkie-talkie. Press the button.

"Simon," I say.

Static. "What's happening? Everything okay?"

"Yeah. We're almost there. Going silent for a bit."

"Talk to you on the other side."

I turn the unit off as Chase takes a slow breath and straightens.

We pick our way to the edge of a field, hoist up and over the chain-link fence.

And take off running, once more, through the weeds.

11:37 P.M.

The Store-More self-storage facility is lit up like day by two portable towers in opposite corners: three long buildings running east and west, garage-size units around its perimeter. One north-south unit interspersed with so many regular metal doors it looks like a motel.

Or a compound.

The facility's long buildings and barbed wire atop the chain-link fence aren't so different from the barrows and walls of the enclave I grew up in. The sliding gate not dissimilar to the one that ground open the day I was sent out like a thing returned to the wild. Not to fly free and thrive but to be devoured.

The fuel tanker sits in a pool of light, fifty feet from several vehicles and a couple campers in the back.

We crouch against the side of a metal building with a wood beam portico on the opposite corner across the street. It's got one of those letter signs out front, most of the tiles missing except for those listing service times. It's the church Simon mentioned when he told us to steer clear of the houses, where Elcannon's men had rigged the yard with traps.

From here I can see that some of the garage doors are open, the interiors set up like apartments with bookshelves and beds, sofas and grills sitting out front beneath makeshift awnings that cast eerie shadows in the artificial light like something from the surface of the moon.

What we can't see is how many men are inside. There's a guard coming down the near side past the ends of the east-west buildings as the one at the entrance five seconds ago disappears around the motel.

Chase glances at his watch.

"How long do you think we have?" I murmur.

He shakes his head. "They gotta know by now there's nothing they can do about the fire but point fingers."

We're running out of time.

I study the fence, the mechanics of the gate. I still have scars from my last run-in with barbed wire, including a faint one on my cheek. Am not eager to tangle with it again.

Chase points to a patch of fence twenty feet from the light tower, near the corner. Or, rather, the ground beneath it, where it's been washed out and slopes away toward the ditch. The earth is dry enough I know that can't be from rain. Judging from the smell wafting toward us, I have a pretty good idea what it is.

Sewer services and that's the best he can come up with?

I grimace, but nod as the guard comes around the end of the nearest building.

The last time I saw one of Elcannon's inner circle orderlies, he had sunglasses on above his dust mask. This time the shades are gone, the mask pulled down to his neck.

Still, there's something familiar about that camouflage bandanna, the dark splotch of a tattoo on his arm that I suddenly know to be a helmeted skull.

Buckeye.

Chase leans forward beside me. "Is that—"

"Yeah."

"Want me to shoot him?" he mutters.

He has no idea how much I want to say yes.

Instead, I count the seconds as Buckeye rounds the corner and strolls along the south side to stand at the gate, looking out in the direction of the fire.

Move. Go.

He rolls his shoulders and stretches his neck. Spits on the ground.

Chase lowers his head, drawing a slow breath in through his nose as I glance at my watch. What if what Buckeye is looking at isn't the glow of the blaze, but a caravan of headlights headed back this way?

Buckeye reaches for his walkie-talkie, adjusts a knob. Staticky chatter fills the air, urgent questions and shouted commands I can't quite make out over the rattle of the light tower's generator. He switches the channel as he finally starts back this way, murmuring into the handset.

An electronic rasp issues from somewhere across the property. Stops when he lowers the unit.

The reply comes a few seconds later, loud enough for us to hear: "Car's not here, but no way he'd take off. Probably back at the fire."

I blink as two thoughts crash through my mind at once:

First, that they're talking about Simon.

Second, that if they're only talking to each other . . .

"There's only two," Chase hisses, leaping up.

Buckeye rounds the near building, heads back up the southern side in conversation on the walkie-talkie, his voice rasping from the far side of the compound on the other guard's handset, closer than before.

"Go!" Chase says.

We run low, across the street, and leap the ditch. Chase covers his nose with his arm and I fight back the urge to gag as we drop down beside the fence, the retreating Buckeye directly in our line of sight.

Chase hooks his fingers through the chain link and tugs it up. I unsling my rifle, push it on the ground in front of me as I crawl through on my stomach in the muck, eyes on Buckeye's back as he returns the walkie-talkie to his belt. I get to my feet, turn, and grab the wire links. Chase drags himself through beneath my legs and then covers me as I slowly lower the fence, grimace at the squeak of metal on metal as I let it go.

An instant later, we're flat against the building facing the street.

"Ready?"

I nod. And then he's sprinting across the concrete past the gate to the motel block where the second guard should be rounding the corner any instant.

He glances at me and nods.

I bolt to the light tower, search the closest side, edge around it, bent low. Find the weathered switch.

Kill it.

The generator rattles to a halt.

Half the facility fades into darkness.

Across the compound, a walkie-talkie crackles.

". . . run out of gas again?" Buckeye's voice comes through the unit on the other side of the motel.

The swift clip of boot soles rounds the building. "I'm on—"

A sick crunch cuts him short.

A few seconds later, Chase returns, dragging the man by the vest with one hand. I grab the guard's rifle, sling it over my shoulder, find a sidearm on a thigh holster, and hand it to Chase. Lastly, I unhook the sheathed knife from the man's belt as Chase tosses the walkie-talkie beneath the silent generator.

We drop him in one of the open units. Pull the door down with a clang.

Static, from the concrete. "You get the gas?" Buckeye.

"Wait for me around the side," Chase whispers, checking the pistol as I slide the door bolt and snap the padlock dangling from it shut. And then he's edging down the building toward the corner.

As I round the other side, I'm already looking down the middle of the compound, trying to make out unit numbers in the fringe of the other tower's light. Simon said he thought the Warden kept most of the meds in C Block—the building he'd appropriated for himself along the inside and out of sight of anyone receiving rations at the gate.

Which means that anything else of value is presumably there as well.

The walkie-talkie crackles from the direction of the dark light tower.

"Munson. You there? Come in."

With the generator out, the sound carries clearly in the still night air.

I glance at the "motel" building facing me. D Block. I'm on the end of A. We dumped the guard in Unit 6—where one of the trucks had presumably been parked.

Three buildings, twelve units on each side, four on each end. That's ninety-six in A through C alone, not even counting the motel.

I tamp down panic.

There's too many. We'll never find the meds in time to get out before the orderlies return.

And Simon . . . but Simon and his daughter are safe and waiting for us at the rendezvous point. Worst case, we walk far enough from town for him to safely circle back and get us.

No. Worst case, we get back to the silo without the meds and find Julie alive.

I stare wildly around, try to come up with some kind of strategy.

And then I notice: not all of the doors have padlocks. That narrows it down, but not enough. We'll have to get lucky—fast.

Footsteps stride down the far side of the complex toward the corner at last.

I drop to a knee. Lower one of the rifles to the ground. Lift the other in my hands, ready to bash open every padlock on C Block if I have to.

I close my eyes, bent over the automatic like a runner waiting for the gun at the start of a race—not to fire, but to connect with Buckeye's head as Chase intercepts him at the opposite corner.

But it doesn't come.

What does, are steps—too close, rushing toward me.

11:52 P.M.

M y eyes fly open as Buckeye emerges from the side of the building twenty feet from me, moving far more quietly than someone his size should be able to, rifle in his hands.

He stops abruptly, eclipsing the glow of the tower. Clearly not having expected to find someone here, let alone kneeling on the concrete.

He squints as though trying to make out my features, or place how he knows me.

"You," he says strangely. His eyes flick toward the rifle on the ground beside me. "How's your retard friend?"

The question's a ruse. I know because the tower light from the back corner has thrown his entire right side into stark relief.

Including his thumb as it slips down the safety.

Like mine did when I opened my eyes in his shadow.

Running steps come from the front of the building, gaining speed.

Buckeye raises the rifle and I straighten.

"Wynter!" Chase screams as he emerges behind me.

The rifle kicks in my arms as a shot punches the air—followed in quick succession by two more.

Buckeye doubles over and then spins to his side. Goes sprawling on the concrete, weapon crashing to the ground beside him.

I push up unsteadily, barrel trained on the form writhing fifteen feet away.

"Are you hurt? Are you okay?" Chase says, coming to stand beside me, pistol still raised in front of him.

"I'm fine," I say, lowering the rifle, and then notice the trickle of blood slipping down his cheek.

"Chase, you're bleeding," I say, panicking as I search his face, his torso, but find nothing.

"Just a little spray," he says, swiping at it as though it were an insect. And then I see the place missing several shards of concrete as he moves to kick the rifle away from the orderly sucking in a breath like a drowning person breaching the surface. He curses and tries to push up, two new holes in his Kevlar vest.

"This guy won't quit," Chase mutters.

"Gonna kill you," he grits out. "And if I don't, the Warden will." He grins then.

Until Chase cracks him across the jaw.

DAY 183: OPEN DAY

We go after the most durable-looking padlocks first. Discover two vintage cars, a motorcycle that makes Chase take a step back with an appreciative sigh. Units stocked with alcohol, pallets of canned food that remind me of the storage level in the silo. MREs, sacks of rice labeled in Chinese, buckets of prepper food—including more cheesy pasta. Inventory sheets stuck to the inside walls list dates and running tallies, all in the same hand.

When we discover the bottled water, we tear the first case open. It doesn't matter that it's warm enough to take a bath in—we each drink two bottles in quick succession as the walkie-talkie sputters volleyed orders from the fire, orderlies looking for more fire extinguishers. Someone saying they're trying to raise Munson but he isn't answering.

And then we drag a Coleman lantern from a stash in C4 to each successive unit—including one set up as a break room, complete with a coffee percolator and stack of mugs and a big orange watercooler like they have on construction sites.

We search a collection of radios, flashlights, road flares, and walkie-talkies. An entire unit of Snap-on tools. Tents, kerosene lanterns and cooktops, sleeping bags, and fishing gear. Tugging things from shelves, toppling rubber totes, and upending bins. There is no art to desperation. Just the white noise of purpose that drowns out all else.

My heart leaps when I come across a stash of red emergency aid backpacks and first aid kits, but falters when I find nothing in the way of meds—just bandages, splints, and field dressings.

"Here!" Chase shouts, just seconds after breaking open the next padlocked door. I carry the lantern into the unit. It's lined with bins in alphabetical order.

Allergy . . . Analgesics . . .

Antibiotics.

We grab and drag it into the light.

"I'll get the truck," Chase says as I dig through the box and then dump its contents out on the ground, and swiftly rifle through it.

But it's all blister pill packs and old-looking prescription bottles— including some pink stuff that looks like something a kid would take.

Where are the glass vials? I search the shelves for another bin with the powerful IV meds. I finally go to the inventory on the wall, scan down the page of antibiotics.

They're not listed.

Chase brings the black truck around and gets out, the driver's side door chiming. "Ready?"

He looks at my empty hands.

I shake my head.

Chase scans the shelves again, though I already know it's not here.

"Hey," he says, crouching near the corner. "There's a pit beneath this shelf." He gets to a knee and pulls up a small cooler like the one Julie and Ken packed cans of pop in the time we went to Indiana Dunes. Stares at the label on the lid.

"Insulin!" he says, pulling it open. He lifts out a box, studies it, and then adds the entire cooler to the army green duffel he's dragged from unit to unit and has been filling with supplies. Grabs a package of syringes.

I wander out between B and C Blocks, hands to my head. Trying to think.

Maybe the Warden doesn't want anyone to know he brought in a fresh haul. Or he hasn't had time to inventory it. He could have stashed it in his personal apartment.

But none of the locked units on this side of C Block was an apartment.

I turn and look behind me, where Chase has started down the end of B Block. Take in the padlock on B6 near the middle, the awning over the door.

From which the Warden would have a perfect view of his resources.

I cross to the lock, rifle raised. Batter it till it breaks. Roll up the door.

I scour the sparsely decorated apartment—from the desk's shallow drawers to the books on the shelf hung behind it to the clothing on the rack, finally dropping down to flip up the blanket from the edge of the bed and drag out the three storage containers beneath it. I pry open their lids.

The first is filled with old letters and pictures. The one on top of Elcannon with a woman in the hospital. Even with a scarf on her head and no eyebrows, she's pretty.

The second is full of shoes.

The last is crammed with ledgers. "Personnel Records." Payments to his orderlies. Who, when, how much.

The one beneath it is a log of every gun, bottle, and bullet in the jail.

I sit back hard, wondering what I've missed.

And then go very still.

The VNA's stash was looted some time between seven-thirty and ten. A window of two and a half hours.

We started the fire less than an hour after that.

I glance at the inventory hanging from the pharmacy wall, pages thick. Carefully crossed out and dated whenever an item comes or goes.

Chase comes back, jaw tight. "Wynter. We're running out of time."

"It's not here," I say, my voice hollow.

"What do you mean? You think he stashed it somewhere else? Or that we missed it at the—"

But the Warden has a meticulous system born of a kind of obsession I understand very well. That doesn't allow for half efforts.

"He hasn't checked it in yet. Because it's still in his car."

Chase stares at me a second, and then turns away, spitting out a curse. He picks a padlock off the ground and hurls it into the pharmacy directly across the drive, where it bounces off the wall and falls inside a bin.

Chatter crackles on the walkie-talkie.

"Weezer's burned pretty bad. He's not looking good."

"—let the fire burn itself out."

Chase comes back as I get to my feet. "We need to go. Now."

I shake my head.

"I can't."

"Wynter, you know he's not going to let that stash out of his sight!"

We've come too far and lost too much to leave empty-handed.

"Take the insulin and food. Get to the rendezvous point," I say, grabbing the bag and pushing it into his arms.

"*What?*" he says, his voice up an octave. "I am not *leaving* you here!"

"I'll hide. I'll get to his truck—" I glance around.

Chase drops the bag and comes toward me. "No. You stay, and he'll kill you. And I will not let that happen."

My gaze falls on a prescription pill bottle. One of the pink liquid ones rolled away from where I dumped out the bin. I blink. Take in the Rx on the label.

Chase steps over the bag and comes toward me. "I'm sorry."

"Wait." I fumble in my front pocket. Terrified for an instant that what I'm looking for is in my old jeans until my fingers close around the folded paper beneath the pistol.

"What's that?" Chase asks.

"A prescription from the doctor in Sidney. In case we couldn't find the other stuff."

I unfold it with trembling fingers.

Trimethoprim
Sulfamethoxazole

I cross to the pharmacy. Check the inventory, find neither. Glance down at the slip as Chase comes to look over my shoulder.

"He said if we can't find anything else, look for this," I say, thumb beside the last drug on the slip.

Dicloxacillin

I flip a page, scan the ledger.

"There," Chase points.

Dicloxacillin (4)

We get to our knees beside the spilled contents of the bin and search.

Dicloxacillin. I barely breathe as I check the contents of the box.

I search for more but find only the one, but it's got four bottles in it.

"Okay," I say. "Let's go."

"That'll do it?" Chase asks, looking confused.

"The doctor called it a fifty-fifty chance."

But it's the only chance we've got.

12:25 A.M.

W e grab every gas can with anything in it, toss them in the back of the truck. Fueling the night, our future.

It's enough to get to Wyoming.

"*YOU KNOW WHAT I THINK?*" Elcannon's voice suddenly cuts through the walkie-talkie on Chase's belt, crisp and clear, sending a chill down my spine.

"What's that, Warden?" someone else says.

"I think someone's been sampling my *PORRIDGE*," Elcannon says.

"Uh, come again?" the orderly says.

"I think *SOMEONE'S* been sitting in my chair . . ."

Static from the other side. "Sir?"

"I think *SOMEONE'S* been in my compound. *AND THEY'RE STILL THERE!*"

Chase and I stare at each other.

"Time to go," Chase says.

I move toward him, closing the distance between us.

Kiss him slow and full on the mouth and then look up at his eyes, his lips still parted as I step back, his walkie-talkie in my hand.

"Gold-i-locks . . ." Elcannon intones over the unmistakable sound of a car door closing. "You're there right now, aren't you, Goldilocks?"

What are you doing? Chase mouths as I lift the handset, eyes on his.

"But it's such *good* porridge," I say, walking to the tanker. I turn the makeshift valve. Hard, as far as it will go. "And such. A *nice*. Chair."

Chase chuckles as gas pours onto the concrete. I cross to the light tower, power it off.

"And such a nice compound!"

I kick it over. Bend down and unscrew the gas cap on the generator tank in the darkness.

I hand Chase my handset set to Simon's channel as I carry his to the truck and get in. High beams on.

And then I'm accelerating toward the entrance, Chase on the Harley behind me.

I blast past the gate, send it flying back on its hinges. Roar down to the corner, turn up the side street, and onto the empty lot beside the compound as Chase pulls in beside me, engine rumbling.

"I'm comin' for you, Goldilocks," the Warden intones. "You've done poked the bear."

I reach into the open duffel and then climb out my door.

I give a slight smile as I pull off the bandolier and load the shell. Clap the breech closed. Aim high.

Fire.

We watch the flare arc up into the darkness like a shooting star.

"You know, you have a bad habit of blowing things up," Chase says, not looking at me.

"Twice is not a habit," I say, as the back end of the compound bursts into flames. Two seconds later the tanker explodes, sending an orange and black fireball into the sky.

Chase and I look at each other, eyes wide.

And then he whoops and turns the bike to the road.

I climb back in the truck and take off after Chase. Pick up the handset.

"For the record, my name isn't Goldilocks. It's Wynter Roth," I say, and then push the button again:

"Come and get me."

12:32 A.M.

"Thank God," Simon says when I raise him on the other channel from the edge of town, a new VOX headset in place on my ear.

"Sorry, we had a slight delay," I say.

"Why do I feel like that happens a lot with you two?"

The night is clear and quiet, Highway 83 unobstructed except for a couple cars on the shoulder, a truck jackknifed across the left lane. I follow the glow of Chase's taillights as he veers past it, scouting for trouble ahead.

"After what we saw here, we're going to need someone out front on the way to Wyoming to make sure we don't run into any more roadblocks," he'd said, and I'd agreed. If one town was doing it, there'd be others, maybe worse. And for as much as I don't relish the thought of Chase riding into a roadblock alone, I like the idea of blindly taking the girls into one even less.

"I just think you really want to ride that Harley," I'd said.

And he'd given me that devastating grin.

It feels good watching him now. Seeing him enjoy himself even if I'd selfishly rather have him sitting beside me. Having a private conversation. He never was the kind of person meant to live behind walls, or stay indoors.

Or drive the limit.

He's the opposite of me in practically every way. Worldly, where I've been sheltered. Wild to my domestication. Testing rules that I kept without question all my life.

I wonder what will happen with us when the lights come back on. When problems can't be solved by blowing up an enemy compound, or skills better suited—as Simon so aptly pointed out—to crime. When the reality of making money and raising a kid who isn't even his and needs clothes and rides to school sets in.

Who are we then?

"It's like he thinks we're Bonnie and Clyde or something," Chase says, bringing me back to the present.

"Those are actually the names I was using for both of you in my head," Simon says. "Until Sylvia told me your real ones."

Ahead of me, I can *see* Chase turning his head to laugh. And am about to say I have no idea who they're talking about when a set of lights flashes to life on my left.

The headlights of a black pickup.

Accelerating toward the intersection, straight for Chase.

I scream and lay on the horn. See him turn to stare right at those high beams—

Before surging ahead with a burst of speed as the truck barrels across the highway.

I touch my brakes just enough to avoid a collision. Hit the gas as the truck slows and pulls over the median.

"Wynter, speed up!" Chase says.

I floor the pedal through the intersection as the truck accelerates around the corner and comes after me.

You told him to come get you, idiot.

"I guess he took you literally," Chase says.

"Guys?" Simon says. "What just happened?"

"The Warden," Chase says.

"What about the Warden?" Simon says, audibly panicked. "And why did he just call you Winter?"

"He's on my tail!" I shout, as headlights flood my mirror.

"You have to outrun him," Chase says.

"No—wait. Is he alone?" Simon.

I glance up. "Yes."

"Then he's not alone!"

"What?"

A shot punches my back window. I scream, swerving.

"I'm coming back," Chase says.

"No! You can't." He's unprotected, an open target. I fumble with the buttons on the left armrest, trying to lower the window. Lower the one behind me and then lock the doors instead.

"I've got a rifle, too," he says.

The truck surges ahead, looming in the crystalline web that is my back window. Nudges my bumper. I grit my teeth. If I scream again, Chase will come back around. I punch the buttons on the door and the window finally goes down. Grab the pistol in my front pocket. Brace the heel of my hand against the steering wheel and chamber a round.

Another shot hits the car, cracks the windshield. I thumb off the safety as the Warden swerves, rushing the left lane.

"It's a trap!" Simon says.

"Where?" Chase says.

A shot flies past me, missing the car entirely.

And then I realize he was shooting at Chase. My eyes narrow and I swing my arm out the window and back. Fire once. Twice at his windshield.

"Did you just go through State Farm?"

"Yes," Chase says. "He came through the intersection from the east. Must've come around the edge of town past the truck stop."

The Warden rams my left side, sending me onto the shoulder. I drop the gun and overcorrect, swerving into the left lane, smashing against his passenger side with the grinding squeal of metal.

"There's a road—like a frontage road, that hooks into Eighty-three—called Dodge Hill Road," Simon says quickly. "It's a blind exit. You won't see them till they're on you. You have to get rid of him now!"

I can see him now, the heavy brow over his glittering eyes like a vulture's. The flag on his camouflage hat.

I feel my lips pull back from my teeth in a grisly smile.

I'm going to kill you.

"I see the sign for it."

"Don't drive past it," Simon says. "They'll be waiting. Oh, my God. You have to—"

I jerk the wheel to the left. Elcannon shoves me back into my lane—and then raises his rifle.

I duck, instinctively tap the brake.

"Waiting with what?" Chase demands.

"Spikes. Guns. Whatever it takes."

A shot whizzes over my head. The passenger window shatters as I fall back.

"There's a line of trees ahead," Chase says. "I'm heading for them. Be behind you in thirty seconds to gun him down."

"No! That's the drive! The road comes out just past it!" Simon says.

I search for the pistol and then grab the rifle instead. But by the time I grasp it, Elcannon's slowed, is raising his gun to fire again.

"Baby, you've got to do it," Chase says.

I see the trees, the break in the pavement ahead.

"You're running out of road!" Chase shouts. "You need to take him off it!"

I tap the brake hard enough to let him surge ahead—

"Wynter, take him out!"

—and then turn straight into his rear tire.

The Warden's truck spins to the right directly in front of me, but instead of maintaining my speed, I hit the accelerator, ramming into the side of the vehicle—

And sending it flying.

I saw a pair of ice skaters once, last November while I was living at Julie's. A couple from China. The girl looked like she was maybe a whole five feet tall. I was amazed at their routine. I hadn't seen ice skating since I was a kid, and I'd never seen it like that—especially when the man threw her into the air and she spun, four times, horizontally, at least five feet over his head.

I hit the brake, conscious of the road connecting to 83 less than fifty feet ahead. Unconsciously counting the truck's rotations as time slows into a lazy spiral.

1 . . .

2 . . .

3 . . .

4 . . .

It lands in the ditch right side up for a fraction of an instant. Before rolling down the embankment and halfway up the other side into a tree.

Call it four and three-quarters.

"Chase!"

I try to pull over the median and into a U-turn, but the truck's losing speed even when I floor the pedal, wheels grinding like there's something stuck underneath.

I go cold, panic turning my limbs to ice.

I have intrusive thoughts like this, waking nightmares my mind doesn't know how to let go of.

"Chase?" I say, my voice terrible.

"Oh, my God," I hear Simon say faintly. "What happened?"

I hear the motorcycle before I see it, coming down the road. He stops beside me.

I fall forward against the steering wheel in relief, my hands shaking.

"Baby, we gotta go," he says, reaching out a hand. "Now."

"The truck, it's not—"

"Your front end's pushed into your wheel wells," he says. "The truck's done."

Shouts from fifty yards away.

I get out, legs like Jell-O. The back of my head stings. I retrieve the duffel and hand it to him before grabbing the rifle and hurrying to the wreck.

"Wynter! What are you doing?"

I run across the road, down through the ditch to the truck in the dark.

The airbags have deployed. There's blood.

Chase pulls up as I lean down, searching the backseat . . .

Then I see it—a soft-sided carrier case. I reach through and grab the strap, pull it toward me.

"Goldi . . ." the voice croaks from the front.

I'm not a killer, then.

Just a liar.

I can live with that.

I unzip the carrier just enough to peer inside.

Bottles and jars of medicine.

My breath leaves me all at once.

Half of them are crushed.

I drop the strap across my body, push the carrier behind me, praying there's enough intact to save Julie. Sling the rifle over my shoulder.

Chase is frowning, but I don't know at what as he helps me on behind him, the duffel across the front of the bike.

"The gas!" I say.

"No room," he says. Someone yells, and a shot splices the air. No time.

I wrap my arms around him as he pulls onto the road, over the median, and into the northbound lane.

"Simon," he says.

"Here," Simon says. "Glad you're both safe."

"Can you lead us there another way?"

"Sure can."

"Hold on, Wynter," Chase says.

I never intended to let go.

I'VE NEVER BEEN on a motorcycle before. I always wondered how people without helmets kept from losing an eye to a flying grasshopper.

Chase lifts one of my hands from his chest and gently slips off the glove. Touches his lips to my fingers. I should tell him not to do that; it isn't safe. I should ask how we'll get to Wyoming now, without even a car we can all fit in.

Instead, I close my eyes, cheek against his shoulder. Hearing nothing but the rumble of the bike, the wind, devoid of smoke, rushing past us with the miles.

He slows a short time later and pulls off onto a county road. Brings the motorcycle to a stop.

"Simon, we're making a quick stop," Chase says. "I need to check something."

"What's wrong?" I say, awkwardly getting up and even more awkwardly getting off the bike.

He guides me to sit, sideways on the leather seat. Opens the duffel and grabs a flashlight, clicks it on and pulls out one of the first aid packs.

"Are you hurt?" I say, alarmed.

"No," he says, tearing the pack open. "You are."

I blink at him and then down at myself. The blood on the strap and front of my overalls. I reach back, but he guides my hand away as he tilts my head forward, parting the hair above my nape while he shines the flashlight on it.

"Oh, thank God," he says, exhaling a sigh.

"Is she okay?" Simon says.

"Wynter—I mean Syl—"

"Chase, give it up," Simon says. "I know who she is."

"No," he says quietly. "You don't know her."

"You're right. I don't. But my daughter's with me. I just need to know before you get here that we'll be safe."

"I can't think of a better person for your daughter to meet."

"Okay. What happened to Wynter?"

"She got grazed in the back of the scalp," he says.

"How bad?"

"She's okay. You're okay," he says, looking at me.

I tilt my forehead against him as he pulls on a pair of gloves and dresses the wound.

"You're okay," he says again as though this time for himself.

1:13 A.M.

Simon breaks down when Chase opens the cooler just outside Wallace. He covers his face with his hand and then grabs each of us in a fierce hug.

"Hi," I say, leaning down to smile from behind my mask at his daughter. She's barely bigger than Truly, though she's two years older, with large brown eyes. The sight of her fills me with longing to get back to the silo and pull Truly into my arms.

We load the insulin, a stack of MREs, flashlights, batteries, and other gear in the back of the car.

"There's antibiotics and some other things in case either one of you gets sick," Chase says.

"What happened to uh . . ." I gesture to the trunk, not wanting to say "the guys we tied up and threw in here before setting the sheriff's office on fire" in front of Keira.

"Craziest thing," Simon says, looking at his daughter. "We pulled over on our way out of town because we kept hearing this *thump thump* in the back."

Keira nods, somberly. "It was loud."

"Really," I say, eyes wide.

"And there were these two guys tied up in the back!" Simon says. "So weird, right? So we untied their legs, but before I could even untie their hands, they took off running."

"That's crazy," I agree and then look at Simon. "Where will you go?"

"I have family in the Black Hills, South Dakota," he says. "Or at least, hope I still do. Guess we'll find out."

"Be careful," Chase says, shaking his hand.

I drop the carrier strap across my shoulders and we get back on the bike.

"Oh, wait—" Simon says, and rushes to the car. He returns with something in his hands.

Otto's sketchbook.

"Thank you," I say, and clasp it to me as we pull onto the interstate.

2:16 A.M.

I switch channels as we near Sidney.

"Micah?" I say. "Irwin?"

Nothing.

"Micah," I try again, heart drumming. "Delaney."

"It's the middle of the night," Chase says, head turned so I can hear him. "They might be sleeping."

I tell myself he's right. But a part of me had just assumed someone would be manning a headset at all hours.

I keep trying anyhow, all the way to Gurley.

2:55 A.M.

I squint in the darkness, heart hammering as we reach the corner of the Peterson place, searching for flashlights, the glow of a walkie-talkie's LED light, moonlight on a gun barrel near the entrance.

Chase pulls out his pistol and slows as we reach the gate. And then my heart stops.

Even in the dark I can see that it's not only unmanned, but open.

"No," I say, struggling, irrationally, to get off. "No—"

"Stay on," Chase says, turning up the driveway.

"Go!"

I unsling the carrier and am off the bike the minute he reaches the rubble of the barn.

"Wynter, wait!" he says.

But I've waited too long already to get back.

Rifle in one hand, stick-on light in the other, I kick open the silo door.

It swings back with a dull clang that echoes all the way down the stairs.

"Hold up!" Chase hisses, pushing past me onto the landing, beam of his flashlight shining down below us.

The door of the atrium is open.

We pound down the metal grate to the concrete. Standing at Chase's shoulder, I steel myself for what we might find, already knowing I won't be prepared for it, already losing myself to panic.

Chase moves into the atrium, the powerful flashlight illuminating it like a lamp. He goes to the wall, tries the light switch.

Nothing.

"Truly?" I say. "Lauren!"

"Wynter—"

I push past him, through the tunnel, and then I'm screaming their names as I hurtle down the spiral stairs to the empty dining room. Barely registering the random mugs and plates still on the tables. Past the kitchen and down, following the concrete wall of the silo itself past the first dormitory level to the second, where I burst through the door.

The beds are empty. The living quarters dark.

"Truly!" I shout. "Lauren!"

I lift my hand to my mouth as Chase comes in behind me.

"Where are they?" I cry. "*Where is everyone?*"

I pitch forward, hurry to my living quarters. Shove through the door, and stop.

It's exactly the way I left it, the drawer still open, shirts hanging over the edge from when I rifled through it as I dressed to leave for town.

"Wynter," Chase calls from the common bunk.

I walk out and find him at the end of the room, standing near a bed different from the others that I recognize as one from the infirmary.

Two of the single beds have been pushed together to form one large one near it, Truly's coloring book on the comforter. One of Lauren's hairbands on the pillow beside her earbuds.

I grab them and turn to Chase. Hold them up. She would never willingly leave them behind.

He turns slowly, obviously baffled.

"I haven't seen any signs of a struggle. It's like they just . . ." He goes still. "Ezra."

We hurry down the stairs to the infirmary.

"Stay back," I say as I reach the landing first. He does, a step behind me, as he trains the flashlight through the door.

There's a sign taped to it I've seen too many times:

INFECTED
DO NOT ENTER

I don't have to search to find Ezra; he's splayed on the infirmary floor, a red splatter on the front of the nurses' station, gun a foot from his body.

I crane to see past the edge of the window, but he's the only one there. I note that the pharmaceutical cupboard is empty.

We check the storage level just to be thorough, not expecting to find anything in the space cleared out of all the supplies that sustained us for six months, only empty containers left behind.

"But we made it in time!" I shout, voice echoing. "How could they—why would they go and take the girls? Why would the girls go with them?"

Chase shakes his head, looking lost. "I don't know. Unless something happened and it wasn't safe, or . . ."

"The colony in Sidney," I say. "That doctor figured out where I'd been!"

But they aren't here and the place hasn't been looted.

I follow Chase up to the dorms again, shell-shocked. Feeling as though some vital organ has been torn from my gut, not knowing how I'll get it back or get past the pain.

We search each level again, looking not for people this time, but for answers.

We find them in a kitchen devoid of food, the dishes left out, but not enough of them.

Which means some people left before the ones who used these plates.

But they knew we were out there, that we'd have no idea what was going on. How could Micah, Delaney, Irwin—everyone who'd been in contact with us—just pick up and go without a word? They knew we'd come back!

Unless they thought we wouldn't.

Empty dresser drawers in the dorms. They don't explain Lauren's earbuds, or the fact that her clothes—and Truly's, and Julie's as well—are still here.

I don't like to think what that may mean.

"Maybe Julie . . ." Chase hesitates, lowers his head a moment, and then just says it. "If Julie died and Irwin and Nelise felt they had to leave sooner for some reason—"

"No. They'd have taken their things. They would have needed their things!" I say angrily. I pick up an empty water glass from a dresser and throw it. "They would have had to take their things!" I grab the comforter from the bed beside it and tear it off, and then hold it to me, lower my head, and start crying.

Chase wraps his arms around me, head bowed against mine.

"We'll find them," he whispers.

But I know what the world has become. How quickly a person can disappear—in it, or in themselves because of it—and never return.

A little while later, after we've spent an hour sitting in a stupor, he extricates himself, saying something about checking outside.

He's going to look for the graves.

To see if Julie's name is on one of them.

I drift upstairs after him. Not wanting to stay in the dorm. It feels eerie, like an abandoned asylum.

Up in the library, I take in the table where I held school. It hurts to look at it. I wander back out through the tunnel to the atrium, with its pixelated wall I used to think of as a wonder until its predictable utopia made me long for the imperfect, real world.

"Wynter!" Chase shouts from the exit stairwell as I hear him run back down the stairs.

I look at him blankly when he comes striding in with a paper in his hand, piece of tape stuck to the top, which I've come to associate with only one thing.

"Where was it?" I say, already assuming it's an infection warning about Ezra.

"On the back of the silo door."

The back of the door? "That's not a very helpful place to—"

"Look!" he says, holding it up.

I do, and then snatch it from him.

It isn't a sign. It's a note.

_____ and _____ (you know who you are ☺),
Came for Open Day to collect you and T. Some wild
rumors recently in the news. Worried about your safety—
_____'s especially, because of J's ex.
  Would have waited, but found (the other) J in a bad way.
We have the medicine she needs (a lot has changed). Don't
know if she'll make it—only chance was to leave right away.
"Ann"

I look up in wonder. Exhale a short breath of relief that might be a laugh. Relief such a foreign emotion that it practically feels like ecstasy.

"They're safe. She has medicine," I say, looking up at him. And then: "How—*why*—do they have medicine?"

"So this *is* a note to us," Chase says.

"Yes!" I translate: "'Wynter and Chase. Came for Open Day to collect you and Truly. Some wild rumors recently in the news. Worried about your safety—Truly's especially, because of who her dad is.'" I don't have to explain his ties to the original disease samples or work on the vaccine; Chase nearly died helping me get them to Ashley.

"'Would have waited, but found Julie in a bad way. We have what she needs . . .' You get the rest." I lower the note. "All we have to do is go. Did you see if they left us any fuel? Because we could be there by—"

"Wynter!" Chase says. "Who's Ann?"

I stop, realizing I never told him about the alias she used in an online exposé about Magnus.

"Kestral," I say. "She's taking Julie and the girls to the Enclave."

3:41 A.M.

The ark has changed in the space of an hour, this place that has been my shelter and my prison.

The beds, so eerie before, now seem thanklessly rumpled. The dishes forgotten on the dining hall tables no longer ominous, but discarded. The books on the library shelves left to gather dust now that their spines have been cracked so many times.

Each book, each dish, each bedsheet the last effects of the man who provided them. Dying in an asylum and prison of his own.

There's no fresh water except in the yard; a shower will have to wait. I've changed out of the stinky and bloodstained clothes and now stand in front of the open drawers of my dresser, trying to decide what to take.

I stack clean jeans, T-shirts, and underwear in a backpack on top of Otto's sketchbook. Women aren't allowed to wear pants in the Enclave, but I don't own any skirts. Have been allergic to them ever since being cast out.

I'll just have to borrow one of Kestral's, as my mom did fifteen years ago.

I grab Truly's coloring book, Julie's purse, and Lauren's earbuds, my comb, toothbrush, and whatever toothpaste and toiletries are left. Add the last of the OCD prescription, the box of dicloxacillin, and the meds that survived the Warden's crash—only one bottle of vancomycin among them, the bottom of the carrier a pharmaceutical Molotov cocktail of drugs and glass.

Last, I slip into a fresh pair of sneakers.

And think of Otto.

Shoeless and lying in a creek bed.

I'm ready—desperate, even—to leave. To rejoin Truly, Lauren, and Julie and see Kestral again.

For the first time in my life, I miss the Enclave. Not for its oppressive routine and endless precepts or the rules that regularly landed me in Penitence, but for the false sense of security they gave me. That we were safe and somehow set apart from a world bent on devouring us.

I even miss the walls.

Because I have been—devoured. By the very world Magnus cast me out into when he branded me a heretic and delivered me to Satan.

I find Chase in the mechanical room trying to siphon fuel from the generator.

"They didn't leave any in the tank?" I ask, incredulous.

"They didn't leave any in the generators, either," he says, shaking his head.

Despite the fact that we weren't exactly friends, I didn't quite expect them to screw us over.

I turn and kick the open door of the empty weapons locker. Scream every obscenity I've ever heard. And then scream again, this time at God, for sending the same solutionless problems over and over again like some obsessive loop from Hell.

I stop when I notice Chase holding his head in his hands.

"Sorry," I say.

He finally looks up, lips pursed. And then bursts out laughing.

"This isn't funny," I say, but can't help the laugh that escapes me like a hiccup—not at the situation, but at him.

"That is . . . not how you use those words."

I roll my eyes and lean back heavily against the wall, just now realizing how exhausted I am.

He shrugs. "I'm just saying, if you're going to shoot people with AR-15s from the hip or roll them off the road—which, that was my move, by the way—you should probably . . ." He pauses, fighting to keep a straight face. And then his expression smoothes.

"I love you," he says simply, stormy eyes fixed on me. "There isn't anyone I'd rather be locked in a silo with, stealing stuff, getting shot at, or committing grand arson with."

I look away, wanting to ask what happens when that's all over. Because it will be, one day—if not this year, or the next.

"Wynter," he says.

"I know. I just—" I stop, startled, as his head snaps toward the mechanical room entrance. He straightens as he turns off his flashlight, mine still illuminating the room as he picks up his rifle.

He moves to the side of the door, weapon trained on the staircase below where my rifle rests on the library table.

"What?" I whisper. He points to my flashlight, still lit.

"Put that out," he says, low.

I do, as the atrium door bursts open with a *boom*.

4:35 A.M.

The door crashes back against the wall, the sound echoing through the tunnel.

I close my eyes and strain in the silence until someone says: "Clear."

There's only one group—one person—who has enough reason to track us all the way here with the means to do it.

I wait for the voice. The intonation like an evil clown from a bad horror movie.

Gold-i-locks . . .

Glow of light from below. Whoever it is moves with unsettling quiet.

I can just make out the line of Chase's jaw, his shoulder, as he peers around the jamb. There's no way anyone's coming up those stairs without getting shot. Strategically speaking, there's no better room to be holed up in; Chase can defend this eagle's nest all day.

Which is why I wonder which one of us has finally caught the crazy when I see him lower his rifle.

He steps back, turns the flashlight on, stands it on the HVAC unit with a soft metallic thud, illuminating the room.

"What are you doing?" I hiss.

Shouts issue from below.

"Move where I can see you! Drop your weapon!"

I stare as he lays aside the rifle.

"Chase!"

"It's okay," he says, looking at me as he moves into the doorway, hands in the air.

It's not okay. I'm not ready to surrender.

But the fact that he's laying down his rifle tells me it's hopeless. That whether I'm ready or not, it's time.

I've never told him I love him.

"Semper Fi, brothers," he says with a nod.

A hesitation, and then: "Semper Fi. Name?"

"Chase Miller. 0321."

"Are you alone?"

"There's someone up here with me," Chase says.

"Their name?"

Chase turns and looks at me, eyes asking me to trust him.

"Wynter Roth."

I shake my head, not understanding what he's doing.

"Roth is with you," the man says, as though making sure he heard right.

"Yes," Chase says.

"She's here," someone says into a radio.

The first man says: "Where are the others?"

"Gone," Chase says.

"You're alone."

Chase nods and glances at me.

I look away.

A voice calls up from below.

"Wynter? Are you there? Where's Truly?"

I look up with a start. Because I know that voice.

Ashley.

4:45 A.M.

The change in Truly's biological father is so dramatic, I'm glad I heard his voice before I saw him or I might have mistaken him for a stranger.

The long hair's gone. He's thinner, something sharper about his eyes, which are still Truly's though there's a fresh scar across his nose he didn't have before.

He's here with four men in camouflage—and not the salvage store wannabe variety, either—whom Chase immediately shook hands with like they were old friends even as he learned their names.

I'm so confused.

Ashley pulls me into a tight hug and then steps back and tugs his mask off as he looks around.

"Where is she?" he asks, and there's only one person he can mean.

I glance at the others at the mention of Truly. Suddenly protective of my niece, even if she is his biological daughter. Wondering why he's come with these men. Why would he, if not to take her away?

"She's not here," I say. Not sure if I should muster a lie, or if Truly will be safer in these men's hands.

"Oh." He glances down, his brows working. He looks crest-fallen.

"But she's fine," I say quickly, realizing how that might have sounded. "She's with friends."

His head snaps up. "Where? Why aren't you with her?"

"We were on our way to her. Maybe you can help us."

"'We'?"

"Ashley, this is Chase," I say.

Chase comes to shake his hand.

"*The* Chase?" he says, glancing at me, and then taking Chase's hand. "You survived!" The last time Ashley saw me, I was mourning Chase, thinking I'd lost him.

"That's the rumor," Chase says with a slight smile.

"How can you be the only ones here? The silo just opened a few hours ago," Ashley says, looking as confused as I feel.

"There was a mechanical failure. It's been open for three days." I glance around at the Marines clearly deferring to one of their own, that man—whichever one he is—seeming to wait for Ashley to say something, Ashley obviously wanting answers about Truly first.

"Ashley, what are you doing here?" I say. "Is Truly in danger? Does someone *know* who she is?" After all I've done and Noah's done to keep it quiet?

"No," he says. "Only these men and another team prepared to get her somewhere safe."

"Why does she need two teams of *Marines*?" I say.

"She doesn't," he says quietly. "These men are here for you."

A chill crab-walks down my spine.

I stare at him.

I've expected betrayal from many sides. But I did not expect it from him.

"What do you mean?" Chase says, coming at him. One of the Marines grabs him by the shoulder and he jerks away, his expression as betrayed as mine must have been in the mechanical room, and twice as desperate. "You *know* she didn't do the things she's accused of! She didn't put the nation at risk—she put her life on the line to *save it*!"

Panic washes over me. If they take me away now, I may never see Truly again.

But Truly's safe. Which is all that matters.

As long as that's true, I won't even resist. Because there's no chance I'll fight my way out of this one, even with Chase.

"I know," Ashley says, shaking his head slightly as he turns to me. And I wait for him to say that it doesn't matter—for whatever reason.

"Which is why I'm sorry," he says, "to ask you to do it again."

I pause. "What?"

"You wouldn't have heard yet, but right now there is no vaccine."

"I'm aware," I say, and glance at the other men, wondering what they're here for if not to take me to prison.

"There will be a widespread vaccine very soon. Just not here in the United States."

"I don't understand. I saw you fly right over me with the National Guard as I was driving your Camaro down I-80 to go get Truly."

"No, you didn't."

"Ashley—" I snap.

"That was *me*," he says slowly. "I flew over you—saw you, even—but that wasn't the National Guard. The last thing I actually remember is waving at you from the sky. Two days later, I woke up in a prison cell."

"What? *Where?*"

"For the first two months, I had no idea. They were very careful not to talk in front of me. The third month, I learned I was in Russia. As far as we can tell, the message I sent to the CDC about the samples was intercepted. It had just been attacked, remember?"

Of course I remember.

"The Russians have the samples," Chase says slowly.

I turn away with a bitter laugh. "Which was always the plan, at least as far as Magnus was concerned." He'd been in the process of trying to exchange the samples for some three-million-year-old life-extending bacteria a Russian scientist had found frozen in Siberia. An exchange that involved my sister, Jackie, who brought them to me, instead.

Which got her killed.

"And now they're manufacturing a vaccine," Ashley says. "With which they can hold the rest of the world hostage."

"They just let you go?"

"No," he says. "I befriended one of my guards. He helped me escape. I made my way to Ukraine, where I spent days finding someone who would listen to me, more days proving I wasn't crazy, and even more trying to contact someone in the American government."

He sounds worn, tired, and not a little bitter.

"I got back two weeks ago. Spent ten days in Alaska trying to find remnants of the animal the samples were taken from. Doing everything—and anything—I could to keep from having to come here and force the silo open or in any way publicly acknowledge my ties to you. Not for your sake, but for Truly's. Because I know we want the same thing: for her to be safe. And that means no one can ever know who she is to me, what makes her special."

He looks intently at me. I understand his meaning.

"What do you need me to do?" I ask.

"We can't sequence the virus from someone who's sick," he says. "The antigens, which are like puzzle pieces, aren't all there. It's why the original samples were so valuable. Without the samples or the original carcasses, there's only one . . ." he says, his eyes begging me not to correct him, "other source."

"Me," I say.

He nods. "I gave them all to you before you left Colorado so you could keep Truly safe. The best and only way I could take care of her."

"Where do we go so I can give them back?"

"The only place in the U.S. with power other than Hawaii," he says. "Puerto Rico."

5:35 A.M.

The sun is just breaking free of the horizon as I emerge from the silo for the last time, my hair whipping up around me from the rotors of the helicopter already spinning so fast that it looks like they're moving in slow motion.

I glance at Chase, who used to tell a story about a stranded man, a rowboat, a motorboat, and a helicopter, each sent by God to save a drowning man.

I mouth the words: *Who's the helicopter now?*

He chuckles, and I know the sound is throaty and warm, though I can't hear it. But mostly he looks relieved and also strangely more alive than an hour ago. I think: *he misses this*. And wonder again what happens when the lights come back on and the Wynter Roth born of fear and desperation with the so-called bad habit of blowing things up (that might just be an anger problem or further evidence of other, latent issues) goes away.

I know nothing about the military, the "SOCOM," "Force Recon," and "Camp Lejeune" being bandied about as Chase and the others explain some connection between them that Ashley understands but that is lost on me altogether. I know nothing about a lot of things in the outside world I've been a part of less than ninety days as an adult. I don't count the months in the silo—a place and kind of life in which I was far more in my element.

So I feel woefully inadequate and awkward at best as one of the Marines introduces the others, including a Navy medic, and they each shake my hand.

I cut a glance to Chase, wondering if I salute or something.

"Thank you for your service," I finally say.

"Thank you for yours. I have two kids. So thank you," the captain, Jon "Preying" Yantiss, says. He searches my eyes as he says it, like he's looking for something in them. No longer an operator in uniform, but someone's son, husband, and father.

I nod. Because I at least know something about going to extraordinary lengths to protect the ones I love.

"I'm fine," I said when Doc asked to look me over.

"That weapon clean?" he asked, up-nodding my rifle.

"It's clean," Chase says.

I had only two conditions before we left. One, that Chase come with me. They've already called in the second team to find Kestral and the girls and make sure they arrive at the Enclave safely, which was the other.

The chopper's loud, and all I can think about is how easily those rotors can dice a head, a hand, or a wayward tree. Yantiss is in the pilot's seat as Staff Sergeant Jonas hands me a helmet and ushers me into the CH-53E Super Stallion, buckling me in like a kid.

I'm self-conscious, having never been so fussed over in my life, like some package secured for delivery.

The helicopter's inside is industrial and raw, like the innards of an alien dragonfly. My hand is sweaty as Chase takes it. I'm nervous; I've never flown—in anything. But as we lift into the air, I feel like I am floating as the country sections below fall away into a green and brown patchwork.

Nervous, too, because we're stopping in Chicago.

"We'll meet our plane at O'Hare," Corporal Nance, "Nancy," said before we left.

"I thought there weren't any more flights?" I'd said, confused. Not once in the last two days have I seen an aircraft cross the sky. And none those last days before we entered the silo in December.

"Not commercial ones," he'd said. "Only military. This one's bringing aid into Chicago, and taking us out."

I haven't been in the city for fifteen years—since Mom packed Jackie and me up in the middle of the night and loaded us in the old Buick parked behind our building. We drove till morning, sleeping for a while in the car at an Iowa rest stop. Eating the last hamburger—or any meat—I've had since at a Denny's in Ames.

I haven't been back to Naperville, either, since the night Jackie showed up at Julie's and gave me the samples, telling me to get them to Ashley. The same night Ken told us to flee the city. I'd called out that I loved her as she ran away. Can still hear the sound of her heels on the pavement.

Chase studies our clasped hands and strokes my knuckles. He's already clarified with Ashley—twice—to make sure that what's required of me isn't more blood than I can part with and live.

A thought I wouldn't relish, but would do if I had to—as he would, too.

Because there's no choice when it comes to the right thing.

He points and I look out. Can see I-80 winding beneath us and—there! North Platte. I recognize the wreckage of cars on the cloverleaf exit. The charred mark where the Store-More's C Block and half of D used to be.

Chase turns to tell Nance the story as I study Ashley. He stares out, chin in his palm. And I wonder if he's reliving the moment he last saw me driving his car on the interstate below as he got knocked out or jabbed with a needle. It happened right about here.

No such drama this time. No drama at all. To the point that the four—technically five—man Marine squad seems like overkill.

Until I remember that as far as the rest of the world knows, I'm the "only" one with the antigens key to our next cold war with Russia.

In which case I'd treat me as a nonrenewable resource, too.

"In-flight meal?" Doc says, offering Chase and then me an MRE, which I start to refuse until I see the words *veggie burger* on the label beneath the ever-appealing "Meal 12."

"You're vegetarian?" I say, taking it. He strikes me as more of a kill-and-grill-it type.

"Ma'am, I'm from Oklahoma. Where the vegetarian option is chicken," he says wryly.

"You know this disease started with bacon, don't you?"

"I can still say with all honesty it'll be a cold day in Hell before I eat one of those."

I smile slightly as he chuckles.

"I brought that for you," he says.

"What else do you know about me?" I say, opening it.

He reaches into a pack and holds out a bottle of hand sanitizer.

"That's scary," I murmur, and pull off my gloves to accept a pump.

8:49 A.M.

I doze and wake over Iowa. Am shocked at the ruin of the city below, interrupting the interstate that used to run through it—and even more so when I realize it has to be Des Moines.

The city was burning the night I returned to the Enclave at last to rescue Truly.

I search for the Enclave north of the splatter in the patchwork that is Ames, but can't make out the walls past a line of trees on the horizon.

I wonder who's gotten sick there. If I know anyone else who's died. How the storeroom's holding up. How Ara is, and her baby, Magnus's son. How Kestral left to go get them.

Most of all, I hope Truly and Lauren are safe. That Julie's alive, and that they know I love and didn't abandon them.

I wave as we fly overhead, and pretend that they see me.

10:09 A.M.

When I see Lake Michigan in the distance, I am as awed as I was the day Ken and Julie took the family to Indiana Dunes. How can an ocean be any bigger than that blue water stretching to the horizon?

I smell the smoke before I see the plumes feeding the haze that hovers over the city. Stare down on blocks with no usable roads, the pavement covered in trash, cars, and rubble. Buildings singed black or boarded up and pieced together into slums.

Smoke and garbage—the twin hallmarks of destruction—everywhere.

I look out toward the skyline, which is the same, except this is the Chicago of nightmares.

Chase sits in somber silence.

He's seen war zones before.

I remember thinking what a major undertaking it would be to repair the Sidney med center. What it would take, and how many people, to clean up an entire town, wash it clean of the stink of decay and despair to something habitable again.

I also remember thinking that when the lights came back on in the North Platte hospital and the disease died out, the building might need to be demolished. That there was no rehabilitating a place so permeated with the reek of madness and death inside it, like furniture in a house fire.

Now, looking out, I think: *it's impossible.* There is no fixing or cleaning it up. No way to put it back to even South Side standards. Only thing to do is demolish it with a bulldozer the size of the hand of God.

What had that old woman said on her porch in North Platte?

The end of the world. When everything dies after all the good is gone. So it can start over pure.

I'd thought it a terrible, deranged thing to say. But now I finally understand.

We bank toward O'Hare. I can see the colossal airport from here, the giant runways crisscrossed like an ancient code etched into the ground.

Jonas leans over and points. "There's our plane."

I crane to see it. It's gray and huge—nothing like the sleek-bodied Southwest Airlines planes I used to watch come in so low sometimes it looked like they'd take off the top of a house—and impossibly graceful as it swoops northwest to meet us.

And then I catch my breath.

A cloud of red parachutes drifts out of its back bay like a giant bouquet of balloons. They catch the air and glide toward the ground. I watch them in wonder, can't help but think of *Charlotte's Web*, which I read to Truly, and the spider babies who fly away on the breeze.

"What are they dropping?" I ask.

"Food and water," Jonas says.

They fall in yards and snag in trees, landing on rooftops and high-ways.

As we come in I hear a pop. A crackling burst sounds from below. It reminds me of the ammo going off as we left the sheriff's office. Movement on the tollway, which is littered with cars: people like ants, dashing toward something from both directions, shooting one another over it.

A red parachute.

One of the ant people drops, lies flat in the middle of the lane. Unmoving as the others grab the box and run away. He doesn't get up, and no one comes back, leaving him like one more abandoned car on the expressway.

"A man just died," I say, to no one in particular.

It's not *Charlotte's Web*. It's *The Hunger Games*.

As we get closer, I can see the fence, the soldiers, and Humvees around the airport's perimeter, holding it like a fortress.

The cargo plane comes in toward a massive runway, and we float down toward a pad near the other end.

Something's wrong. The plane tilts. It's coming in too fast, start-ing to roll almost lazily to the side.

Chase shouts and Jonas yells something to Yantiss. We abruptly reverse, pulling up as the plane's wing catches the tarmac.

The aircraft bounces like a toy, and I scream as it comes cart-wheeling right for us, billowing black smoke. Chase throws his arms around me as far as his harness will allow.

Something punches our tail. Sends us spinning up and away from the airport like a flying top.

Sky. Ground. Smoke. Sun. Flickering like a film reel interspersed with the grimaces of the men across from me. I don't scream; I can't catch my breath.

"Hold on to your harness!" Chase says, and pushes my head forward. I do, eyes squeezed shut, as he pushes back in his seat.

The Stallion skips, fighting to stay upright. Skids to the tarmac, colliding with the earth.

Growing up in a doomsday cult, I'd been prepared, any day, to die. I had looked forward to crossing that threshold, even, eager to get on with what waited on the other side. My only fear was about the pain—how much it would hurt to crack my mortal shell and leave it behind.

But this moment—the last of my life—all I can think is: *I'm ready.*

Yesterday I would have felt cheated of all our plans—for the future we've been waiting to begin. The life we might have had.

The ocean I've dreamt of seeing.

I'll see it still, I'm certain. With Chase and Otto, Jackie, Mom, and Noah. And it will be more beautiful because of them.

But this life—in this world—is too hard. Too filled with sorrow.

And too far gone. The lights that made it worth saving blinking out like stars.

There's only one thing I would regret not doing.

"I love you!" I say, the words ripped from my mouth by the sound of the rotors biting into cement.

I reach for his hand, his fumbling as it finds mine.

I love you. I say it in my heart, trusting he can hear it over the crash of breaking steel.

THE QUIET IS like a vacuum. The way a voice sounds in a padded room.

No barking dogs. No air-conditioning unit kicking in.

You're not aware of your limbs because you have none. You feel no hunger because you need no food.

And see no color because you have no eyes.

But you *see* with your entire being as you remember the secret name God called you and that you answered to.

Before you forgot everything.

I wait for it.

The *"Oh, yes, I remember!"*

For the name that fits like a favorite pair of jeans.

I'm patient.

I can wait all unending day.

The quiet is wrong. Too silent and not silent enough.

Filled with tension like humidity, sticky with fear.

And smoke like a bloody tang.

Someone slaps my cheeks. "Hey, look at me."

Doc.

I pry open my eyes to find Chase leaning at an odd angle, firing his rifle out the door beside me.

Who's he firing at? The airport is under military control.

I reach for my harness, fumble with the latch. Across the cabin, unsteadily gets to his feet and staggers. The back of the chopper is open, Jonas and Nance crouched on opposite sides of the cargo bay, rifles trained down the ramp.

A metal boom sounds outside. A door crashes back on its hinges.

"Can you stand?" Doc asks, kneeling in front of me. I nod and shove up as he stands and grabs me under the arm.

And then promptly sit back, hard. Bend over and puke on his shoes.

"Sorry," I cough, as another wave of nausea hits me. Lean to the side and vomit again.

He looks down. "Yup. Never eating a veggie burger."

TURNS OUT WE'RE not on the tarmac or even at O'Hare, but on top of a twenty-story building half a mile away, where the Stallion crashed into a safety wall after spinning out of control.

Shots burst at random intervals like the last popcorn kernels in a microwave bag as Chase, Jonas, and Nance run beside and behind me to the rooftop door and down the stairs to where Ashley and Doc wait below.

Yantiss comes last of all.

It feels weird after the last two days to have what amounts to a cadre of bodyguards. Who don't care about the fact I hate being treated like I'm fragile because the mission isn't about me.

I wait with Chase, Doc, and Ashley in the stairwell of what's apparently a hotel as the others scout options. The plan is to hole up till dark. But first: get away from the $100 million chopper drawing attention.

"At least with the drop," Doc says, "everyone's too preoccupied Easter egg hunting to come after our food and gear."

"People do that even when they see that you're armed?"

Doc snorts. "I saw a lady attack a Marine with nothing but a rock for the crackers in his MRE."

A few minutes later Nance comes racing up the stairs, the light on his helmet shining in our eyes.

"Let's go."

They clear the service stairs all the way down to the basement, where we emerge into a hallway littered with metal carts and broken plates. Pass through a kitchen strewn with rotting garbage, out back to a delivery dock that somehow still smells faintly of all the cigarettes that have been smoked here, even with the haze in the air.

Shouts issue from somewhere around front in some foreign language. An answering shout from above. They're already on the roof.

We hug the back wall all the way down the concrete ramp to a parking garage, stopping and starting, Jonas and Nance pulling me into a crouch and then dragging me back up when it's time to run.

12:21 P.M.

I've forgotten how to sleep.

Set up in a classroom of some kind of technical college as the operators take turns keeping watch, we have nothing to do while we wait. For dark. For a plane. A vaccine. Electricity.

The delusion that life will return to normal.

But it won't—even with all those things. Not after seeing what we've seen. Or, in Ashley's case, living through whatever it is that holds him hostage behind his own eyes. Sucking him back to whatever memory is drowning him like a whirlpool.

I was terse with him when he showed up. Worried about Truly and what his arrival at the silo meant. But as far as I can tell, he's also protected her.

"What happened to you in Russia?" I ask quietly while Chase is talking to Jonas, who recognized him as Cutter Buck, the MMA fighter Chase used to be.

Ashley glances up, hesitates a minute, as though waiting for the echo of my words, not having heard them in the maelstrom of his own thoughts.

He tilts his head and, after a minute, says, "I spent weeks in the dark, alone. Not knowing what day or time it was. Not having anyone to talk to. Sleeping. Going crazy.

"Things came back to me—things I thought I'd forgotten from the past, had been able to avoid thinking much about, too busy with life. Until I wasn't in prison alone, but locked up with all my demons. And let me tell you: it was crowded."

When I don't say anything, he says, "That sounds crazy, doesn't it."

"No," I say.

God knows I've spent plenty of days and nights locked in a cell myself under far better circumstances.

"You think a lot when you think you're about to die," he says. "It's like you want to make some kind of accounting of your life and what you did and whether any of it mattered. But all I could think about was every regret I had. The things I wish I'd said to my dad before he died. The things I did say, which should never be any son's last words to a father." He pauses, scratching a fingernail at the carpet.

"I thought about my high school girlfriend who got pregnant the summer before college. We decided to terminate. I have never stopped thinking about that. Wondering who that person would have grown up to be. How Shelly seemed to go on with her life and be okay when I definitely, at times, was not. Thinking I should have tried harder to reach out to her after she quit taking my calls.

"When I found out about Truly I was shocked, and then happy—so happy. But the months I was in prison, not knowing if I'd live another hour, let alone make it back home to ever meet her, I figured it was just what I deserved. And I would've been okay with never meeting her if I thought, at least, that I'd done *something* to give her a better world to live in. To feel that I'd been a good father, if in the only way I could. But I'd only been a part of making it worse."

"It wasn't your fault, Ashley," I say.

"There's other stuff," he says, shaking his head. "I had to do things to get out and in exchange for help to have even a shot at making this right. Things I know I have to live with, but don't know if I can." He looks at me, gives a simple shrug.

"I'm sorry," I say. For all of it. For what happened to him, and the obvious torment he's in.

"The thing is, every time I go back to the moment of any of those decisions—to who I was and what I knew then—"

"You can't change it," I say.

He looks away. "But I keep trying to," he says softly. "And that *is* crazy."

I consider him a moment.

"Come back to the Enclave with us after Puerto Rico," I say.

He shakes his head. "I wouldn't want the person I am today as a father. Or want Truly to know these kinds of things about the man who's supposed to be her hero."

I think of my own father the last time I saw him, waving a gun at my mother, threatening to shoot us all.

I give him a small smile. "Come with us and meet her. So someday when you're ready to tell her, you'll already be her friend."

He sits back then. "Okay." He nods and looks away, biting his lips together, his eyes filled with tears.

DOC ENDS UP stitching the graze in the back of my head, which came open again in the crash. He says I'll need antibiotics.

"What do you recommend?" I say, opening my pack.

I do sleep, finally, after eating something and taking a pain pill.

7:51 P.M.

When I wake up, Chase is propped up on an elbow looking at me. His eyes so turbulent I might be staring at the sky.

Ashley sits alone beyond him, not moving, fist folded against his mouth. Doc and Jonas nap, hats over their faces, rucksacks behind their heads.

"I invited Ashley to come back with us to the Enclave," I say.

Chase glances at him, chewing the inside of his lip. "You sure that's a good idea?"

I consider the muscle tightening against his jaw.

"I think he needs it," I say.

"What about Truly?"

"I don't think now is the time to tell her."

"Was he always like that?" Chase asks, tilting his head in Ashley's direction.

"Not the few days I knew him before."

"Being held prisoner can really mess some people up."

"He'll be fine," I say. "We'll keep an eye on him." And then I smile.

"What?"

"You really love her."

"I do," he says. "Now Lauren—I love her, too, but she's a pain in the ass."

"Yes, she can be."

He goes quiet a moment, toying with a tendril of my hair, and then says, "You know, I had the craziest crash dream a few hours ago."

"Oh really."

He looks alive, more comfortable in his own skin than he's seemed since I met him. It's been cool and not only a little sexy to see him in his element. I've even made a bet with myself that he's considering reenlisting.

"I could've sworn you were saying you loved me."

I feel my lips curve into a smile.

"You know, I was thinking . . ."

"Mm-hmm?" I say, brows raised, wondering if I'm about to win a bet with myself. Thinking I should have put money on it, if only on principle.

"Would you two get a room already?" Jonas mutters from beneath his hat.

Yantiss leans into the room. "Getting dark," he says. "Gear up."

10:31 P.M.

Fires burn throughout the city like sinister constellations. Gunshots crack the night, the sound carrying farther in the dark.

We hear them, moving in packs. Shouting and calling out enemies in a variety of languages. Raiding houses and buildings, demanding "parachutes." Somehow the plane drop, rather than sustaining life, has only endangered it even more, the presence of food stoking primal hunger.

Yantiss moves first and we follow. Jonas brings up the rear.

I feel as cumbersome as our armored helicopter with my new vest and protection detail. Slow and ungainly as we make our way from the industrial park where we've spent the last twelve hours through a neighborhood along the route Nance scoped out earlier and we reviewed for over an hour.

"By now, the entire city knows there are passengers of a downed military chopper somewhere outside the airport perimeter trying to get back in," Yantiss had said.

I've heard Yantiss fire five times so far. Which I assume equates to five dead in the name of saving lives.

Even in a city this size, the houses tell the same story: broken windows like put-out eyes, burn barrels in some of the backyards. The only difference is there are too many doors to mark. Some bear the X we've seen in Nebraska. Others simply hang open.

I force one foot in front of the other as we reach the tollway. My entire body hurts, the pain pill from earlier having worn off

Here, there's no more cover but the darkness itself as we slip past the refuse of wrecks and fires.

A hundred yards from the fence, a shot pierces the air. Flies so close to my head it sounds like an insect.

Chase drags me down behind the concrete reinforcement wall as Nance and Doc return fire.

"Where's it coming from?" Jonas calls out.

"Parking garage over there." Yantiss.

I can't do this.

I don't want a world like this for Truly. I don't want her to live in fear. Watching the good disappear like the last fireflies of the evening.

A vaccine won't bring back the light.

It'll only extend the darkness.

"Anybody see him?" Nance.

"Yup," Yantiss says, sliding the barrel of his rifle over the concrete block and slowly adjusting a dial.

He curses a second later.

"Lost him."

"Probably went to call his friends," Jonas says, turning to survey the wooded area between us and the airport fence.

A shot hits the pavement behind us.

"New shooter—building beside the garage."

"Friends are coming," Jonas says. "Four o'clock."

Another minute and they'll cut off our exit through the woods.

"Jonas, Miller, Nancy," Yantiss says. "Get ready to move your asset. Ashley, Doc, with me."

"Right beside you," Chase says.

We crouch, shuffling low on the pavement.

And then we're bolting toward the first abandoned car as Yantiss and Doc fire in the opposite direction behind us.

We stop behind the bumper of an SUV and then run again, lurching across the tollway from cover to cover. Chase on my right. Nance in front, Jonas on the left, both firing toward the incoming others.

We reach the woods and run twenty yards in, drop down in a small clearing ready to provide cover fire.

Someone shouts—more gunshots.

"Prof's been hit," Jonas says. "Get ready!"

The heat leaves my hands and face.

Prof. The Professor. Ashley.

"What?" I straighten, and Nance pulls me back down as Yantiss enters the woods dragging Ashley with him, firing in his wake.

"Hostiles coming in fast!" Doc shouts, running in after him.

I scramble for Ashley. He's leaning back on one arm, blood seeping through the fingers over his abdomen below his vest.

Yantiss lets him go and Nance grabs him. Doc takes a quick look at the wound as Chase and Yantiss form up around me. We prepare for a last sprint to the fence while Jonas and Nance cover our retreat.

"Is he okay?" I say. "Is he gonna be okay?"

"You won't make it if you have to drag me," Ashley says. He pulls out his pistol. Trains it toward the incoming pursuers.

"Ashley, no!" I say.

"We don't leave men behind," Yantiss says.

Ashley glances back at us. "I'm not a Marine. I'm a father." His eyes fall on me.

"No!" I buck against Doc as Yantiss grabs me by the vest.

"Move!" Yantiss shouts as Chase brings up the back.

I scream as Ashley opens fire. Glance back in time to see the weapon fall from his arms as he slumps to the side.

And then we're running for the airport perimeter.

DAY 184
1:12 A.M.

The only plane out of O'Hare is too small to make it to San Juan. It flies our team instead to Rantoul, a decommissioned Illinois base recommissioned during the crisis. A plane has been diverted to meet us there.

Chase holds me and I pretend to sleep, lulled by the drone of the engines. But I can't stop thinking about what Ashley told me when we spoke earlier. Unsure if he died killing the darkness inside himself, or to keep the light alive.

"I'm sorry about the Prof," Yantiss says sometime later when Chase is asleep. "He was a good man."

I nod, unable to summon words. I finally manage: "He reminds me of our friend Noah."

"The silo guy?" Yantiss asks.

I nod.

"What happened to him, anyway?"

I think of Noah and his mural inside the asylum. That wall is the one thing of beauty that could make the place worth saving.

I give a small smile. "He's off helping others."

What will I tell Truly about her father?

I'll tell her he was a hero.

I fall asleep searching the darkness below for the Atlantic I know to be there.

And wake to a runway filled with light.

DAY 190

"You're probably the first person to have their own designated sharps container," Chase says as we wait inside the Rodriguez Army Health Clinic, following my gaze to a cart full of vials, gloves, syringes, and a red container with a biohazard sign on it that's been marked with a black *X*.

He doesn't know that I'm really looking at the wall behind it. Trying to imagine the beige paint covered with a Vietnamese village, a girl carrying pails of water hanging from a pole across her shoulders.

We've spent the last week watching the news from our room here, in Fort Buchanan, stunned by the headlines. The estimated 100 million dead, the vast majority of the casualties in the United States. The alarming infection rate in South America and growing number of sick in Europe and Asia. Russia's state-sponsored doping program turning to the distribution of IV "vitamins" to boost immunity against the disease. The U.S. battleships surrounding the islands of Puerto Rico, where frantic research is rumored to be underway on a vaccine.

I want to marvel at the palm trees. At the exotic and sometimes star-shaped fruits that arrive with lunch and cooked bananas Chase says are plantains. At being so close to the ocean I can practically taste it on the air.

But I have no idea if Julie's still alive.

I trust that Truly is safe with Kestral. For all I know she's ecstatic to be back in the only real home she's ever known. But Lauren, I worry about. She's almost seventeen.

Marriage material by New Earth standards.

Meanwhile, the hot showers, air-conditioning, fresh clothes, clean linens, twenty-four-hour television, and regular meals we've had since we arrived haven't felt so much luxurious as disconcerting. The sounds of the vehicles inside the army base too frequent, the electric lights too many.

I'm not allowed to go anywhere without an armed escort, and then only to visit the medical center, where I spent the entire first day submitting to examinations, tests, and blood draws.

My first day here they said it could be eight weeks before I'm allowed to leave. To protect not just their ready supply of blood samples should the pharmaceutical companies here or in the United Kingdom require more from Donor X, but my anonymity, should another country get the idea to abduct me for similar purposes.

I've asked for only two things since we arrived: for Julie, Lauren, and Truly to be brought here as soon as Julie's well enough to travel, and to talk to them via satellite phone in the meantime, as soon as possible.

Also, to visit the beach.

CHASE, AT LEAST, was able to reach his family in France our second day here and reassure them that he was okay as he talked to them for an hour. I was glad for him, and to hear my name brought up in conversation, but also envious at how much lighter he seemed afterward.

A knock, and the door opens. But instead of Dr. Acheson, who oversees the clinic, or Dustin, the sole phlebotomist allowed to draw my blood, it's a member of my detail.

"For you," she says, handing me a phone with a thick antenna.

My heart jumps.

"Hello?" I say, the instant she steps back out.

"Sylvia?" a man on the other end says.

It's my mother's name, and the one I've agreed to go by—for this conversation, and any other interactions while I'm here.

"Yes. Who's this?" I say.

"Just a moment," he says. And then, to someone else: "She's on the line."

The phone changes hands.

"*Sylvia?*"

Kestral.

"Hi!" I say, getting off the end of the exam table and turning to look at Chase.

"Oh, it's so good to hear your voice!"

"Yours, too. How's Julie?"

"She's doing great. She responded to the antibiotics right away. Here, hold on."

A few seconds later, Julie says, "W—Sylvia? Oh, my God. Are you okay?"

"I've been so worried about you!" I say, voice tightening as my vision blurs. "We got the antibiotics—we found some in North Platte, but by the time we got back, you were already gone . . ."

"Are you okay? Tell me you're okay. I can only imagine everything you've gone through!"

"I'm fine." I look around at the medical equipment plugged into the wall, the lights on overhead. By all accounts, I'm far better off than they are. "Is Truly—"

"Truly's fine," she says.

"I just want to know you're all right. All of you."

"Lauren's good, Truly's good. I'm up and moving around—a little slowly, but hey. They don't let me do too much."

I cover my mouth, on the verge of bawling in relief.

"And you're doing okay." And what I mean is: inside the compound. I've wondered who's taken over Magnus's position, how much stricter things have gotten in the middle of what I know they regard as the final cataclysm. Wonder how Julie and Lauren are dealing with all the talk of Final Day, or faring inside a community I know Julie considers as crazy as the deranged outside world. But for all I know they've taken this call inside the (rebuilt) administrative building and can't speak freely.

"You're repeating yourself," she says. "And yes. I promise. I just hate that you're by yourself," she says, and then lowers her voice. "Is Ashley with you, at least?"

"No, he, um, couldn't make it," I say, not wanting to talk about it on the phone. "But Chase is."

"Oh *really*," she says, and I can hear her smile.

"And you and Lauren and Truly will be, soon as you're healthy enough to travel. Kestral, too, if she wants."

For a moment, she doesn't answer.

"Julie? You still there?" I say.

"Yes," she says. And then: "Wynter . . . I think we should stay."

"What?" I say, thinking I must have heard her wrong.

I think back to the way we were enveloped with friendship and acceptance on our arrival fifteen years ago. "Love bombing," they call it in the articles I read after I got out. But Julie hates New Earth for what it did to my mother, Jackie, and me. Is far too cynical for it to work on her. Isn't she?

It hasn't even been two weeks!

"Truly and Lauren are happy here," she says.

No. No, no, no.

"Julie, I know it might seem like—"

"And I am, too."

"But you hate them!" I say, feeling strangely betrayed.

"A lot's changed since you were here. We're needed here. Also, the military people who brought the satellite phone said maybe they can help me get in contact with the boys. Hon, I've spent the last six months wondering if they're still alive. I need to know. And if they are, I want to bring them here."

"They can come here, too!"

"Wyn—Sylvia. I've been to Puerto Rico. I've seen it—and a lot of places. But I've never seen anything like this."

I start to argue with her, angry panic rising inside me, but then Kestral gets back on the phone.

"Sylvia, what's an island but just one more enclave cut off from the rest of the world?" she says gently. "You could probably insist that they put Truly on a plane—"

"Yes! I can!"

"But she'd be terrified. And I'm telling you, she doesn't want to leave."

I cover my eyes as tears slip down my cheeks. Because I don't understand. Don't see how or why Julie would want to stay. I feel betrayed by them both.

"You promise she's safe," I say, my voice breaking.

"I promise. What's more, she's happy here. And I think you would be, too."

I chuff a laugh.

"Just . . . come when you can and see for yourself. If you want to leave with Truly then, no one will stop you."

DAY 192

Last night they let us into the army base's bowling alley after hours, where we had the entire facility to ourselves and Chase taught me how to bowl and I had my first—and last—beer.

The night before, it was a Bollywood movie at the community center. Which I might have enjoyed except that I couldn't stop thinking about Julie. Hoping her sons, whom I grew up playing with, are safe. Worried her health might take a turn for the worse. Wishing I'd insisted on talking to Truly. All reasons I insisted on a weekly phone call until I'm allowed to leave.

"Do you have everything you need?" I asked Dr. Acheson this morning. "Because I can't keep doing this. I appreciate the movie and the bowling, but I'm going crazy."

Crazy from the news, crazy from being indoors, even though they change our room every two days. Crazy from wondering why Julie would possibly want to bring her boys to the Enclave, if a bunch of girls Lauren's age are love bombing her into thinking she's happy. If I'll have to rescue Truly again once this is over.

"We do. Though we'd like to keep you close," Dr. Acheson said. "But I'd definitely say you've earned some R and R."

TONIGHT AS I step inside the boat, I can smell the salt of the black expanse before us beneath the sickle moon. Can hear the waves on the nearby beach, rolling in like a breath and away like an exhale, as though the ocean were breathing. Can taste the spray as we pull from the dock and head out into open water.

"I love you," Chase murmurs against my shoulder, wrapping his arms around me.

It's an hour to the island of Vieques, where the boat drives right up onto the beach. I take off my shoes as Chase gets out, the duffel of our new belongings over his shoulder. He offers me a hand and I climb out, barefoot, just in time for a wave to wash over my toes.

I gasp and then squeal like a kid.

"It's there," the lieutenant who drove us here says, pointing to a yellow house with a porch light shining over the front door.

We thank him and Chase gives the boat a push into the water. But all I can think is I'm standing on the edge of the thing I've wanted to see my whole life. It's here. Out there in the inky night.

I linger in wonder long after Chase has fished the key from the envelope in his pocket and taken our things inside. Eventually he returns with two plastic chairs and sets them in the sand, where we sit through the night, and later doze to the sound of the surf.

Chase is asleep when I wake, a blanket similar to the one covering me around his shoulders like a shawl. Gold glows in the eastern sky, gilding the clouds, throwing the palm trees along the cove into stark relief.

Ripples line the sand; the waves that lapped at my toes last night have moved out with the tide. I watch as the water turns from denim to turquoise beneath the rising sun. I wonder how many miles it is to the U.S. mainland from here, to South America, Africa, Europe, and even Russia. This water called the Caribbean Sea doesn't care where it's supposed to become the Atlantic but flows against every ocean shore. Connecting all the continents it supposedly separates. Too vast to be understood, too wild to be contained, beautiful and fearsome at once. The waves rolling to that rhythmic breath that seems to say, *Be still. Know that I Am.*

I spent fifteen years seeking God inside a compound. In rules, locked in a white penitent's cell. Shunning the wider world as dangerous at best and evil at worst. Which it is—more than I ever imagined. But it is also where I found Noah and Otto, Ashley and Chase in some of its darkest corners.

I can't stop thinking about what Kestral said.

What's an island but just one more enclave cut off from the rest of the world?

I'd wanted to shout that it's a safe place.

But looking out at the ocean now, I realize that every time I ever met God, I was nowhere safe.

DAY 229

Our last morning in Vieques, we eat breakfast on the beach.

Chase is trying to read the newspaper we picked up in Esperanza. He's been claiming for days the Spanish he learned while stationed in Honduras is finally coming back to him.

"'U.S. Accuses Russia of Acts of War,'" he translates. "'The U.S. has formally accused Russia of war acts including attacks on the United States' electrical grid, the December attack on the Centers for Disease Control, and the kidnapping and false imprisonment of Colorado State University professor Dr. Ashley Neal in order to obtain stolen samples of the original disease . . .'"

He scans down the front and flips to the inside. "'Puerto Rico Ships First Doses of Vaccine as U.K. and Switzerland Ramp Up Production . . . Germany Sends Additional Aid . . .' Ah, here, way down in the corner of page 3: 'Wynter Roth, the twenty-two-year-old fugitive—'"

"Twenty-three," I say.

He glances at me. The Puerto Rican sun has turned the sultry cocktail of his Native and African American and Middle Eastern genes a dark bronze.

Meanwhile, it's taken me nearly two weeks to get a decent tan after I peeled like a lizard.

"Twenty-three? When did this happen?" He blinks.

"In Chicago," I say, picking at the sweet Mallorca bread left over from my egg and cheese sandwich. "Keep reading."

He picks up the paper again.

"'The *twenty-three*-year-old'—" He looks at me, flicking the newspaper. "I should write to the paper and make them correct it. This is just bad journalism. 'Fugitive wanted for murder in the December 11 death of Jaclyn Theisen has been exonerated as new forensic evidence points to Theisen's husband, New Earth cult leader Magnus Theisen. In a signed statement before his death, Dr. Ashley Neal testified that the samples were retrieved and delivered to him by a do-gooder who wishes to remain anonymous, hailing that person as a national hero.'"

He puts the paper down.

"Wow," I say.

He turns and pulls me into his arms. "I'm holding a national hero," he whispers against my ear.

I laugh as he nuzzles my neck and then turns me toward him so he can look at me.

"So, I've been thinking," he says.

"Yes?" I loop my arms around his neck, having expected the question about his reenlisting for days—weeks—now. Especially since he and the Doomsday team have stayed in communication.

"When we get back to the U.S. . . . ." His gaze softens. "I want you to marry me."

I blink, and then laugh. "Oh, really?"

"Don't you want to? If not right away . . . eventually?" he says, the smile faltering.

"We've only known each other six months."

"And a half. Almost seven. In apocalypse time, that's like, five years."

I tuck a tendril of hair behind his ear. I'm going to miss it when he reenlists.

"Practically a lifetime," I say.

"Lifetimes being in short supply during apocalypses and all." He looks up and I follow his gaze out toward the water where the boat is coming to ferry us back to the mainland.

"Where are you going to find a preacher?"

"I'm a Marine. I'll find a preacher."

"Where are you going to find a ring?" I tilt my head.

He lifts his brows. "I've never seen you wear jewelry."

We never had such things in the Enclave. But I've tried Julie's on in secret.

"Diamonds look good on me."

"Well then, I should probably do two things," he says, reaching over for the duffel as the boat comes to shore. "First, tell you I'm thinking of reenlisting."

"And the second?"

"Start shopping for rings worthy of a hero."

"Oorah," I say with a smile.

DAY 231

As we pull up the gravel drive I remember so vividly, I lean forward and gape.

The walls are gone. The new guard towers torn down.

Chase stares. "What the . . ."

We pull up to a hand-painted sign in the parking lot.

WELCOME! VISITORS' CENTER ➜

The sign points to the old administrative building. Or, rather, a new building where the old one used to be.

I get out and look around. The front parking lot, where the Select gathered for my casting out, has been turned into a playground. The barrows have been painted bright colors.

Julie was right—and wrong. Because it isn't just that a lot's changed.

The Enclave I remember is no more.

The few fragments of wall left standing support grape and sweet pea vines and vertical gardens.

Another's been turned into a climbing wall. The girl on it leaps down and comes running toward us.

"Hi," she says. "Can I help you?"

She's wearing jeans.

"Um, yes. Thank you," I say. "I'm looking for Kestral."

"I'll get her!" she calls, running off.

I walk up the path toward Percepta Hall, and stare at a signpost with brightly painted boards pointing in different directions.

HUNGRY? ↗

↖ PRAYER CHAPEL (ALL WELCOME!)

VISITORS' CENTER →

← SCHOOL

↖ PLAYGROUND

CLINIC ↑

↓ VOLUNTEER

COUNSELING OFFICE ↘

↙ CLOTHING CENTER,

NEED HELP?? ASK ANYONE!

"I take it it wasn't like this before," Chase says.

"No," I say, faintly.

A figure comes running down the path. Kestral, her face tanned, hair caught back in a scarf. Work gloves on her hands.

"You're here!" she shouts, catching us up in big hugs. "We've been waiting for you forever!"

I used to think she was pretty. Angelic, even. But she's radiant now.

And then—

I let her go and catch my breath at the figure behind her. Practically fall into Julie's arms.

She's thinner, her hair grown out its natural gray. But she looks healthy—and more than that, happy.

I follow her and Kestral to the school as Kestral talks about the medical clinic in the new facility. It takes me a moment to realize she means the building Magnus meant to turn into a quarantine for those seeking refuge from the disease.

"We'll be a licensed vaccination center in the next few weeks," she says.

"And . . . Magnus?" I say.

"Buried beneath the gravel drive," she says dispassionately as we reach the school. "Along with his legacy."

She opens the door to what used to be the Farm—the boys' dorm.

"Winnie!" Truly shouts, getting up from her desk and running to grab me around the waist. I grab her up, vowing this time I will not let her go. Not again. Not ever. We're joined by Lauren, who hugs me and then walks with Chase as we follow Kestral to the warehouse.

"The seed bank is the only thing we kept," Kestral says. "Because I think we'll need it in the days to come." She opens the door and we step inside. "Visitors!" she shouts.

They come to greet us, and I'm astonished to see their faces. To recognize so many I knew before—including Ara, who is smiling for the first time I can remember.

"You made it!" a male voice says. I look over Lauren's head to see Mel shaking Chase's hand, and Zach waiting his turn.

But there's one who simply won't wait. He comes charging through the crowd from the direction of the office, an exuberant streak of white and brown that leaps at Chase.

"Buddy!" Chase laughs and grabs him up into his arms as he did the night we found him.

"Come!" Kestral says, taking me by the arm. "Come see, and then we'll go eat."

We walk from building to building—each of them so changed as to be unrecognizable. Except for Percepta Hall with its steeple, which is now a prayer chapel with unlocked meditation rooms below and a new chaplain. When Kestral takes me inside to her office, I stop in shock.

"Reverend Carolyn!" I say, before rushing to hug her.

"I went on a pilgrimage when I left the silo," she says. "It was a long, convoluted adventure."

I want to say: *Aren't they all?*

"But the long and short of it is that it led me here." She smiles, and it's like she's a new person.

"Hey, do you by chance do weddings?" I hear Chase ask as I continue the tour.

KESTRAL EXPLAINS THAT parcel next to this one.

"We have a brand-new building going up there, a new model for community living," she says. "With better space efficiency to accommodate more people. And more jobs. And look," she says, gesturing inside the storehouse where Jaclyn once slipped me a note to trust her. "The storehouse is nearly empty."

"What are you going to do?" I say. I've seen at least three hundred people more than the five hundred who lived in the Enclave before.

"No, you don't understand," she says, beaming. "That's the goal. We want our shelves to be empty. We want our walls removed. We don't defend—we welcome and accept. We have nothing for anyone to steal, because we give it freely." Her eyes shine. "We don't hide here—we work here for the means to go out and feed others."

My expression crumples. I swipe at my eyes, vision blurring as I take in the empty shelves, adding the image to my collection of beautiful things.

Noah's wall.

Otto's drawings.

Chase's smile.

The wide blue sea.

Beauty to inspire new beginnings. A new start.

A new Earth.

ACKNOWLEDGMENTS

During the final edits for this book, a "bomb cyclone" hit my home state of Nebraska, delivering devastating blizzards to the west and water to the east. Seventy-nine thousand miles of waterways swelled in what would become the most widespread destruction in our state's history. As the National Guard rolled in, Black Hawk helicopters flew rescue missions, and the town closest to our farm ran out of fuel, I was filled with eerie déjà vu, having included similar scenes in *The Line Between*.

As I write these acknowledgments, many of our roadways and bridges remain unusable, if not washed out altogether. Ranchers, farmers, and entire communities throughout the Midwest are still reeling in the aftermath of the blizzard, ice dams, and floods that cost some their livelihoods, many their homes, and a few their lives.

Thank you to the first responders, volunteers, and everyone who have donated their time, funds, skills, supplies, and simple elbow grease to those here in need. As the daughter of a native Nebraskan and great-great-great granddaughter of one of Nebraska's first women homesteaders (a widow with four children, no less!), I can attest we are a resilient people who value hard work and we take care of our neighbors. Thank you to the neighbors here, and in other states, who have taken care of us during these weeks and months.

Please continue to keep Nebraska—and the entire Midwest—in your prayers.

Meanwhile, thank you, as always, to my readers for going on yet another adventure with me. (Given the weird real-life stuff that has ensued since writing this book—and the influenza A I got while writing the first one in the series—not to mention the fact that I learned while writing *The Progeny* that I was distantly related to Elizabeth Bathory . . . I take it you won't mind if I pause to write a story about a novelist who wins the lottery??) Thank you to my amazing launch team for not only helping to release this story into the wild, but also making it far more fun.

Thank you to Marine veterans Craig Conger and Bill Dieckman for your time, patience with my questions, and thoughtful answers—and most of all, for your service.

Special shout-out to Carolyn M. Richel, MS Ed, after whom Reverend Richel is named in this story. Thank you, Carolyn, for your generosity through Compassion Connect, and for the special and important work you do in hospice.

Jennifer Jackson, thank you for reading an early draft of this story and for being an advocate of books and authors like me—as a bookseller and a librarian. Thank you to all the booksellers and librarians who help readers connect with new books, authors, and their next great adventure.

Thank you to the indispensible Cindy Conger and Stephen Parolini, my publicist Mickey Mikkelson, agent Dan Raines, and the entire team at Simon & Schuster. Thank you, Michael Napoliello,

Maria Frisk, and Ted Fields of Radar Pictures, and Aaron Lubin and Ed Burns of Marlboro Road Gang Productions, for being such fabulous partners and having great taste in stories.

Thank you to my growing family, which I am so blessed to have more of today than ever. And to my boys—Kayl, Gage, and Kole— for being so understanding of my weird hours and the Cool Ranch nachos that disappear during the night. I might have lied when I said I didn't know what happened to them . . . all five times.

Thank you, Bryan, for the great gift of your love, gentleness, humor, wisdom, and imagination. I've struggled to put into adequate words how much I love you, and have finally concluded I'm not that good of a writer. But it won't stop me from making cheesy attempts in public, and earnest ones in private.

Thank you, first and last of all, to the Ultimate Author. Yes.
You were right.

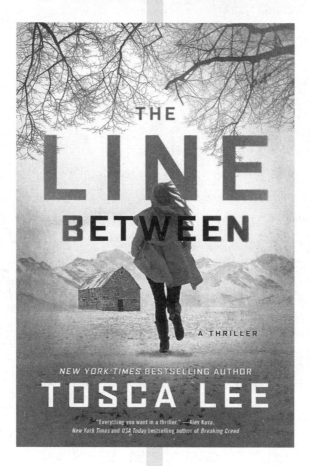

THE HOUSE OF BATHORY
DUOLOGY

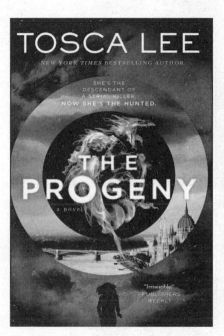

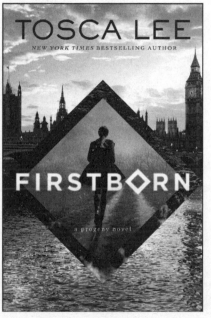

PICK UP OR DOWNLOAD YOUR COPIES TODAY!

HOWARD BOOKS
An Imprint of Simon & Schuster
A CBS COMPANY

67408

ALSO *by* TOSCA LEE

Pick up or download your copies today!

β²